STALKING

Steven

Fidelity Investigations #2

JENNA BENNETT

Fresh from solving her late husband's murder, Gina Beaufort Kelley is dealing with her first case as a licensed PI: stalking Steven Morton, the husband of Gina's divorce attorney, Diana Morton.

University professor Steven is spending significant time with a beautiful, blond Russian young enough to be his daughter, which sets all of Gina's antennae quivering. But what is supposed to be a simple case of philandering soon turns sinister when the nosy neighbor of the young Russian girl is murdered, and Steven and the young woman are nowhere to be found.

Add in a ransom note for Steven's return, a bloody attack on Gina's associate Zachary when he asks questions about the Russian girl, and the newest addition to the firm—a Boston Terrier that used to belong to the murder victim—and the newly licensed PI has her hands full.

Can Gina find Steven, avenge Zachary, and discover a killer before it's case closed… for good?

STALKING STEVEN
Fidelity Investigations Case 2

This is a work of fiction. Names, characters, places and incidents either are the product of the author's imagination or are used fictitiously, and any resemblance to actual persons, living or dead, business establishments, events or locales is entirely coincidental.

ISBN: 9781942939122

Magpie Ink

Chapter One

I was minding my own business, sitting in my incognito black SUV, innocently parked on a quiet street in what's called 'an established neighborhood,' when a sudden rap on the window made me jump in my seat. My heart leapt up onto my tongue and kept banging there, and it took some effort to get it back down where it belonged.

When I turned in the direction of the rapper, I was faced with a badge and an ID-card, held against the window.

The badge was shiny, and had *Metropolitan Nashville Police Department* stamped on it.

The ID card next to it was almost equally shiny. The picture showed a man in his early thirties, with black hair and the frozen expression people have in official photos. Although he looked considerably less handsome in the picture than I knew him to be in life, I didn't need to check the name on the card to recognize him.

I powered down my window, as the badge and ID disappeared into the pocket of a very nice suit. Armani. "Detective," I said politely. "Long time, no see."

"Three weeks," Jaime Mendoza answered, putting an arm on the top of my car and leaning down to peer inside. "What are you doing, Mrs. Kelly?"

Eyes the color of melting chocolate took in the interior of my car. Empty back seat—cream colored leather—and a passenger seat with a manila folder, a notebook and pen, a digital camera, and a textbook. The name on the book was *Private Investigating for Dummies*.

"You're kidding me," Mendoza said.

I had known this was coming. Diana Morton—my divorce attorney and current client, and the reason I was sitting here on this quiet street in the middle of the afternoon—had warned me that Mendoza didn't approve of PIs. Something about his ex-wife hiring one, and then marrying him.

The PI, not Mendoza.

I didn't know all the details, and had resisted the temptation to use my newly-acquired skills to figure them out. But I'd been waiting for this. Diana had told me that Mendoza would be unhappy when he heard about my new career.

"No, Detective," I told him. "I'm not kidding. I qualified for my license last week. I'm turning David's office on Music Row into a PI firm. Fidelity Investigations."

His mouth curved at that. "That'll serve him right."

I smiled back. "I think of it as poetic justice."

David, who became my late husband just in time to avoid becoming my ex, had left me for a twenty-five-year-old Salma Hayek lookalike a few months ago, and had managed to get himself killed shortly afterwards. Mendoza had been the homicide detective in charge of the case, which was how we met. I'd been the obvious suspect, and I'll always be grateful to him for digging deeper instead of just slapping handcuffs on me.

"Rachel is helping me run the office," I added. "David's administrative assistant, remember? And Zachary is doing the computer searching and online marketing and such."

"I thought he was waiting to apply to the police academy when he turns twenty-one," Mendoza said.

I nodded. "He still wants to do that. But he figures working for a private investigator will look better on his resume than being the doorman at the Apex."

Mendoza looked doubtful, and considering that the PI in question—me—had had her license for all of six days, maybe he had cause.

"We have our first case," I added. "Diana hired me to stalk... I mean, follow her husband around."

Mendoza arched his brows. "She thinks Steven's cheating?"

"She isn't sure. That's why she wants me to follow him. To find out."

Mendoza nodded.

"So what are you doing here?" I added. "Not that it isn't nice to see you, of course."

That got me a smile, complete with dimples and a corresponding surge of appreciation in my stomach. Mendoza is way too handsome for his own good—or at least too handsome for mine. He's close to a decade younger than me, and even just lusting after him in the privacy of my own mind is questionable. Lusting at all, at forty, might be a no-no.

"A call came in to the 911 hotline," he told me, "about a suspicious vehicle on this street."

"Really?" I looked around. "I've been sitting here for

more than an hour, and I haven't seen anyone suspicious."

Unless he was talking about Steven's car, a nondescript brown sedan that was parked in a driveway a couple houses up from where I was sitting. But it was doing absolutely nothing suspicious that I could see. What Steven was doing inside the house might be another matter, of course, but I hadn't yet dared to leave my own car to investigate. Not in broad daylight.

"Your vehicle," Mendoza said.

My eyes widened. "Someone reported me?"

He nodded, his mouth twitching. I deduced he was working hard to suppress a grin. "Mrs. Grimshaw, up there."

He nodded at the house I was parked outside, a low-slung brick ranch with a big picture window in the front. If I squinted, I could just make out a human figure through the glass.

"She reported me?"

Mendoza nodded. "She called 911 and said a suspicious vehicle had been parked outside her house for more than an hour. Big and black, she said. And I think she may have mentioned the X-files."

"Not really?"

"Probably not," Mendoza admitted. "But she did call 911 and report suspicious activity."

He took a step back to run his gaze along the side of my new-to-me Lexus. "New car?"

"The convertible was too conspicuous."

"That's too bad," Mendoza said.

I shrugged. The SUV was all right. I couldn't drive around with the wind blowing through my hair—not unless I rolled down all the windows and created a sort of whirlwind effect inside the car, which wouldn't do my hair any good—but it was a small price to pay for being inconspicuous. "So what are you doing here? The neighbor called, yes. But you're a homicide detective. Or did they demote you after you got yourself knocked out and stuck in the vault?"

"No," Mendoza said, sounding annoyed, "they didn't demote me. I solved my case, and arrested a murderer and an embezzler. My lieutenant, and the lieutenant in the white collar crime division, are both very happy with me."

"Good for you. So what are you doing here? No one's dead."

"Mrs. Grimshaw used her binoculars to get your license plate number," Mendoza said. "When they put your name into the database, they saw you were flagged as a person of interest in one of my cases. So they tagged me."

"And you volunteered to come out and check on what I was doing?"

He nodded.

"No dead bodies taking up your time today?"

"Not so far." Although his tone intimated that I was in danger of changing that. I deduced I was annoying the detective.

"I'm sorry," I said. "There's nothing going on here. Certainly nothing Mrs. Grimshaw has to worry about. Steven Morton is in that house up there, where the brown sedan is parked. That's his car. As soon as he leaves, I'll be leaving, too."

"It would be better if you left now," Mendoza told

me, "but you're in a public place, and not threatening anyone with your presence, so there isn't much I can do about it if you won't."

No, there wasn't. Although if he really insisted, I'd do as he said. It's always a good idea to stay on friendly terms with the police.

Of course, I'd just park around the corner and wait for Steven to drive by. And then I'd follow Steven home. Or back to the university. Or wherever he was going next.

"Let me give you a piece of advice, though," Mendoza added.

"Sure."

"Next time you're planning to stake out a house for any length of time, give the police a call first. Not 911, just the regular number. Introduce yourself, tell them who you are, give them your license number, and explain what you're doing. That way, if someone like Mrs. Grimshaw calls, they won't have to send anyone out to check."

Good advice. However...

"You didn't have to come out here," I felt compelled to point out. "You knew it was me. And you must have known I wasn't doing anything illegal."

"You had a restraining order filed against you last month," Mendoza reminded me.

"She was my husband's mistress! I had the right to know what she looked like!"

"You didn't have the right to park outside her apartment for hours at a time and stare at her through your binoculars."

"I didn't!" And he knew that, because I'd told him

so before. I inhaled a deep breath through my nose. "You have my phone number. Why didn't you just call?"

Was it possible—*be still, my heart!*—that he had taken the opportunity to drive out to see me?

"I have to go tell Mrs. Grimshaw that she's safe," Mendoza said. And added, as I deflated, "Plus, I wanted to make sure you weren't stalking someone else."

He was joking. At least I think he was. Told myself he was.

"I'm stalking Steven," I said. "Legally. His wife hired me. And I have a license to stalk."

"Good for you," Mendoza said. "I hope you and your license will be very happy together."

He straightened, and glanced up at the house. "I should go see Mrs. Grimshaw now."

"Tell her I'm nice. And harmless."

Mendoza snorted.

I thought about getting huffy, but then I smiled sweetly instead. "Be careful, Detective. Don't let any desperate criminals get the drop on you."

"It was an old lady with a golf trophy!" Mendoza said, referring to the woman who had knocked him cold a few weeks ago. The same woman who had locked him in the vault I mentioned earlier. And she hadn't been all that old. Older than Mendoza, certainly, by a lot of years. Older than me, too, but not by as many.

"Mrs. Grimshaw is probably an old lady, too." Unless she wasn't. Maybe she was a hot divorcée in her thirties with an interest in Hispanic cops.

"Probably." Mendoza gave me a nod. "Stay out of trouble, Mrs. Kelly."

"You too, Detective," I told him, and watched as he

headed up the driveway. He passed the picture window on the way, and the outline moved away and headed in the direction of the front door.

Mendoza stepped up on the stoop and knocked. A second later—someone had definitely been waiting—the door opened. A small black-and-white-and-brown shape darted out of the crack, yapping hysterically, and threw itself at Mendoza's knees.

He staggered. I giggled. And although there was no way he could have heard me—I was a football field's width away, on the other side of the lawn, with my windows up—he scowled in my direction.

The small shape—dog, obviously—kept dancing around his feet. It was moving so fast I couldn't get a good look at it, but eventually it collapsed on the toes of Mendoza's shoes and stuck four stubby legs in the air. He leaned down to scratch its belly.

Must be a girl dog. He has that effect on me, too. All I want to do when I see him, is roll over and beg.

But I digress.

After scratching for a second, Mendoza straightened. The dog stayed where it was, obviously hoping for more, and when no more was forthcoming, it rolled to its feet and trotted inside, bat ears flapping. Mendoza talked to the open door for another minute before walking away. The door closed. Moments later, the figure reappeared in the picture window.

I waited for Mendoza to come back down the driveway and over to my car window before I told him, "You made a new friend!"

He glanced back at the house. "It wasn't me she had the problem with. I'm the good guy. You're the one 'sitting out here in your big, black car, looking suspicious."

"I wasn't talking about Mrs. Grimshaw," I said. "I couldn't see Mrs. Grimshaw. I meant the rat."

"Dog."

I rolled my eyes. "I know it's a dog, Detective. What happened to your sense of humor?"

"I left it at the office," Mendoza told me. "When they called to tell me you were out here, acting suspicious."

He looked up at the sound of a car engine starting up the street. "Here comes Steven."

I looked up, too, away from Mendoza. It was harder than it should have been. He's just so nice to look at. But yes, the brown sedan was backing out of the driveway and onto the street.

I reached for my key. "That's my cue to get out of here."

"Give him a minute," Mendoza said, leaning down to rest his arms in my open window. "You don't want him to make you."

I glanced at the sedan. "I don't want to lose him, either."

"He's either going home or back to work," Mendoza said. "Is this your first time tailing him?"

I nodded.

"Next time, find somewhere else to park. Nobody else is parked on the side of the road here."

No, they weren't. It was the kind of neighborhood where the properties were large and had long driveways. Mrs. Grimshaw, for instance, could easily accommodate ten cars nose to back.

"I can't park on someone else's property!"

"You can if you want to look like you belong," Mendoza said, as Steven rolled by. "Just pick a driveway where everyone's at work, and nobody'll ever know you were there."

I turned my head to watch Steven's progress, and Mendoza added, "Look at me."

"Why?"

"So he can't see your face," Mendoza said, watching the sedan move past on the other side of the car. "With any luck, he'll think we're just two neighbors who happened to meet on the street, and stopped to have a conversation."

Sure. "You're driving a cop car. Government plates and extra antennas."

"Antennae," Mendoza said. "The kind bugs have."

"The kind cop cars have."

He shrugged. "I can't help that. And anyway, why would it matter to him? Infidelity isn't a crime."

Very true. Although it ought to be.

I watched in the rearview mirror as the brown sedan slowed, signaled, and then took a left onto the side street, bound for the nearest interstate. Or so I assumed.

"Is it OK if I leave now?" I asked. "Before he gets away?"

"Sure." Mendoza removed his arms from my window and straightened as I cranked the key over in the ignition. The Lexus purred to life. "Don't drive too fast trying to catch up. I don't wanna have to pull you over for speeding."

"I'm sure you don't." I reached for the window control. "Have a nice day, Detective."

"You too, Mrs. Kelly," Mendoza told me, and took a step back. I made a highly illegal U-turn and sped off down the street, hoping to catch Steven before he got to the highway. When I glanced in the rearview mirror on my way around the corner, Mendoza was still standing in the same spot with his hands on his hips, and I didn't have to see his face to know he was scowling after me.

Chapter Two

My late husband, David Kelly, before he left me for Jackie-with-a-q and then got himself murdered, was one of two partners in a financial firm that had its offices on Music Row in midtown Nashville. David and his business partner Farley started the company a few years before David and I got married, while David was still married to his previous wife Sandra, although when you walk into the lobby, you'd swear that the place has been in business for more than half a century. It was an impression David had gone to great lengths to cultivate, mainly by lining the walls with framed, signed photographs of some of country music's greats, many of whom had died while he and Farley were in diapers. Patsy Cline, Jim Reeves, Hank Williams Senior, Johnny Cash, all smiled—or in Johnny's case, glowered—down from the walls of the lobby. All of them—save Johnny—dead before David had started grade school.

Not one of them had ever been a client of either David's or Farley's.

Rachel looked up from arranging an array of

magazines on the table in the corner. "Gina. How did it go?"

I dropped my purse on the nearest chair and walked over to inspect the magazines. "Tailing someone is harder than I thought. Why do we suddenly subscribe to *Guns & Ammo* and *Shooting Times*?"

"We don't," Rachel said, aligning the corners with razor sharp precision. "Zachary brought them in. They're from his personal collection. He said they'd set the tone for any walk-in clients."

"I guess they would. If any clients happened to walk in."

And I wasn't holding my breath.

Our current case was a favor for a friend. Diana Morton had handled my divorce from David, the one he had died in the middle of, and it was thanks to her that I still owned the house in Hillwood (that I would sell, as soon as the damage from a recent fire was repaired), the luxury penthouse in the Gulch (David's love nest, that I lived in now), the Lexus I had gotten when I traded in my convertible, and the building we were standing in. She'd offered to pay me for stalking Steven, but I was more than happy to do it gratis. It seemed the least I could do, and anyway, once I proved myself, I hoped she'd refer clients my way. A lot of wives, when they first suspect their husbands of straying, are willing to pay to have that suspicion confirmed.

Just look at Jaime Mendoza's ex-wife.

"Any new calls?"

Rachel shook her head. "We've only just started, Gina. It takes time to build a business."

Of course it did. But in the meantime, I had two

employees and no income.

Actually, Rachel wasn't so much employee as partner. And she had a severance packet that she could live on for a couple of months, until we—hopefully—got some money coming in. But Zachary had quit his job at the Apex—the building where David's penthouse was— and he was working for Fidelity Investigations full time. And he had to eat and put gas in his car. Unless we got some actual paying clients through the door in the next couple of weeks, I'd be paying Zachary's salary out of my savings account.

"Is Zach here?"

"He's working on the website," Rachel said, with a glance toward the rear of the building, where the offices were. "Search engine optimization, he said."

Excellent. "I need him to do something for me. Steven left the university and drove to a house in Crieve Hall. He spent almost two hours inside, and then he drove home."

Rachel nodded.

"I want a look at whoever lives there. So I want Zachary to deliver a pizza."

"Pizza?"

"It's a classic ploy. *Private Investigating for Dummies* says so. You knock on the door with a pizza and say you have a delivery. They tell you they didn't order a pizza. You double check the address. They insist they didn't order the pizza. You offer to give them the pizza anyway, since your boss will be angry if you bring it back. They open the door and take the pizza, since nobody turns down a free pizza, and..."

I broke off. "You know, never mind. That's for

process servers. But I bet it would work for us, too."

"Can't hurt to try," Rachel agreed.

"Can't hurt to try what?" Zachary asked. He must have heard us talking, and come in from his own office. Now he was lounging in the doorway, looking from one to the other of us.

He's adorable, in a very young, freckled way. Barely taller than me—I'm five-nine—and as bright-eyed and bushy-tailed as the proverbial squirrel. I think he was as excited about working for a PI firm as I was. Maybe more so, since he didn't have any of the financial worries.

I told him where Steven had gone this afternoon. "We need someone to get a look at who lives there. You're our best bet. You can deliver a pizza."

Nobody would believe that I, at my age, was a pizza delivery person. And Rachel was even older than I was.

Zachary flushed excitedly, from the neck of his blue T-shirt all the way up to the roots of his carroty hair. "You mean I get to go undercover?"

Rachel opened her mouth, probably to tell him not to get carried away, and I got in first.

"Yes! Exactly. You'd go undercover as a pizza delivery person. I'd need you to bribe someone at the pizza place to let you borrow a uniform shirt or hat and one of those lighted signs they put on their roofs. And then I need you to go to the house and see if you can get someone to open the door. Most people will open the door for a free pizza."

Zachary nodded. "I've read the book."

"Then you know what to do."

"Now?"

"Finish up what you were doing first. And give me a chance to go to the bathroom. I've been in the car a long time."

"You're coming, too?" It sounded like he wasn't entirely sure whether he was excited or the opposite about going out in the field with the boss.

"Just in the car," I said. "If you get them to open the door, I want to see what they look like. And try to get a photograph. You can't do that if you're holding the pizza. But you'll be on your own at the door. And inside the pizza parlor."

He nodded. "I'll go shut down the computer."

"I'm going to the bathroom." I headed down the hallway while he went back into his own office.

By the time I came back out to the lobby, Zachary had finished what he had to do, and was waiting for me, twitchy with excitement. Rachel was there, as well, twitchy with worry. "Do you want me to wait until you come back? Just in case?"

"In case of what?" Zachary wanted to know. "We're just delivering a pizza!"

I was less impatient—and less cocksure. "I don't think that's necessary, Rachel. It's almost five anyway. And Zachary's right. Even if somebody in the house is having an affair with Steven Morton, nobody's going to come after Zachary with a shotgun. He's just a kid delivering a pizza."

Rachel nodded, but was clearly not convinced. "Will you call me and tell me that everything went well?"

"Of course," I said. "But I don't expect any trouble."

"Still." Rachel headed out the door. Zachary

followed, and I brought up the rear so I could lock up behind us.

"Which pizza place would you like to work for?" I asked when Rachel had gotten in her car and was pulling out of the parking lot. "Little Caesar's? Papa John's? CiCi's? Domino's?"

"Michelangelo's," Zachary said, maybe in hopes that he'd end up eating the pizza after this was over. When it came to eating, Michelangelo's pizza was far superior to anything else. Twice the price, too, of course, but tasty. "I have a buddy who works there. He'll let me borrow a shirt and hat."

"I'll meet you there." I got into my Lexus. Zachary got into his beat-up Honda and led the way.

At Michelangelo's, I stayed in the car and let him take the lead. I figured he'd appreciate it, and that I'd probably just be in the way while he sweet-talked the girl behind the counter. He came out five minutes later with a pizza, wearing a black shirt with Michelangelo's stitched on the chest, and a black baseball cap, ditto.

"No car light," he told me. "The real drivers need them."

No problem. "The uniform will be enough. Let's take your car."

Mine was five years old and not in perfect shape, but his still looked more like something a pizza delivery guy would drive.

"Sure," Zachary said. "Um... it's sort of messy."

"That's all right. I'm only going to be in it for a few minutes." And I really wasn't old enough that he needed to treat me like his honored grandmother. I was only... well, twice his age. Old enough to be his mother, technically. Although not with David. But still. "And I've seen it before. You drove me back to the Apex three weeks ago, remember?"

"Sure," Zachary said, although he sounded less than sure. "Just don't say I didn't warn you."

I promised I wouldn't, and got into the passenger seat, while he gently placed the pizza box on top of a pile of what might be laundry in the back seat. It looked like every piece of clothing Zachary owned.

He got behind the wheel. "Where's this place we're going to?"

I told him it was in Crieve Hall, and gave him directions for how to get there. Ten minutes later, we took the turn into the driveway on two wheels and came to a shuddering stop. Zachary drove like a twenty-year-old on speed, the perfect camouflage for pretending he was a pizza delivery guy to whom time was money. I was grateful we hadn't mowed down any pedestrians on the way. And while the pizza box had shimmied on top of the mountain of clothes, it hadn't slid down the side.

The street was quiet. Darkness had settled, and there was the flicker of blue screens from inside several of the houses we passed. Windows were lit, and here and there we saw families gathered around dining room tables. At Mrs. Grimshaw's house next door, the living room light was on, and I could see the outline of the small dog at the window, big bat ears quivering.

The house where Steven had spent the afternoon was mostly dark. The outside light above the door was on, but nothing else that I could see.

"Looks empty," Zachary said.

I nodded.

He glanced at me. "Do I get to eat the pizza if they aren't here?"

"Sure." It would adhere directly to my thighs, so I certainly didn't want it. "Check first, though."

"No problem." He adjusted the Michelangelo's hat on his head and opened the car door. The interior light stayed off, for which I was grateful. Better if nobody noticed that the pizza delivery guy had a passenger. Someone might think it strange.

Zachary opened the back door and grabbed the box off the top of the mountain of clothes.

"Good luck," I told him.

He didn't answer—*good boy*—just slammed the car door behind him and bounced up the walk to the front door.

I watched as he knocked and stepped back. And knocked again.

Just as I thought he would give up and come back to the car, the door opened.

Unfortunately, I wasn't able to see much. The door opened on the wrong side. Zachary got an eyeful, but I saw very little. She—I assumed it was a woman—stayed out of sight while Zachary explained his errand, and then offered the pizza box.

She didn't step forward to take it.

Zachary moved closer and tried to make her take it, and got the door slammed in his face for his trouble. The noise made me jump, and Zachary jumped too, backward.

He stayed on the stoop for a moment—in character. I could hear his voice yelling at the closed door. "Can't you just take the damn pizza? Now I'm gonna have to eat it myself. I can't bring it back and tell my boss we got the address wrong. He's gonna take it out of my salary!"

The door didn't reopen, so after a few seconds, Zachary stomped off the stoop and down along the walkway to the car. He opened the back door—"Stay in character," I told him softly—and tossed the pizza inside, angrily. Then he slammed the door, and got behind the wheel, muttering. The car squealed backward down the driveway and burned rubber up the street.

"Slow down," I told him when we were around the corner and out of sight.

He glanced in the rearview mirror. "Nobody following us?"

I did the same. "Doesn't look that way. Did you do something that might make someone follow you?"

"I don't think so," Zachary said, taking off the ball cap and tossing it into the backseat, on top of the pizza box, before running his hand through his hair. "Although she seemed upset."

"Why?"

"No idea." He slowed down for a second to check traffic, before merging. "I guess maybe she didn't want to be disturbed. And she didn't want the pizza."

"I noticed. I guess you get pizza for dinner tonight."

He shot me a look. "I'll pay you for it if you want."

"That's OK," I said. I probably had more money than he did, and anyway, there might come a time soon when I wouldn't be able to keep up with his salary. The pizza might get me brownie points for later. "So tell me about it."

Zachary shrugged. "I knocked. Nobody answered. I knocked again. I was about to leave when She opened the door."

The way he pronounced the word, gave it a distinct capital letter.

"I didn't get a good look at her," I said. "What did she look like?"

"Tall and blond," Zachary said with a dreamy expression. "Like a goddess. Or a swimsuit model."

"The kind of girl a sedate university professor might throw his wife over for?"

"The kind of girl any man in his right mind would throw his wife under a train for," Zachary said. He pulled into a parking space outside Michelangelo's with a squeal of tires, and stopped the car. "She looked like she was maybe twenty-two or -three. And real pretty. If I was her professor and she came on to me, I wouldn't say no."

I nodded. "Tomorrow, maybe you can do some computer research. See if you can find any kind of connection between the house in Crieve Hall and Steven Morton. For all we know he might own it—an investment property—and the girl is a potential tenant." I reached for my door handle, and hesitated. "And if you wanted, you could hang around the campus for a bit. Undercover. Pretend to be a student. See if you see her again."

Zachary nodded.

"Head over there in the morning. Take a look around. See what you can see. And then come into the office in the afternoon. I'll take over the surveillance then."

"Works for me," Zachary said. "You sure you don't want the pizza?"

"I'm positive. But thanks for asking." I pushed the door open and got out. "Give Rachel a call and tell her you're all right. See you tomorrow."

"Take care," Zachary said, and buzzed off.

I walked the few feet to the door of the Lexus, and hesitated. There was nothing to eat at home. And here I was, standing outside a pizza parlor. Artisanal pizza, no less. Hand-tossed, with gourmet toppings. The smell wrapped around me, yeasty and delicious, permeating my clothes and hair, making my mouth water.

I hadn't wanted the lion's share of a pepperoni pizza sitting in my refrigerator, calling my name. Much safer to let Zachary take it with him. He was twenty; he could eat most of a pizza tonight and not be five pounds heavier tomorrow. At forty, those days were past me. But I wouldn't mind a slice of pizza for dinner. Maybe something with vegetables on it, to make me feel more virtuous about the grease and cheese and fat.

Did Michelangelo's sell pizza by the slice, by any chance?

They didn't, as it turned out. But they made individual gourmet pizzas with four slices. That'd only be half the amount of dough and cheese sitting in my fridge, calling my name. I ordered one, with a virtuous amount of mushrooms and red onions, olives and feta, and took it home. And ate it. All of it.

Hey, at least the leftovers wouldn't sit in the fridge and tempt me.

Chapter Three

As penance for the pizza, I did an extra twenty minutes on the elliptical the next morning.

David's building—my building now—had a gym on the first floor, so I had given up my membership to the Green Hills YMCA. I didn't even have to brave the elements to exercise anymore. I could just take the elevator from the 14th floor to the 1st, do my time, and then take the elevator back to the 14th floor and my own shower again.

It was nice and convenient, although it took away any excuse I might have had when I didn't feel like working out.

Since Zachary was covering Steven Morton, there was no point in my going over to the university. Besides, Diana had told me he usually had lectures and appointments in the mornings. And there was nothing at the office I needed to tend to. I decided to drive over to Crieve Hall instead, and scope out the house next door to Mrs. Grimshaw's in daylight.

If the young woman Zachary had met last night was

a student, maybe she wouldn't be home this morning.

Maybe the house would be empty, so I could take a look around.

It isn't a long drive, so it was less than fifteen minutes later that I swung down the street where I'd spent so much time yesterday.

Things looked as quiet now as they had then. This was a solid middle class neighborhood, and most people had probably gone to work and school already. A woman was jogging down the street with a dog, and in a driveway, another was strapping a toddler into a car seat.

As soon as I slowed down in front of the house, I realized why the place had looked dark last night. There were heavy curtains covering every window, even the one in the door. Either these people were vampires, or they really liked their privacy.

There were no cars in the driveway. I thought about getting out and walking around the house, but if the windows were covered, what would be the point? And since Steven wasn't here anyway, pressing my nose to perfect strangers' windows seemed a little out of line.

Tampering with the mail is a federal offense, but I figured no one would really mind if I just took a look. Sure, my heart was knocking a little extra hard against my ribs as I slid out of the car and opened the mailbox... but I did it. And all for nothing. The box was empty.

According to *Private Investigating for Dummies*, you can learn a lot about someone from their trash. Diana surely had Steven's trash covered, since she lived with him. And I wasn't about to break into the university's recyclers to try to get at his office trash. But would it be worth my while to peek into the trash can? If nothing else, I might learn the name of the lady of the house. Or the sister or daughter or whoever Steven had been seeing.

My nose wrinkled involuntarily at the thought of digging through garbage. Toilet paper rolls and used tissues and empty cans and leftover food.

Maybe I could just take the trash bags back to the office and make Zachary dig through them? Wasn't that the kind of thing I was paying him for?

I decided it was.

The trash cans must be behind the house. It wasn't trash day, since nobody's cans had been rolled down to the street. That would have made things much easier. But with the curtains closed anyway, I might be safe in driving up to the parking pad, emptying the trash bags into the trunk of the Lexus, and driving off with them. It would only take a minute.

I did it. My heart was knocking against my ribs, but I scooted the car up the driveway and behind the house, into an open parking area. It was empty. Unless they had cars parked in the garage, the house appeared to be empty, too.

The garage doors were solid, with no windows, so there was no way to look in. And like in the front, all the windows were covered with curtains back here, too.

One tan trash can and one green recycling can were parked by the wall next to the garage door. I opened the recycling can first. It was empty. Most people try to recycle something—cardboard, if nothing else; maybe plastic—but maybe the tenants weren't that environmentally conscious.

I took a step sideways and lifted the lid of the trash can instead, wrinkling my nose against the expected odor. It was October, not July, so it wasn't like the garbage had been cooking in the midsummer heat, but I still expected it to smell.

And it did, but not as badly as I had expected. The reason was obvious once I peered inside. The odor was residual. There was nothing inside the can. No trash, and nothing else, either.

I blinked.

Not recycling is one thing. Not throwing anything away is quite another.

What kind of people don't generate trash?

There was nothing I could do about it, though, so I just drove the Lexus back down the driveway again.

I was passing Mrs. Grimshaw's house when I saw movement out of the corner of my eye, and stepped on the brake the way you do when a squirrel is about to jump in front of the car.

There was no squirrel, but the small, spotted dog was moving through the grass close to the road. I glanced at the house, expecting to see Mrs. Grimshaw on the stoop, watching it, but the front door was closed. I squinted, but didn't see a figure behind the glass in the picture window, either.

Of course, that was Mrs. Grimshaw's business. The dog was on her property, and might even be safe behind an invisible electronic fence.

Nonetheless, I didn't like it being loose so close to the street. The last thing I wanted was for it to dart out suddenly, in pursuit of a squirrel, in front of a car, and get turned into roadkill. Those short legs probably couldn't move very fast.

I pulled into the bottom of Mrs. Grimshaw's driveway, parked the car, and got out. "Hi, sweetheart."

The dog stopped rooting through the grass to look up at me. It had round black eyes set wide apart in a broad face with a flattish snout, two big, black bat ears, and a white blaze down the middle of its nose. Some sort of small bulldog or boxer mix, maybe. Not a pug, but similar.

"What are you doing out here by yourself?" I asked.

It didn't answer, of course. But after a second, it abandoned the ditch and trotted up the grassy yard toward the house. I watched it go. After a few seconds, it stopped to look at me over its shoulder.

Do dogs have shoulders?

I've never had a dog. David didn't want anything that might ruin his expensively decorated house, and before that, it was just my mother and me, before I went off to college. We had enough trouble feeding ourselves. We couldn't afford a dog.

Anyway, they don't have arms, so it doesn't make sense that they'd have shoulders. But they probably don't have two sets of hips, either.

At any rate, the dog looked back at me, clearly expecting me to follow.

"Fine," I said, and headed up the driveway.

Instead of going to the front door, the dog headed for the rear. I turned the back corner in time to see its hind quarters, with a tiny stub of a tail, disappear through a pet flap into the house.

So that explained how the dog had gotten out, and why Mrs. Grimshaw wasn't watching it. For all I knew, it might be doing this every morning.

For all I knew, Mrs. Grimshaw was ninety-five, and much too decrepit to walk her dog. This trip into the front yard might be the animal's daily constitutional.

At any rate, there was clearly no point in knocking on the door and telling her that her dog was loose. Not only was it not loose anymore, but it was obvious that she must know about the dog's coming and going, since presumably she knew about the pet flap that was attached to her house.

I was about to turn around and go back to my car when something struck me.

There were tiny doggie footprints coming out of and going into the house. But it hadn't rained for days. So why were the dog's paws wet?

I moved closer, squinting in the darkness under the carport.

Only to stop short when I realized that the paw prints weren't black, like water. They were red.

"Shit."

I fumbled for my phone with hands that shook. And stopped with it in my hand. Talk about jumping to conclusions.

Maybe Mrs. Grimshaw was an artist and the dog had stepped in red paint.

Or maybe there was a broken can of marinara sauce on the kitchen floor and the dog had walked through it before Mrs. G could shoo it away.

Or hell, maybe it really was blood, but all that had happened was that the dog had stepped on the glass from the broken jar and cut itself.

Even if it was blood, that didn't mean that Mrs.

Grimshaw was lying inside in a pool of it, with her throat cut.

Before I caused an alarm, I should probably endeavor to find out whether there was cause for alarm.

I walked to the back door and knocked. "Mrs. Grimshaw? Can you hear me?"

There was no answer. I cupped my hands over my eyes and peered through the glass in the door.

All I could see was a washer and dryer, and an ironing board. No Mrs. Grimshaw. No blood. The door was locked. The knob rattled in my hand, but it didn't turn and the door didn't budge.

I made my way around the house, peering into the windows I could reach. The first room I came to was a den, paneled in mid-century knotty pine. It was empty, of people and of blood.

Beyond that were a couple of bedrooms, the beds made and pristine. Guest rooms, I assumed. A small window between them, too high for me to reach, was probably a Jack-and-Jill bathroom.

The master bedroom was on the far end of the house, and pristine, also. The bed was sort of halfway made: the pillows stacked on the floor, the comforter smooth, but folded down. Mrs. G had either started to turn it down last night, and stopped before getting into bed, or she had started to make the bed this morning, but had stopped before finishing the job.

There was no sign of her in the bedroom. The light was on in the adjacent master bath, which struck me as a little peculiar when it was bright and sunny outside, but it wasn't necessarily sinister. She might not have been into the bedroom since earlier, and might not realize the light was still on.

In the front of the house was a dining room, with what looked like a carved mahogany dining room set, and then the front door and picture window.

I went up on the stoop and knocked again. There were three small windows in the top of the door, too high for me to see in.

There was no answer, but the dog started barking. A second later, it threw itself at the panes in the picture window, yipping hysterically.

I left the stoop and waded through the flower bed over to the window, pushing my way through prickly holly bushes and taking care not to step on flowering mums. The dog went crazy, hopping stiff-legged inside the window. Funny, when it hadn't barked at me outside earlier.

Must be a protective thing. It was inside the house now, and it had to protect its territory.

The picture window was huge. Almost floor to ceiling. I could see the hardwoods a foot below the window inside, and when I peered up, the ceiling wasn't very high above the window frame, either.

There was some very nice morning light in Mrs. Grimshaw's formal living room.

Enough light to let me see, clearly, hundreds of tiny red paw prints meandering back and forth in front of the window.

I cupped my hands over my eyes again and peered inside.

Flowered chintz furniture, dark coffee table with a glass top. Small TV on a stand against the wall. Small, rabid dog jumping up and down, bat ears flapping.

And a pair of feet, toes pointing at the ceiling. One wore a fuzzy, pink slipper; the other nothing. Another fuzzy pink slipper lay a foot or two away. The rest of the body—Mrs. Grimshaw's, I assumed—was out of sight behind an upholstered wingback chair.

I stepped out of the flowerbed and away from the window, fumbling for my phone.

I gave the 911 operator my name and Mrs. Grimshaw's address, and explained that I could see her through the window, lying on the floor, and that there was a lot of bloody paw prints on the floor, but I couldn't see anything else.

"Have you gone inside the house?" the operator inquired.

I said I hadn't. "The back door was locked. I haven't tried the front door. I can do it now."

"No," the operator said. "Wait for the police."

"But what if she's still alive? What if there's something I can do, and I'm just standing here?"

"There's an ambulance on the way," the operator told me. "Stay on the line with me until it gets there."

I could already hear the sirens in the distance. The nearest fire station must be nearby. "I can't," I told her. "I have to call someone. Sorry."

I hung up. And then I called Mendoza.

The phone rang twice, and then he came on. "Mrs. Kelly." It was impossible to say whether he was happy, exasperated, or something else, to hear from me.

"You have to come out here," I told him, through chattering teeth. "Something's happened to Mrs. Grimshaw."

"Who?"

"The lady who called you yesterday. About the suspicious car. The one with the little dog. Something's wrong."

Immediately he was all business. "What?"

"There's blood on the floor. The dog stepped in it. It was outside in the street. When I followed it back up to the house, I saw bloody paw prints. So I started looking through the windows. She's in the living room. On the floor. On her back. And there are bloody paw prints all over the room."

"Are you there now?" Mendoza asked.

I nodded. "Uh-huh."

"Have you called 911?"

"Uh-huh. I can hear them."

"Stay there," Mendoza said. "Don't touch anything. I'm on my way."

He hung up before I had a chance to tell him that I had no plans of touching anything whatsoever.

While I waited, I got back into my car, still parked at the bottom of the driveway, and drove it up and around the corner to the carport. No sense in blocking access for the ambulance—or for Mendoza, once he arrived. And as he'd mentioned yesterday, cars parked on the street were conspicuous around here. The neighbors would notice the ruckus once the ambulance and police cars arrived, assuming there was anyone home on the street to notice, but there was no sense in attracting their attention sooner.

And then I sat there and waited for someone to arrive. It was tempting to call someone—like Rachel—to tell her what was going on, and to whimper against her shoulder long distance, but Mendoza was coming—with better shoulders—and besides, I didn't know that Mrs. Grimshaw was actually dead. Blubbering might be premature. So I just sat there and concentrated on breathing deeply while I listened to the sirens coming closer.

It wasn't a long wait. Two minutes, maybe three, and then a vehicle came screaming up the driveway and stopped with a squeal of brakes. I got out of my car and peeked around the corner. It was the ambulance, having come to a quivering stop by the front walkway. Two paramedics jumped out. I went to greet them.

Mendoza zoomed into the driveway about five minutes later, in the same gray sedan he'd been driving yesterday. The same gray sedan he'd been driving every time I'd seen him. I figured he must have a personal vehicle, and in my spare time I amused myself by trying to imagine what it might be—pickup truck? Jeep Wrangler? Maserati?—but I had no real expectation that I'd ever find out. We didn't have a personal relationship. I only saw the detective when he was on duty.

By that point, the ambulance personnel had determined that the front door was open, or rather unlocked. They had gone inside and had examined Mrs. Grimshaw, and determined that life was extinct—or in layman's terms, that Mrs. G was dead. I didn't get a good look at her—nor did I want one—but her chest was a bloody mess. I assumed she'd been shot, or maybe stabbed. It wasn't natural causes; I could tell that much.

And then Mendoza swept through the door and looked around. "This the way she was when you found her?"

The paramedics nodded. He glanced at me. I

nodded too. "This is where she was lying when I looked through the window."

Mendoza nodded. "You can go," he told the paramedics. "Nothing you can do here. I'll call the ME's office and get them out here to remove the body. Thanks for your help."

They gathered up their equipment and filed out. Mendoza turned to me. "You can go, too."

"Do I have to?"

"This is a crime scene. I can't let you wander around and compromise evidence."

"That's ridiculous," I told him. "The crime scene is the area between the door and where the body is. The whole rest of the house is available."

Including the patch of floor where I was standing, out of the direct line between the door and the body.

His brows arched. They're nice brows, thick and dark and elegantly shaped. "Your PI classes tell you that?"

"No," I said, annoyed. "Logic told me that. The door was unlocked. She didn't strike me as the type to be careless, so I don't think she would have left it that way." Not the woman who had called the cops because of a suspicious car on her street yesterday. "She's lying on the floor in front of the door. It looks like she was shot. My guess is, someone knocked on the door. Probably last night sometime. Late. After dark. She opened it, so it might have been someone she knew. Whoever was outside shot her, and then pulled the door shut so it wouldn't look suspicious. Then he—or she—walked away."

Mendoza's lips had started quirking when I was

about halfway through my reasoning. "Not bad for your first time. But not necessarily accurate. We don't know why someone wanted Mrs. Grimshaw dead. Whoever shot her might have been looking for something. If so, he—or she—might have come inside after the shooting, to look around. The entire house could be a crime scene."

I hadn't thought of that. Now I did, and shuddered at the idea that someone had shot this poor old lady, and then, while she was lying on the floor dead or dying, had callously stepped over the body to ransack the house.

"Murder isn't pretty," Mendoza told me. "Please, Mrs. Kelly. Go home and let me do my job. And take this—" He bent and scooped up the small dog with a hand under its belly, "with you."

He dropped it into my arms. It almost ended up on the floor before I got a good grip on it. And I'm sure it was leaving nasty, red paw prints all over my nice silk blouse as it scrabbled for purchase. "I can't take it!"

"She can't stay here alone," Mendoza pointed out. "And she can't go with the body."

I shifted the small, quivering body to a better hold. "Why don't you take it?"

"It's a she. Her name is Edwina. And my kid's allergic."

Mendoza had a son. Five years old. Elias. All of which I knew because Mendoza had told me, not because I'd ever met Elias. He lived with his mother and the PI, but sometimes he stayed with Mendoza. If Elias was allergic to dogs, then no, Edwina couldn't go home with Mendoza. She'd probably prefer it—she was eying him with adoration, even from my arms—but she'd have to put up with me. At least until I could figure something else out. I wasn't even sure the Apex allowed pets.

"Maybe Rachel wants a dog. Or Zachary." Although if Zachary wanted a dog, it would probably be something bigger than this. Rachel might enjoy her, though.

"That's the spirit," Mendoza said. "Now take her away and let me work."

I stayed where I was. "Will you call me later and tell me what you find out? I feel…" I hesitated, looking for the right word. Not responsible, because what had happened to Mrs. Grimshaw had nothing to do with me, but… something.

"I'll do my best," Mendoza said. "Please, Mrs. Kelly. The longer you stand there, the longer before I can concentrate on figuring out what happened here."

I withdrew. With a final, "Call me." Mendoza didn't respond.

I put the dog in the passenger seat and walked around the car to the driver's side. By the time I had backed down the driveway and was headed up the street, the dog was standing on my thighs with her nose against the window. I had one arm snaked over her back, and the other in front of her chest, with her head on top of my arm. It made turning the steering wheel difficult.

"This isn't going to work," I told her.

She ignored me, in favor of watching the world go by. Her nose was making a damp spot on the window.

I dumped her back in the passenger seat. She gave me a wounded look before turning to the other window.

"Oh, dammit!"

Those bloody little paws were leaving marks on my cream leather seat. And worse, they had marked my linen slacks, too. Blood's impossible to get out, unless you do it right away.

"That does it," I told the dog. "We're going home. You can walk around in the bathtub while I soak my shirt."

She didn't answer, of course. Just kept looking out the window. Although I swear she was grinning.

Chapter Four

When David left me for Jacquie —actually, before David left me for Jacquie—he bought himself a love nest on the top floor of the Apex, one of the new high-rise condo buildings in the Gulch, a neighborhood on the south end of downtown. I stayed on in the house in Hillwood, even after David died. Until someone set fire to the family room, directly below the master bedroom, and I had to jump out a second story window to save myself. I moved into the Apex after that. It was available, and felt safe, and the house needed repair before I could move back into it.

At this point, I thought I might not want to move back in. I had spent eighteen years in Hillwood, as David's trophy wife. Now that I was single again, I just wanted to put my marriage behind me. What better way than to sell the house we'd shared and take over possession of David's bachelor pad?

When I sailed through the front doors with Edwina under my arm, short legs scrabbling for purchase on my hip, there was a new guy behind the desk in the lobby, where Zachary used to sit. He didn't say a word to me. I'm not sure he even saw the dog. All he did was glance up, confirm that I was someone whose face he knew, nod, and go back to whatever he was reading behind the desk. *Penthouse, Marvel Comics*, or the *National Enquirer*.

I made my way through the lobby and up in the elevator. The first thing I did was fill the big tub with two inches of water and drop the dog in. The sides were too tall for her to climb back out—or so I hoped—and she could waddle around in the shallow water and clean the blood from her paws.

While she did that, I headed into the bedroom and stripped out of my clothes, which also had to soak. By the time I had changed into new clothes, and left the old ones in the utility sink in the laundry room, the dog had managed to roll in the water and get wet everywhere. I had to lift her out and wrap her in a towel—which she didn't like; she barked at me—and then dry her with the hair dryer, which she liked less. By the time she was mostly dry, I was wet again, and had to change clothes for the second time that day. By now I had caught on to the fact that life with a dog was likely to keep me in a perpetual state of disarray, so I compromised by putting on a pair of jeans and a colorful tunic. Hopefully there was nothing too bad the dog could do to it in the next few hours.

That done, Edwina and I headed back downstairs to the garage. I put her in the backseat—which lasted about two minutes before she figured out how to jump over the console to the front—and we drove to the office. It didn't take more than five minutes, but by the time we got there, I was already exhausted from keeping the dog off my lap and telling her not to drool on the windows.

I carried her inside and put her on the sofa in the lobby. "Do you know anything about dogs?"

"Not much," Rachel said, eyeing Edwina. "I'm really more of a cat person."

Me, too. Or if I had to choose, I'd probably say I liked cats better than dogs. Not that I'd had much experience with either. But dogs seemed like a lot of work. "What about Zachary?"

"He isn't here," Rachel said.

I had noticed the absence of his car in the lot. "I told him to go check out the university this morning. See if he could find the girl from yesterday and get an identity on her. He should be back soon." I'd told him I'd relieve him in the afternoon.

Unless he'd found the girl and had struck up a conversation with her. Then he might not be back until dinnertime.

"Where did the dog come from?" Rachel asked. Edwina had jumped down from the couch and was investigating the corners of the office.

"Her name is Edwina. Mendoza gave her to me."

Rachel got a funny look on her face. "Not what I'd call a romantic gift."

Me, either. However—

I shook my head. "Not a gift. And not romantic. We're dog-sitting the witness to a murder. Edwina's owner was shot last night. Mrs. Grimshaw. In the house next door to Steven Morton's mistress. Or whatever she is."

Rachel arched her brows. "That's interesting."

Was it? "How so?"

"I'm not sure," Rachel admitted, "but it seems coincidental, doesn't it? Yesterday you followed Steven over there, and last night the woman next door was shot?"

Maybe so. But— "I'm sure a coincidence is all it is. Even if Steven is having an affair with the girl, why would either of them kill Mrs. Grimshaw because of it?"

"She called the police," Rachel said.

"On me. It had nothing to do with them."

"They wouldn't know that," Rachel pointed out. "There you were, looking very official in your black SUV. Official enough that Mrs. Grimshaw calls the police to report you. And here's Mendoza, in his cop car. He talks to you, and he talks to Mrs. Grimshaw, and then Steven leaves and you follow him."

I nodded. "But why would they worry about any of it? Sleeping around isn't a crime. Mrs. Grimshaw can call anyone she wants. If all they're doing is cheating on Diana, there's nothing I or anyone else can do about it."

"Steven might not think about it that way," Rachel said. "He might have recognized you and figured you were spying on him for Mrs. Morton."

"But if so, wouldn't he shoot me and not Mrs. Grimshaw?"

Unpleasant idea. It gave me a little frisson of fear down the back of my spine. It wasn't that long ago that I'd found myself facing the business end of a pistol. I had no desire to repeat the experience.

Rachel shrugged. "Maybe he didn't recognize you. Maybe he recognized Detective Mendoza and thought the detective would tell Diana."

"Same question," I said. "Why shoot Mrs. Grimshaw

and not Mendoza?"

"Maybe he's planning to shoot Mendoza. Maybe Mrs. Grimshaw was just the beginning."

It had a crazy, overblown sort of logic. "Maybe I should call Mendoza," I said.

Rachel nodded. "I think you should."

"I'll go do that right now. Keep an eye on—" I looked around. "Where is she?"

"She went that way," Rachel said, jerking her thumb down the hallway toward the offices.

"And you didn't think to mention it?"

I scurried down the hallway after the dog.

She wasn't in my office. She wasn't in the spare room, where Farley and David had kept their files. She wasn't in the bathroom or the kitchen. I finally tracked her down in Zachary's office. At first I didn't think she was there, either, but then I heard a snuffling, wet sort of noise, and followed it to find her hidden in the space under Zachary's desk, flat nose buried in a pizza box. The wet, snuffling noise was the sound of her licking at the grease and cheese stuck to the bottom of the box.

It looked like the Michelangelo's box from last night. Maybe Zachary had brought in the leftovers to have for lunch. Hopefully the dog hadn't eaten them.

I disposed of the box in the kitchen, and took the dog into my office, where I dropped her on the sofa. "Take a nap."

She gave me a look.

"Or you can just stay there. As long as you're quiet and don't get into any trouble."

Fat chance, her expression said. She was kind of cute, in an annoyingly pop-eyed, flat-nosed way. Or she would be, if I were in the market for a dog. As it was, she would probably end up going to Mrs. Grimshaw's next of kin. She must have been married at some point—or she'd be Miss or Ms. Grimshaw, not Mrs.—so there might be a child or children who'd inherit everything, including the dog.

Maybe the murder had nothing at all to do with Steven and the girl next door. Maybe Mrs. Grimshaw was obscenely wealthy, or even moderately wealthy, and her next of kin had killed her for the inheritance. It happens.

Nonetheless, I called Mendoza. Just in case it wasn't the next of kin and someone had it in for him.

Or me.

The phone rang a couple of times, and then he answered. "Mrs. Kelly."

He obviously had my name and number programmed in his cell phone. I wondered whether I should feel encouraged by that, or whether he did it for all his suspects. I wasn't a suspect this time—at least I couldn't think of a reason why I would be—but I had been one not too long ago.

"Detective," I said. "I just wanted to update you." And hopefully get an update in return. "The dog is clean. She's here at the office with me. I've had to change my clothes twice."

I could hear amusement in his voice. "Am I supposed to feel sorry for you?"

"She's a pain in my butt. How long do I have to keep her?"

"Not sure," Mendoza said. "I haven't done anything about notifying next of kin yet. I'm not sure who next of kin is. But by the end of the day I should know whether one of Mrs. Grimshaw's relatives will be willing to take the dog or whether it'll have to go to the pound."

The pound? I glanced across the room at the little thing, sniffing the crevices of the sofa, snuffling in the folds of leather. "I don't feel great about that."

"It's life," Mendoza said. "If the relatives don't want the dog, and we can't find someone else willing to take it, it'll end up at the pound. Someone might see it and adopt it."

And someone might not. It wasn't a puppy. I have very little experience with or knowledge of dogs, but I could tell it was fully grown. It even had a few gray hairs among the black and white on the snout and batty ears. Most people don't like to adopt older dogs.

"I'll keep it for now. Her. Although I'm not sure I can bring myself to call it Edwina."

"Call it anything you want," Mendoza said. "Who's going to know the difference?"

The dog might. But before I could say so, I heard a sound in the background, on his end of the phone, not mine, and then he came back. "I have to go."

"Just one more thing."

"The ME just showed up to take the body. I don't have time for chit-chat."

I could understand that. "I just wanted to tell you to be careful. Just in case Mrs. Grimshaw was shot because of what happened yesterday."

"What happened yesterday?" Mendoza said.

"She called you. And reported me."

"Unless you shot her," Mendoza said, "I doubt it applies. Goodbye, Mrs. Kelly."

He hung up without giving me the chance to explain what Rachel had said. I resisted the temptation to stick my tongue out at the phone, and merely put it down on the desk. Over on the sofa, the dog turned in a circle, twice, and settled down in the corner of the pillows with her snout on her back legs and an almost human-sounding sigh.

I decided then and there that she would go to the pound over my dead body. If Mrs. Grimshaw's relatives didn't want her, I'd figure something else out.

Out front, the door opened and closed. "Morning, Rachel," Zachary's voice said.

"It's afternoon," Rachel answered. "Good of you to join us."

"Gina said to spend the morning at the university." His voice got louder as he passed her and came down the hallway toward the offices. A second later, his head appeared around the door jamb to my office. "Morning, boss."

"Afternoon," I said. Over on the sofa, the dog uncoiled enough to lift its head and inspect Zachary. He must have passed, because there was no growling. However, Edwina didn't fall in instant love the way she had with Mendoza, either.

Zachary looked at her. "We have a dog?"

"Temporarily." I told him what had happened. "Mendoza said if one of Mrs. Grimshaw's relatives doesn't want her, she'll end up at the pound."

"Or she can stay here," Zachary said, "and guard the place."

I guess she could. Not that she looked very guard-like. Or sounded it, either.

I tried to imagine myself saying, "Down, Edwina!" and failed.

"I think she may have eaten your lunch," I told Zachary. "I found her in your office earlier with her nose in a pizza box. If there was anything left in it, it's probably in her stomach by now."

"Oh." He flushed. "That's all right. But we should probably get her some real dog food. I don't think pizza is good for her."

Probably not. "I should drive back to Mrs. Grimshaw's house and see what's there. There must be a leash and some food, at least." Unless Mrs. Grimshaw hadn't actually walked her dog, but had merely let it wander in the yard to do its business and get exercise. But even so, she had to have fed it. "Mendoza dumped her on me so fast I didn't think to ask for anything she might need."

"I'll watch her while you go," Zachary said. "I have a report to write. And that internet search to do."

"What happened at the university this morning?"

He shook his head. "Nothing. I walked around for a couple of hours, and looked for the girl. I didn't see her. Eventually, I decided to go look for Steven Morton, but he wasn't in his office. So I came back here."

"He wasn't at work today?"

Normally that wouldn't strike me as strange at all. I wouldn't think anything of it. Maybe he didn't have any classes this morning. Or any appointments. Maybe he'd taken the opportunity to sleep in and make love to his wife.

Or maybe he'd left home early and gone to make love to his mistress instead.

"He wasn't at work when I looked for him," Zachary said.

Except when I'd been there earlier, the house had looked empty. And then there was the murder next door.

Yes, it was definitely worth mentioning that Steven wasn't where he was supposed to be this morning.

"I need to talk to Mendoza," I said, pushing my chair back.

Zachary nodded. "We'll hold down the fort. Does the dog need to go out?"

Edwina had decided he was no threat and had gone back to sleep, curled into a circle. She snored gently. Although when she heard the word 'out,' she raised her head to look at him.

"It's probably best to wait until we have a leash to put her on," I said. "I'd hate to have her run away. She isn't familiar with this neighborhood, and we don't have a fenced yard."

Zachary nodded. "If she gets desperate, I'll see about finding a piece of string I can tie to her collar."

That would work. I grabbed my purse from the hook by the door. "I'll be back as soon as I can."

"We'll be fine," Zachary said and glanced at the dog. "Won't we?"

Edwina lowered her head and rested her snout on her legs.

I walked out.

Like yesterday, it was a short drive from Music Row to Crieve Hall. Fifteen minutes later, I pulled to a stop outside Mrs. Grimshaw's house.

Or more accurately, I pulled into the driveway next door, where Steven's car had been parked yesterday, because Mrs. Grimshaw's driveway was full.

The paramedics had taken their ambulance and left. As Mendoza had told them, there was nothing they could do for Mrs. G. But his gray sedan was still there. So was a white crime scene van from the Metropolitan Nashville Police Department. Behind it, a black-and-white squad car. And the most recent arrival, the hearse from the morgue. Just before it, wedged between the hearse and the squad car, a TV van from Channel Six, bristling with antennae, even more so than Mendoza's car. A young anchor woman, blond and gorgeous in a power-red suit, was touching up her lipstick in the side mirror of the van, while a camera man was hauling a TV camera up on his shoulder.

As the front door opened and the staff from the ME's office started wheeling the gurney out, they both straightened, and the young woman turned to the camera, teeth on display. She had a lot of them, and they were blindingly white. I could see her mouth start to move, although I was too far away to hear what she said.

And then Mendoza bounded out of the house and across the grass, waving the morgue people to a stop on his way past.

I couldn't hear what he said either, but I didn't have to. He was clearly unhappy about the camera being there. He expostulated with the camera operator, who kept filming until Mendoza got right in his face—or in the camera lens—and presumably threatened him with dire consequences if he didn't cease and desist immediately.

The camera was lowered, and Mendoza waved to the morgue crew to continue. They came out of the house with a gurney topped by a black bag, and navigated the couple of steps down to ground level carefully. Once they were on the walkway, they put the gurney down and started wheeling it toward the morgue van.

The news anchor, meanwhile, was talking to Mendoza. Flirting, unless my eyes deceived me. It was a little difficult to see from this distance, but she was smiling, and flipping her hair, and putting her hand on his arm. It might just have been a typically feminine tactic to get her way, but I did get the impression that she enjoyed it.

It might even have worked. If she was trying to get permission to turn the camera back on, she got it. Not until the morgue van had tucked its sad burden out of sight, but once it started backing down the driveway and onto the street, he must have told her she could go back to filming, because the camera came back up. Mendoza must have even agreed to take a couple of questions, because he stayed there, in front of the camera, for a couple of minutes, and made nice. I could see his smile flash, and the young woman in red practically had to wipe drool off her chin.

Then he gave her a final, dazzling smile before walking back up the driveway and into the house. The young lady spent another minute finishing up the broadcast, and then she and the camera man piled into the news van and reversed out of the driveway after the van from the morgue. I waited until they, too, had disappeared up the street before I made my way across

Mrs. Grimshaw's lawn to the front door.

Chapter Five

Mendoza did not look happy to see me, although he was polite as he blocked the door into the house. "Mrs. Kelly."

"Detective," I said, peering over his shoulder. I'm as tall as he is in heels. When I'm wearing heels, I'm as tall as Mendoza is without, I mean.

He shifted to block my view. "What can I do for you?"

I turned my attention from what was behind him to his face. Between you and me, it was no hardship. I was interested in what was going on inside the house, but Mendoza is just so pretty it's no problem to look at him. "Two things. I need the dog's food and leash. Unless you want me to go out and buy food and a leash for her. But I figure there is probably already some of that here, and it makes more sense that I just pick it up."

Mendoza sighed. "That's what you're doing here?"

"That, and I wanted to tell you something." I peered over his other shoulder.

He shifted again. "What's that?"

I subsided. "Zachary just came back to the office. I sent him to the university this morning, to see if he could find the girl from next door."

Mendoza nodded.

"She wasn't there. Or if she was, he didn't see her."

"OK," Mendoza said. "So maybe she's not a student."

"Maybe not. But Zachary said Steven wasn't there either."

"Maybe he took the morning off."

Maybe he had. "I'm not saying there's anything suspicious about it. He could be home with his wife." Or next door with this girl. Although if he was, his car wasn't parked in the driveway today. "It just occurred to me that one unusual incident might be connected to another."

"First," Mendoza said, "we don't know that Steven's absence is unusual. Maybe he always comes in late on Wednesdays."

Maybe.

"And secondly, even if it is unusual for Steven to miss work, we don't know that it has anything to do with Mrs. Grimshaw's murder. Which happened last night between ten and midnight, by the way. Do you know where Steven was then?"

I shook my head. I had no idea. "I assumed home with his wife."

"Have you spoken to Diana?"

I said I hadn't.

"Call her," Mendoza said.

"Why do I have to call her? It's your murder case."

"We don't know that Steven's involved in my

murder case," Mendoza told me. "It's your cheating husband case. And you're working for Diana. She won't think anything of it if you call to see whether Steven's home. If I call, she'll wonder why."

He had a point. I pulled out my phone and dialed.

It was the middle of the workday, and Diana was a busy divorce attorney. I thought it was possible that she was talking to a client, or having lunch with a colleague. Part of me wished she wouldn't answer the phone, so I wouldn't have to tell her what Steven had been doing yesterday. You'll notice I hadn't written up a report or filled in my client yet. There was a reason for that. Diana wasn't just a client. She was a friend. And I didn't want to give her bad news.

She was available to talk, though. The phone rang once, then twice, and then her voice came on. "Gina."

"Diana," I said. And didn't know what else to say. I could hear the tension in her voice, and I didn't know what to do about it.

"He's cheating, isn't he?"

"I don't know," I said honestly. "I followed him from the university yesterday afternoon. He drove to a house in Crieve Hall. Do you know where that is?"

"Neighborhood south of Nashville," Diana said. "Lots of ranch houses."

"Do you know anyone who lives there?"

"I can't think of anyone. What was he doing there?"

"He went inside a house," I said. "Spent more than an hour there. Then he left and drove back to the university."

"Who lives there?"

"We're trying to figure that out," I said. "Zachary

knocked on the door last night, with a pizza, and said the girl who opened the door was around twenty-two or twenty-three, blond and very pretty."

Diana moaned softly.

"But that was later. There could be other people living in the house, as well."

Diana didn't answer. Mendoza waved at me to go on.

"The reason I'm calling," I said, turning my back on him, "is that I can't find Steven this morning. Zachary went to the university to see if he could track down the blonde. We thought maybe she was one of Steven's students. But he didn't see her. He also said that Steven wasn't around."

I waited for her to tell me that Steven was home, in bed, with a bucket next to him.

She didn't. "That's strange. I talked to him this morning. He didn't say anything about not going to work."

If his absence from the university had anything to do with the girl, then he probably wouldn't mention it to his wife. But now at least we knew he really wasn't where he was supposed to be. "Maybe you could call him? Try to figure out where he is, so I can pick up his trail?"

"I can do that," Diana said. "I'll call you back."

She was gone before I even had the chance to say goodbye, let alone mention anything about Mrs. Grimshaw's murder. I turned back to Mendoza. "She doesn't know where he is. She's going to call him and get back to me."

Mendoza nodded.

"So Mrs. Grimshaw was shot between ten and midnight last night?"

"That's the ME's preliminary determination. It could change upon further examination, but it's probably pretty close."

"I was home by then," I said. "I have no idea what happened."

"I didn't think you would," Mendoza told me.

"Have you spoken to the neighbors?" I glanced at the house next door, where Steven had been yesterday.

"There are two uniformed officers going door to door asking if anyone saw or heard anything last night."

"And did anyone see or hear anything?"

"Not so far," Mendoza said.

"Was anyone home next door?"

He didn't answer, and I added, "I didn't tell you this, but this morning, before I saw the dog and discovered Mrs. Grimshaw, I checked the trash cans outside the house next door."

Mendoza's lips twitched. It was the first time they'd done that during this conversation. "The trash cans?"

"*Private Investigating for Dummies* says you can learn a lot about someone from their trash."

The twitch became more pronounced. Practically a grin. "What did you learn?"

"That they don't care about the environment."

He looked blank, and I added, "They don't recycle. And apparently they don't generate trash, either. All the cans were empty."

"That's interesting," Mendoza said.

I had thought it was. Until I forgot all about it in the horror of discovering that Mrs. Grimshaw was dead.

"Come on," I told Mendoza. "I'll show you."

I'm sure he was capable of walking across the lawn to the trash cans on his own, to look for himself, but he didn't say so. Instead he just followed as I led the way across the grass to the next driveway and around the house. "There." I pointed to the trash can and recycling bin lined up under the carport. "Empty. Just like I told you."

Mendoza checked for himself, wrinkling his nose at the residual stench, just as I had. I did my best not to admire his rear view, but I didn't succeed very well.

Once he had satisfied his curiosity and turned back to me, I gestured to the house. "All the curtains are drawn. I'm sure you noticed. There's no way to look inside."

Mendoza nodded.

"If Mrs. Grimshaw had been living here instead of next door, I wouldn't have seen her through the window. She could have been lying there for days before anyone noticed she was dead."

Mendoza gave me a look. He was clearly following the train of my thoughts. "Do you have any reason to suspect that the inhabitant of this house has been shot?"

"Not a reason," I admitted, "per se. But if you consider that the inhabitant of the house next door was shot, and the inhabitant of this one isn't answering the door, I think it bears looking into."

Mendoza contemplated me for a second. "You just want a look inside."

I did. But— "I'm still right."

"You might be," Mendoza said. "It's a long shot. But under the circumstances, I can make a case for opening the door and taking a look."

"Great." I refrained from rubbing my hands together gleefully.

He eyed me. "I said *I* can take a look. Not you."

"That's mean," I said.

His lips twitched. "Just stay back."

I made a face, but I stayed out of the way as he pulled a key chain out of his pocket and chose what I assumed was a universal key. The first thing he did, was knock on the back door. "Hello? Anybody home?"

Nobody answered, of course. So Mendoza called out again. "This is the police. If you're in there, please answer the door."

Nobody answered the door. Mendoza inserted the key in the lock and twisted it. "Metro Nashville PD," he called out again as he pushed it open with one hand and dropped the keys into his pocket with the other. "I'm coming in."

He pushed the suit jacket aside to pull a gun from the holster at his hip. My breath caught in my throat. He looks like a matinee idol to begin with, with that gorgeous face and sleek, black hair. Add in the gun and the heroic expression, and it was like watching James Bond in action, right in front of me.

Mendoza slipped through the door. I followed, all the way up to the threshold, and stuck my head into the room.

The back door opened into a kitchen, circa 1950s vintage. Original to the house. Wood, slab-front cabinets, Formica counters with an aluminum edge, and fake brick vinyl on the floor.

There was no sign of occupancy. No dirty dishes in

the sink or on the counter, no trash in the can I spied sitting next to the plain, white fridge.

Mendoza had disappeared through the doorway to the right and couldn't see me. I slithered through the open kitchen door and into the house.

When he came back three minutes later, he found me standing in the middle of the kitchen floor. "I didn't go beyond this point," I told him. "I know you said to stay outside, so I only went as far as the kitchen."

He didn't answer, just holstered the pistol.

"I didn't hear you scream, or shoot anyone, so I guess the place is empty?"

"You could say that," Mendoza said. "Come and take a look."

"Really?" I stuck my hands in my pockets. "Thank you. And don't worry, I won't touch anything."

"I'm not worried," Mendoza said and led the way through the door into the dining room.

I could see why. There was nothing to touch. As we moved from room to empty room, our footsteps echoed hollowly.

"I don't understand," I said when we were back in the kitchen. "There's nothing here."

No furniture, no carpets, no pictures on the walls. No beds and no bedding. When I yanked open one of the kitchen cabinets, there were no dishes or glasses. No food in the pantry.

"No one lives here," Mendoza said.

"I can see that. Unless... You don't think there's any chance that they moved out overnight, do you?"

"Someone would have noticed that," Mendoza said.

"Maybe not. Nobody noticed the neighbor getting

shot."

"It probably took all of three minutes to shoot Mrs. Grimshaw, including the time it took the shooter to walk from his car to the house and back. But you don't empty a whole house of furniture in a couple of minutes. If someone pulled a moving van into the driveway and started carrying out furniture, someone would have noticed. And they couldn't have done it in the dark. If it was dark, they would have needed flood lights to see what they were doing."

All good points.

"Maybe Mrs. Grimshaw noticed," I said. "And that's why they shot her."

Mendoza didn't answer. I looked around again. "The girl was here yesterday. So was Steven. For more than an hour. And there isn't even a bed in here!"

Mendoza's mouth quirked. "There are other ways, you know. Ways that don't require a bed."

I'm sure there were. "For more than an hour, though? That can't be comfortable. And Steven must be close to David's age, wouldn't you say? Fifty, at least."

Well past the age of picking anyone up, propping her against the wall, and proceeding to have his way with her. Or so one would think.

"Nothing to sit on here," Mendoza said with a look around. "No bed. No sofa. Not even a table."

There was the kitchen counter. But that was hard to imagine too, frankly.

"So what were they doing for more than an hour?" I asked.

"Maybe she was a real estate agent," Mendoza suggested, "and she was showing him the house."

It made as much sense as anything else. None, in other words. "Hard to see how anyone would spend an hour and a half looking at half a dozen empty rooms. And there's no sign in the yard."

"Maybe it's for rent and not for sale," Mendoza said. "Or maybe they sat on the floor and pretended to have a picnic."

Maybe. At this point, I'd accept almost any explanation. "At least no one's dead in here."

Mendoza shook his head. "And nobody's likely to complain that we took a look, either. We didn't invade anyone's privacy. Time to go."

He gestured to the back door. I headed in that direction, and waited for him to close and lock the door behind us. "You don't think Steven had anything to do with what happened to Mrs. Grimshaw, do you?"

Mendoza gave me a look out of the corner of his eye. "Do you?"

"I don't know him well. Although I wouldn't think so. He's a normal person. A university professor. Married to a lawyer. Not the kind of person who'd go around shooting someone for no reason."

"I'm sure he had a reason," Mendoza said, "whoever he was."

"Or she."

He nodded. "Tell me more about the girl who was in the house last night."

I couldn't tell him anything beyond what I'd already told him, and said so. "You'd have to talk to Zachary about her. He was the one who took the pizza up to the door and actually spoke to her. I was waiting in the car, and the angle was wrong. I didn't get a good look. All I know is that she had long, blond hair. Zachary said she was very pretty, and maybe a couple of years older than him. But he capitalized her pronoun when he came back to the car, so I'm sure he'd be able to give you a good description."

Mendoza's eyebrows had elevated. "Excuse me?"

"She," I said. "When he said 'she,' it sounded like it had a capital S. She obviously made an impression on him."

"Ah." Mendoza's lips quirked. I kept amusing him, it seemed. I tried to tell myself that it was a good thing, but honestly, I wasn't sure. He might be laughing *at* me instead of *with* me.

This seemed like a good segue to ask about the blond newscaster, but I wasn't sure how to bring up the subject without sounding like I was jealous. And before I could figure it out, we had reached the front steps of Mrs. Grimshaw's house.

"Stay here," Mendoza instructed me. "I'll get you the dog stuff."

"Thank you." I had no desire to go inside. I had already seen the blood on the floor, and I had no need to look at it up close and personal. Mendoza got paid to deal with it. Let him.

He disappeared inside, and I waited. When my phone rang, I pulled it out and glanced at the display. "Diana."

"Gina." Her voice was tight. "Steven isn't answering his phone. I called the university, and his assistant said she hadn't seen him today."

"The assistant doesn't happen to be blond and beautiful, does she?"

"No," Diana said. "Black girl. Very professional. Not at all the type to sleep with her boss."

Good to know. "So you have no idea where he is?"

I imagined her shaking her head. There was a faint clicking noise, as if an earring was hitting the speaker. "I left messages. With Jeanette. With the office. At home. On Steven's cell. I'll let you know if I hear from him. And now I'm driving home, to make sure he hasn't had a heart attack and is dead on the floor."

"I'll meet you there," I said. "I'm just about to leave where I am. I can be there in about twenty minutes."

Diana said she'd see me there, and hung up. I turned toward the door as Mendoza came out, a bag of dog food under one arm, and a plastic bag in the other hand. "Food and water bowls," he told me, lifting it. "And a leash. There are some chew toys in there, too, and a bag of dog treats."

I reached for it, but he shook his head. "I'll carry it to your car."

"That's kind of you." And hopefully it wasn't because he looked at me and thought I was too old to carry my own dog food. Not that I particularly wanted to haul the bag, but I'm forty, not eighty-five. I can still pull my weight.

"No problem," Mendoza said and set off across the grass. If nothing else, he wasn't worried about me being too decrepit to keep up. "Did I hear your phone ring?"

"Diana called back." I told him what she'd said as we made our way across the lawn. "I'm going over to their house to meet her. Just in case something's wrong, I don't want her there alone."

Mendoza nodded, and waited for me to open the

trunk of the Lexus. It slid up elegantly with the push of a button. Mendoza dumped the dog food and plastic bag into the back. He straightened. "Call me if you find anything. Or even if you don't."

I said I would. "Let me know what you find out about the dog. If any of the relatives want her. And if Steven's name comes up anywhere in your investigation."

I opened my car door. Mendoza made sure all of me was safely inside the car before he shut it. Then he set off across the grass toward Mrs. Grimshaw's house once more, while I reversed down the neighbor's driveway and headed up the street.

Chapter Six

The Mortons live in a big, old foursquare house in Richland. The neighborhood isn't too far from the house I shared with David in Hillwood, but a mile or two closer to downtown, and fifty years or so older. The houses are all early twentieth-century: foursquares, Tudors, and big Craftsman bungalows, on neat rectangular lots spaced precisely seventy-five feet apart. Nothing like the rambling hillsides of Hillwood, but very pretty and quite affluent. Full of doctors and lawyers and university professors.

The house is yellow brick, with a stately three-step staircase leading up to a set of double doors and a sitting porch. A concrete urn with a curly topiary tree stood on each side of the door. I knocked on the wooden frame and refrained from pressing my nose against the glass. Without going to that extreme, I could make out gleaming wood floors in a high-ceilinged foyer, a Persian rug, and a console table against the wall on the right.

Nobody answered. If Steven was here, he either wasn't conscious, or he didn't want to talk to anyone.

I thought about trying the doorknob, but then I realized that Diana might not be thrilled to drive up and find that I had made myself comfortable in her home.

Better to wait until she got here.

So I sat down in one of the wicker chairs on the porch instead, and no sooner had I gotten comfortable than she pulled up at the curb. I got up again and went to greet her. "I knocked on the door. Nobody answered."

Diana is a few years older than me, an elegant blonde in a cream colored business suit and blue blouse. Small gold studs caught the afternoon sun and glittered in her ears. "That's not good," she told me on her way over to the door, keys already in her hand.

I followed. "I don't think it's bad. It's probably just that he isn't here. He can't answer the door if he isn't home."

Diana nodded. "Just as long as nothing's wrong." She pushed the door open and rushed inside. "Steven? Steven!"

I followed, more slowly. While Diana ran up the stairs to the second floor, I took in the downstairs.

What I could see of it from where I was standing, was lovely. Not ostentatious, but clearly a product of good taste combined with enough money to indulge it.

I grew up poor. It was just my mother and me in a small apartment, and she worked two jobs to make ends meet. I put myself through college—until I met David and he proposed and I dropped out to marry him. Quite the Cinderella story, rags to riches and all that. David also had enough money to make his house look good, but he hadn't trusted my taste to do it; he had hired an interior decorator instead. I still felt a bit inadequate about that, and just a little out of place here. Not that I thought Diana looked down on me for my background— she probably didn't even know about it—but I still felt like I'd climbed above my station in life. While I like antiques and quality furniture, I can't reliably tell the difference between a real Duncan Phyfe sofa and a copy.

Above my head, Diana was running from room to room calling for Steven. Since she was still calling, I assumed she hadn't found him.

I headed up the stairs. When I reached the second floor, Diana came out of a door halfway down the hallway. "He isn't here."

So at least Steven hadn't had a heart attack in bed or the shower this morning. Or God forbid, gone the way of Mrs. Grimshaw. "I don't suppose you checked the closet?"

"Why would he be there?"

I didn't think he was there. "In case he packed a bag," I said.

Diana pressed her lips together in a tight line, but swung on her heel and headed for the closet. She pulled the double doors apart, and I looked in at racks of sedate suits and shirts and neatly aligned shoes along the floor.

"It doesn't look as if anything's missing." There were no obvious gaps or empty hangers where something had been removed.

Diana shook her head.

"Maybe he got a phone call and had to go somewhere in a hurry. Does he have family? Other than you, I mean?"

"His mother's still alive," Diana said. "I should call her. Make sure everything's all right."

I nodded. "Probably a good idea. I'll walk through the downstairs. Maybe he left a note or something."

"Do people leave notes anymore?" Diana was busy

scrolling through her phone, probably looking for her mother-in-law's number. "Don't they just text?"

Usually. Unless Steven had wanted to let Diana know where he was going, but not right away. Texts are immediate. A note left on the kitchen counter is something you don't read until you get home. Giving whoever left it a head start.

Naturally I didn't say any of that. I just headed down the stairs to let her talk to her mother-in-law in peace. Depending on whether the senior Mrs. Morton had heard from Steven or not, I figured it could get ugly.

There was no note downstairs. A lot of lovely furniture and lovelier knick-knacks and artwork of all sorts, but no note. There were snapshots of Diana and Steven in every room, and from what I could see, they looked happy together. Snorkeling somewhere where the water was turquoise and there were palm trees in the background. Sharing a toast at a small outdoor café in what looked like an Italian village. Sitting side by side in rocking chairs on the porch of a cabin. In a few of the pictures, there was a young man included. He resembled Steven, in height and facial features. One of them showed him in a cap and gown, with a beaming Diana and Steven on either side of him.

The kitchen was neat and clean, all white cabinets with glass fronts and marble counters. Very classic and elegant. There was a used bowl in the kitchen sink—looked like someone had had oatmeal for breakfast—so maybe Steven had eaten before he left.

Diana nodded when I pointed it out. "Cholesterol."

Of course. David had eaten his own share of oatmeal in the year or two before he died. "There's no note," I said. "Had his mother heard from him?"

Diana made a face. "No. Although she intimated she'd seen it coming. We've been married fifteen years, and she's been waiting through every one of them for him to realize he can do better."

Sounded like my mother-in-law. "David's mother never liked me, either." After a second, I added, "I think she probably liked Sandra better. Sandra was the first wife, and the mother of the grandchildren. I was the hussy who made David leave his wife and kids."

"Mothers never see their children clearly," Diana said. "I'm sure she thought it was your fault when he left you for Jacquie, too."

"I'm sure she would have. But she wasn't around anymore when that happened. She died a few years ago." And good riddance.

"Anyway," Diana said, "Steven's mother hasn't heard from him. She said she'd let me know if she did, but I'm not sure I trust her to."

I wouldn't have trusted David's mother to, either. "Where does she live?"

"Virginia," Diana said.

"If he's driving, he wouldn't get there for a few hours yet." And anyway, if nothing was wrong with the mother, there was no reason for him to go there. Especially if this had something to do with the young blonde from yesterday. A cheating husband doesn't run away to his mother. "Any other family? Brothers? Sisters? What about his son?"

I figured the young man in the pictures had to be David's son, but not Diana's. Not if they'd only been married fifteen years. The young man had been ten years older than that in some of the photographs.

"David doesn't have any children," Diana said. "And we got married later in life. He spent a long time traveling for work—photojournalist—before he started teaching, and I was busy establishing myself as a lawyer. We were in our thirties when we got married."

"David already had Krystal and Kenny when I entered the picture," I said. "They were ten and twelve, or something like that. He didn't want to start over again with the diaper changes and midnight feedings. And he was probably worried that I'd lose my figure. Or that he wouldn't get enough sex."

I'd been twenty-two when David and I got married. He'd been in his mid-thirties. I didn't fool myself into thinking he'd married me for my intellect.

"Do you regret it?" Diana asked.

I had to think for a moment. "I never had a choice, really. David didn't want more children. If I had insisted, he probably would have left me sooner. Since I didn't, he stayed with me until I was forty."

Diana nodded.

"But now... I don't know. My mother is gone. I never knew my father. My husband's dead. His children never liked me. If I'd had children of my own, at least I wouldn't be alone."

There was a moment of silence. Perhaps Diana was contemplating the possibility that she would now find herself in the same situation. If Steven was gone and not coming back, she might very well do just that.

"You have a lot of pictures of a young man who looks like Steven," I said. "I thought maybe it was your son. Or his son, once you said you'd only been married fifteen years."

Diana shook her head. "That's Trevor. Steven's nephew."

"Have you called him? Maybe he knows where Steven is."

Diana reached for her phone. "I'll do it right now."

"Where's the garage? Do you have one?"

Not everyone in these old neighborhoods do. There were cars parked up and down the streets all over Richland.

"Out back," Diana said, waving toward the rear of the house.

"I'll go see if his car is there while you make your call." I headed off in that direction as she dialed. By the time she started speaking, I had located the double French doors from the family room—surely an addition to the original house—onto the deck, and gone out that way.

The garage was a separate structure at the back of the property. It might have been a carriage house at one point, when the neighborhood was new, or it could have been a later addition made to look like it had always been there.

It opened into the alley. The yard was enclosed with a privacy fence on all sides, so the only way out was through the garage. I tried the side door. It was locked. This time I did press my nose to the glass and peer inside. The garage was empty.

I trudged back through the yard and into the family room. "Nothing."

Diana nodded. "Trevor hasn't heard from Steven. Or so he says."

"Do you have any reason to think he'd be lying?"

She shook her head. "He's in Los Angeles. It isn't likely Steven would go to him."

Probably not. That was even farther than Virginia. "I guess we just have to wait," I said. "At least nothing seems to be wrong. He left of his own accord this morning. Maybe he's just somewhere out of cell phone range. Or he turned off his phone for some reason. Or forgot to charge it last night, so it ran out of juice."

Diana nodded. Although I noticed she had gnawed the lipstick off her bottom lip. "I have another appointment in..." She checked her watch, "forty minutes. I have to go back to the office."

"Let me know if you hear from him," I told her, as we walked out the front door together, and I watched her close and lock it. "I'm sure nothing's wrong. But let me know what you find out."

She nodded. "You do the same."

I promised I would. We got into our respective cars, and I sat and waited until Diana zoomed off, back toward Germantown and the office. Then I pulled out my phone and dialed Mendoza. "I just wanted to update you," I told him when he came on, sounding harried. "Steven Morton wasn't at home, alive or dead. His car's gone. His clothes are all here. He had oatmeal for breakfast and left the bowl in the sink. He didn't leave a note. There's nothing to indicate he left under duress or in a hurry. His mother in Virginia hasn't heard from him, nor has his nephew in California. Or so they both say. Diana is worried, but trying to hold it together. She went back to the office for an appointment."

Mendoza thanked me.

"Anything new on your end?"

"Nothing pertaining to Steven Morton," Mendoza said. "Go walk the dog, Mrs. Kelly."

He hung up. I deduced he was busy.

By the time I got back to the office, poor Edwina was practically crossing her legs on the sofa. "I'm sorry," I told her, as I shook the leash out and snapped the end of it onto her collar. "I'm sure you have to go. Let's take a walk."

She jumped off the sofa, ears flapping. Her nails skidded on the floor as she headed for the hallway. I hurried after, through the lobby and outside. For having such short legs—albeit four of them—she could put on a lot of speed. Behind me, Rachel giggled.

Outside, Edwina made a beeline for the nearest flower bed. I could almost hear the sigh of relief when she squatted among the mostly bare stalks. Then she nosed around for a minute, peed again, and trotted back toward the door.

"This is the office," I told her as we walked. "For the rest of the day," just a couple of hours now, "you'll have to stay here. You'll get very comfortable with that particular flowerbed, I bet. If you stick around, maybe you can come with me when I go places sometimes, but a lot of the time I'll have to try to look inconspicuous, and there's nothing inconspicuous about you."

She turned to look at me, ears at attention.

"You can sleep on the sofa," I continued, "or I'll try to find you a doggie bed. It depends on how long you're staying. Someone else might want you." Someone with a legal claim, like Mrs. Grimshaw's next of kin. "But tonight, unless something changes, you can come home with me. You've already been there. It's where you walked around in the bathtub."

Her little stub of a tail wagged. I don't think she had any idea what I was saying, but maybe she liked being talked to. If it had been just her and Mrs. Grimshaw in the house, chances were Mrs. Grimshaw had talked to her a lot.

Inside, we stopped at Rachel's desk for a moment. When I blew through earlier, in and out, I'd been too busy to stop and talk. Now we lingered as I asked for an update.

"No calls," Rachel said. "Zachary wrote his report and put it on your desk. Then he left again. He said he was going back to the university for afternoon classes."

He was probably just hoping he'd get lucky and catch a glimpse of the blonde, but OK. He'd let me know if Steven showed up. "The house next door to Mrs. Grimshaw is empty. The house where Steven and the blonde spent at least an hour yesterday."

Rachel looked politely inquiring, and I added, "Mendoza let me in." Or rather, Mendoza had opened the door, and I'd walked in. "Nobody lives there. There's no furniture. Not even a rug to sit on. I have no idea what they can have been doing for the hour or more they spent in there."

"That's strange," Rachel said.

I nodded. "See if you can track down contact information for the owners. And see if maybe the house is for sale or for rent, or something like that. Mendoza suggested that maybe the blonde was a real estate agent."

Rachel scribbled notes to herself. "What about you?"

"I'm not quite sure," I told her. "Zachary knows what the blonde looks like. I don't. It won't do me any good to look for her. I wouldn't recognize her if I saw her. And with Steven God knows where, it's not like I can follow him. And I think I've bugged Mendoza enough today. If I show up over at Mrs. Grimshaw's house again, I'm afraid he'll have me arrested for trespassing."

Rachel nodded. "For now, maybe you can just go read Zachary's report. Maybe something will strike you."

Maybe. At the moment I was fresh out of ideas.

"Let me know what you can dig up about the house and the owners," I said. "Edwina and I are going to my office."

"Any word on how long she's sticking around?"

I shook my head. "Mendoza didn't mention anything about having notified next of kin. There might not be anyone to notify. Mrs. Grimshaw lived alone—except for Edwina—so maybe her husband was gone. And not everyone has children. And as old as she was, she might not have parents or siblings left. We could get stuck with the dog."

Rachel peered across the desk at her. Edwina's tongue lolled out of her mouth as she grinned. Her stub of a tail wagged.

"I prefer cats," Rachel said.

"I don't mind her," I answered. "She's not much trouble." And she was a good excuse to stay in touch with Mendoza.

Rachel shrugged. "I'll see what I can find out about

the house. Let me know if you need anything else."

I said I would, and then Edwina and I headed down the hall to my office.

Chapter Seven

Zachary's report was complete and thorough, if perhaps a little overly dramatic. I think he thought I might share it with Mendoza, because it was full of what I guessed to be police slang. Abbreviations like ATL, which seemed to mean attempt to locate, and RO—registered owner—and MUTT, which at first I thought might apply to Edwina, but it seemed to refer to a person Zachary didn't like.

The bottom line was the same thing he'd already told me. Steven hadn't been at the university today, nor had the blonde. We had no way of knowing whether the blonde was ever at the university, of course, but if she was a student, she wasn't in class this morning. Not anywhere where Zachary could have seen her.

I put the report on the desk and my feet next to it, and leaned back, contemplating the ceiling. There was a spot up there, the result of a former roof leak, that looked like Virginia.

For all I knew, Steven was on his way there right now. No reason to think he was, of course. Then again, no reason to think he wasn't, either.

Over on the sofa, Edwina opened her eyes and looked at me for a second, before burrowing her snub nose back into her legs and closing her eyes again.

It wasn't until I heard the front door open that I realized that her sharper ears had picked up what mine hadn't.

"Good afternoon, Rachel," Jaime Mendoza's smooth voice said.

I could imagine Rachel's expression. She thinks Mendoza is handsome. So does every other woman in the world. "Good afternoon, Detective. Are you looking for Gina?"

"I'm looking for the dog," Mendoza said, and dashed my hopes.

"They're both back there." Rachel probably waved a hand. "Go ahead."

A second later, I heard Mendoza's footsteps along the hallway. A second after that, he appeared in the doorway.

"Mrs. Kelly."

"Detective," I said politely, and took my feet off the desk.

He stepped through the opening into the office. "Thinking?"

"It's the only thing I can do at the moment. Steven's gone, so I can't follow him. I don't know who the blonde is, so I can't follow her. I could follow Diana, but I don't know what good that would do, other than give me the impression I'm doing something."

Mendoza nodded. "May I?" He gestured to the spot on the sofa next to Edwina.

"Of course. Have a seat." I straightened and watched as he sat down on the opposite end of the sofa from the dog. She opened an eye and contemplated him. Then she did a sort of doggie double-take, and opened the other eye. Both of them stared at him for a few seconds before she uncoiled, picked her way across the sofa, and collapsed again, this time with her head in Mendoza's lap. She gazed up at him, pop-eyes adoring, and he put a hand on her stomach and rubbed. She wiggled with pleasure.

I wouldn't mind being in that position myself. To distract myself from it, I said, "I heard you tell Rachel you wanted to see the dog. You're not taking her away, are you?"

"Not yet," Mendoza said, while Edwina licked his hand.

"As you can see, she's fine. I took her out earlier. She's not suffering. And I let her get on the furniture. She doesn't have to sleep on the cold, hard floor."

Mendoza's lips twitched. "I'm sure you're doing a fine job."

And so was he. The dog was practically purring.

"So what can I do for you?"

He stopped rubbing, and Edwina looked up at him with big, doleful eyes. When it became obvious that he wasn't going to continue to rub, she settled her chin on his thigh with a disappointed sigh.

"I was actually hoping Zachary would be here."

"Oh." And here I thought he'd been looking for Edwina. "He went back to the university to have another look around. He left me a report of his adventures this morning and last night. Would you like to see it?"

"I wouldn't mind," Mendoza said. I handed over the report, and he sat back in the sofa to read it. I spent the time watching him while he was not watching me do it.

The thing is, he's just so very easy on the eyes. Great bone structure, perfect skin, thick, black hair. Perfect teeth. Dimples. Nice shoulders, good chest, trim waist, and so on, all the way down to his perfect feet.

Not that I've ever seen them, unencased in shoes. If he ever takes his shoes off, it might turn out he has ingrown toenails or hammer toes, but until then, I'll just imagine them as being as perfect as the rest of him.

And if he ever gets to a point where he's getting undressed in my presence, I'm pretty sure I'll have other things to think about than his toes.

The expressions on his face were amusing to watch, too, as he made his way through the report. While I'd found Zachary's abbreviations and slang faintly annoying, Mendoza seemed to find them humorous. By the time he'd finished both reports, he was grinning, perfect, white teeth and dimples on display.

"There's nothing there you didn't already know," I pointed out.

He nodded. "It's still good to read it in his own words. I need him to give me a better description of the blonde, though. Maybe even get him to work with a police artist, to see if we can come up with a face for her."

I leaned forward. "You think she might have had something to do with Mrs. Grimshaw's murder?"

"She was there," Mendoza said. "If nothing else, she might have seen or heard something."

She might. And this was the first time I had

considered that possibility. Because I suspected the blonde of having led Steven astray, I had only thought of her as the villainess. I'd been more than happy to wonder whether she'd shot poor, old Mrs. Grimshaw and left Edwina an orphan, but I hadn't considered that she might be a witness to the crime.

Although that would explain—or would also explain—why she was gone this morning. If I'd seen someone commit cold-blooded murder next door, and I was worried that they might have realized I was there and could identify them, I would have wanted to get away as soon and as far as possible, too.

"I can have Zachary call you when he comes back in," I offered.

Mendoza arched his brows. "Trying to get rid of me?"

I shook my head. *Never.* "I'm sure you must be busy."

"Now that you mention it." He leaned back against the sofa and closed his eyes. "It's been a long day."

"Have you found out anything?"

"Not much." He opened his eyes again. So much for the nap. Edwina gazed up at him adoringly. "I found a business card from a lawyer in Mrs. Grimshaw's desk. When I called, he admitted to having done some work for her. Including drawing up her will. I am headed over there next, to take a look."

"Will you let me know what happens?" Mrs. Grimshaw's next of kin might want Edwina. I would have to give her up. And I was already becoming attached to her.

Mendoza nodded. "Once I've spoken to him, I'll

have a better idea who might have had a reason to want Mrs. Grimshaw out of the way."

He moved Edwina's head off his lap, and pushed up from the sofa with a grunt. Edwina gave him a baleful look.

"Sorry, sweetheart," I told her. I didn't want him to leave, either.

Mendoza's mouth twitched, but he didn't comment. "I'll call you later," he told me. "Take care of the dog."

I promised I would.

"And let me know when Zachary comes back."

"I will. When can I expect to see you—I mean, hear from you—again?"

He glanced at his watch. "I have an appointment with the lawyer in thirty minutes. After that, I should have a better idea what might be going on. I'll call you."

I told him I appreciated it, and watched him walk out the door. He said goodbye to Rachel on his way through the lobby, and then I heard the front door close behind him. A few seconds later, the sound of an engine started in the parking lot. At the same time, Rachel's sensible heels came clicking down the hallway. A moment later, she appeared in the doorway of my office. "If I wasn't an old lady, and he wasn't young enough to be my son, I would jump that man."

"You are not an old lady," I told her, even as I tacitly admitted that the same was true for me. If I wasn't an old lady, I would also jump that man. "And I don't think you're old enough to be his mother. He has to be into his thirties." While Rachel was in her mid fifties. So yes, maybe she was old enough to be his mother. The same way I was old enough to be Zachary's.

She put a piece of paper on my desk. "There's the information you wanted. The house belongs to someone named Araminta Tucker. She has a permanent address in Franklin."

"Kentucky?"

Rachel shook her head. "Tennessee."

Nashville is about sixty miles from the Kentucky border. There's a small town called Franklin just over the border, and another about twenty miles south of us, in Williamson County. Since one of them is about half the distance of the other—not that either is a particularly long drive—I was relieved that she was talking about the closer one.

I pulled the paper closer. "Maybe I'll go talk to her."

Rachel nodded. "I'll hold down the fort."

I got to my feet and grabbed my bag. "If Zachary comes back, tell him to call Mendoza. The detective wants a better description of the blonde."

Edwina watched us walk out of my office, but made no move to jump down from the sofa and follow. "Car ride?" I asked her.

She twitched an ear, but didn't move otherwise.

"I'll see you later," I told her, and followed Rachel down the hallway toward the front door.

Franklin is a nice little town, surrounded by horse farms and the estates of country music stars and record executives. And these days, surrounded by a lot of subdivisions, as well. When I plugged Araminta Tucker's address into the GPS, it directed me to one such. It was called Sheridan Farms, and was located on the south side of Highway 96, not too far from the

Historic Carnton Plantation, a civil war site.

The houses were large and cookie-cutter, in four or five different designs. I saw gothic farmhouses, a couple of different Queen Anne styles, and a modern Eastlake as I followed the GPS directions.

"You have arrived," the deep male voice with the Italian accent said. I had named him Bruno, and sometimes I talked back to him. In this case I told him, "Thank you," and pulled up to the curb and cut the engine, and peered through the windshield at the house.

Or building, rather.

Five stories tall, with at least sixty windows just on the front. A big sign next to the entrance said *Sheridan Farms Assisted Living Community.*

A retirement home. Someone had attempted to give it the same Victorian flair as the surrounding homes, but while it had something of the air of an old turn-of-the-century hotel, they hadn't quite managed to get rid of the institutional. It gave off more of a Victorian insane asylum vibe, if that isn't too politically incorrect a comparison.

I opened the car door and got out. And made my way into the lobby.

At least that looked more like a hotel than an asylum. Lots of green plants and plush sofas. I deduced—from the looks of it, and the fact that it was located in prosperous Williamson County—that only rich old people could afford to live here.

The young woman behind the reception desk was wearing a trim, blue uniform rather than the expected scrubs. "Can I help you?"

"I'm looking for Araminta Tucker," I said.

Her elegant brows drew together. "Are you a relative?"

"Just a friend. Of a friend." Or something like that. "I wanted to talk to her about her neighbor." Former neighbor. "Mrs. Grimshaw."

"Are you with the police?"

I blinked. "No. Have the police been here?"

"She said they'd be coming," the receptionist said.

"Who did? Ms. Tucker?"

She nodded.

"No," I said. "I'm not with the police." Although I supposed there was a chance they might show up. If the blonde was, or became, a suspect in Mrs. Grimshaw's murder.

"Identification?"

It took me a second to realize that she was asking for mine. I dug in my wallet and pulled out my driver's license. She scanned it and handed it back, along with a sticker that said 'visitor' along with a grainy black-and-white depiction of my face. My driver's license photo is bad enough; the grainy copy of it looked like something out of a horror movie.

I peeled the back off and put the sticker on my coat.

"Sign here." She pointed to the empty line at the bottom of a visitor's log. I wrote Araminta Tucker's name down as the person I was visiting, and scrawled my signature next to it.

"Unit 204," the receptionist said. "Second floor. Elevator's down there." She pointed down the hallway.

I thanked her and headed off. And wondered how Araminta Tucker had known that the police might show up to talk to her.

The answer to that, at least, became very clear when I got off the elevator on the second floor and headed down the hall toward unit 204. The closer I got, the louder I could hear the sound of a TV. By the time I stood outside the door—cracked open an inch or two—I could barely hear myself think. There was no chance at all that Ms. Tucker would hear a knock, so I dispensed with politesse and just pushed the door open.

It led into a small living room, with an ornate velvet sofa against one wall, flanked by two equally elegant wingback chairs. The coffee table was glass, and sported an oversize, fake flower arrangement full of spiky gladiolus and what I thought might be moonflowers. The sound was up so high on the TV that the vase rattled against the glass.

Ms. Tucker sat on the sofa, legs tucked up Indian style. She was tiny, with a bouffant hairdo of impossibly black hair, and two beady black eyes in a small, wrinkled face. Her hands were fisted, and she was swearing at the screen like a sergeant major in a military movie.

I looked at the screen. Ice hockey.

Really?

I cleared my throat. She flapped a hand at me. "Hush, girl."

Hush? How had she even been able to hear me with the noise coming from the TV?

And girl? It's been decades since I was a girl. Although to a woman twice my age, maybe I looked younger than I was.

"I'd like to talk to you!" I bellowed.

"There's no need to yell, girl." She reached out and dropped the volume on the TV. "I'm not deaf, you know."

Could have fooled me. Or at least I had assumed she was hard of hearing, with the way she had the sound turned up. The silence was so loud it practically rang in my ears.

I cleared my throat. "My name is Gina Beaufort Kelly."

"Araminta Tucker." She looked me up and down. "You're quite attractive for a police detective, dear."

Hard to tell whether she approved or disapproved.

"I'm sorry to disappoint," I said. "But I'm not with the police."

She hadn't asked me to sit, but I sidled a little farther into the room and positioned myself next to one of the wingback chairs, with my hand sort of casually propped on its back. It was positioned well out of the way of the sofa's view of the TV, I noticed.

She waved me into it, sort of vaguely. "I saw what happened next door. I thought maybe that handsome detective would show up to talk to me."

I perched on the edge of the wingback. "Mendoza?" She must have seen the interview the blonde reporter had done earlier. Hard to blame her for wanting him to stop by.

She nodded. "Such a good-looking boy. My poor husband wasn't much in the looks department, bless his soul. But he was a good provider." She crossed herself.

"If you want to see Mendoza," I told her, "I'd be happy to put in a good word. Do you know something he might want to hear?"

"I knew Griselda Grimshaw," Araminta Tucker said.

Griselda? Really?

I made myself more comfortable in the chair. "Did you used to live in the house next door?"

She nodded. "All through my marriage. Poor Patton, tied to his sister's apron strings his whole life long."

"Wait…" I wasn't sure, but it sounded like… "Mrs. Grimshaw was your sister-in-law?"

She snorted. "Mrs. Grimshaw? If anyone had the right to call herself Mrs. Grimshaw, it was me, dear. Griselda never married. Never found anyone who was good enough for her, Patton used to say. Between you and me, I don't think she found anyone crazy enough to take her on. And so I told him, too. Repeatedly."

"So Mrs. Grimshaw wasn't Mrs. Grimshaw at all. She was Miss Grimshaw."

She nodded.

"But you…?"

"Kept my maiden name," Araminta Tucker said. "Going through life as Araminta Tucker was bad enough. Could you imagine being Araminta Grimshaw?"

I couldn't. It sounded like something out of Harry Potter. As did Griselda Grimshaw. Or Patton Grimshaw, for that matter.

"I took my husband's name," I said. "And tacked it onto my own."

"Nothing wrong with Kelly, dear. Good Irish name."

There'd been something wrong with my husband, though. But before we could wander down that garden path, I dragged the conversation back on track again. "So you and your husband lived next door to Mrs.... um... Griselda. Before you moved here?"

She nodded. The bouffant swayed. "Patton died two years ago. I moved out a week after the funeral. Couldn't stand being near her any longer. And she must have felt the same, because I haven't seen her since. She hasn't visited me even once."

"And you haven't gone back to see her?"

She shook her head. "She despised me, dear. Never failed to tell poor Patton what a rotten choice he'd made."

"That must have been tough." David hadn't had any sisters. His misfit brother Daniel could take me or leave me, but until recently, Daniel had lived in California, so he'd only been a drag on David's finances and not the rest of our lives.

"Oh," Araminta Tucker said brightly, "I wouldn't say that, dear. Every day I wake up and know it's a good day because I don't have to see Griselda Grimshaw today."

OK, then. And now that was permanent. Which didn't seem to bother her much.

"So you saw the footage on the news and recognized the house?"

She nodded. "I lived next to that house for forty-nine years. Not like I could mistake it."

I guess not. "Any idea who might have wanted your sister-in-law dead?"

"Other than me?" She didn't wait for me to answer. "Any number of people, I imagine. She had a positive genius for rubbing people the wrong way. And always sticking her nose in other people's business."

"She called the police on me yesterday," I said.

Her brows, plucked to within an inch of their lives and carefully drawn on, arched. "Did she?"

"I was sitting in my car on the street watching the house next door. She called the police and reported a suspicious vehicle."

Araminta Tucker nodded. "That sounds like something she'd do. I don't suppose you killed her?"

I told her I hadn't. "She died sometime overnight. Ten to midnight, I think Detective Mendoza said. I was at home by then. Asleep."

"And I suppose you can prove that, can't you?" She didn't wait for me to answer. "Why were you watching the house next door?"

"That's what I wanted to talk to you about," I said. "I'm a private investigator—"

I fumbled in my purse for my license while her eyebrows winged up her forehead again. "Why didn't you say so? That's almost as good as the police. Maybe even better." She snatched the license out of my hand and examined it carefully.

"Sorry," I said. "I forgot."

She handed the license back. "That's the kind of thing you lead with, dear. Not something you use as a throwaway line in the middle of a conversation."

I told her I'd keep that in mind. "So about the house…"

"The one you were watching. My house."

I nodded. "I was following a man whose wife hired me to see if he was cheating on her."

"Steven Morton," Araminta Tucker said.

By now I was past surprise. "You know him?"

She shook her head. "Not to say know, dear. He contacted me a few days ago."

He must have known her, then. Or known about her. Or something. "What did he want?"

"To rent my house," Araminta Tucker said. "For his daughter."

Daughter? "Steven doesn't have a daughter."

"You don't say?" Araminta said. And added, "I wasn't born yesterday, dear." She shook her head. "They had different names. Different nationalities. And how many middle-aged men do you know who would pay the rent on a grown woman's apartment out of the goodness of their hearts? Especially one that looks like that?"

Not many. David had contributed to Jacquie's rent and wardrobe and probably wine budget, but it hadn't been altruistic.

"What do you mean, different nationalities?"

"She was Russian," Araminta Tucker said. "Or from somewhere in what we used to call the Soviet Union when I was a girl. He had her cosign the lease. He paid, first and last month's rent, but he insisted she sign the lease."

My heart started beating faster. "Do you have a copy of it?"

"Of course, dear." She shoved a hand under the sofa pillows and pulled out a couple of pieces of paper. "I have the original."

I kept myself from snatching it out of her hand, but it wasn't easy. But I was rewarded when she handed the papers over and I was able to flip to page two and look at the signature. In big, bold letters, nicely rounded and girlish: the name Anastasia Sokolov.

Chapter Eight

I let Ms. Tucker keep the rental contract, and promised her I'd tell Detective Mendoza all about it. And encourage him to take a look for himself, so Araminta Tucker could get a good look at him, up close. She waved me off with all good cheer. I had barely cleared the door before the hockey game came back on, at the same teeth-rattling decibels.

I waited until I was in the car to pull out my phone. And while I was tempted to contact Mendoza first thing, I convinced myself that my first duty was to my client.

She picked up on the first ring. "Gina. Have you heard anything?"

I was actually calling to ask her the same thing. Now I didn't have to. "From Steven? Sorry, no. I guess you haven't, either?"

She hadn't. No surprise there.

"How about we go grab some dinner?" I suggested. It was getting on for that time, or close to it, and I didn't want to tell her about Anastasia Sokolov over the phone.

She hesitated.

"It wouldn't have to be anything fancy. Just a quick bite and a little time to brainstorm in person rather than over the phone."

"I suppose that would be OK..." After a second, she added, "I don't want to stay out too long, though. Just in case Steven comes back."

Which he might. He might show up just as usual, as if nothing was wrong.

And for that matter, nothing might be wrong. Sure, he hadn't been at work today, and he hadn't been answering his phone. Nobody in his life knew where he was, or if they did, they weren't talking. But there was no reason we knew why he might not walk through the door, just like he did every other day, this evening.

"I could pick up some takeout and meet you there," I suggested. It would give me another chance to look around. And to see whether Steven had been home since we'd been through the house earlier today.

"Yes." She sounded like she was thinking about it. Then she came back with a stronger, "Yes, that would be good. Just in case."

I didn't ask in case of what. "What would you like?"

"I'll get it," Diana said and hung up. She probably wanted the line open in case Steven called.

I thought for sure I'd be eating lettuce—we ladies of a certain age have to watch what we eat to keep our girlish figures, especially when we're competing with women half our age for the men in our lives—but Diana must have wanted comfort food. When I walked into the kitchen in Richland, there were four different cartons of Chinese food on the counter.

I saw her car pull into the alley when I turned onto the street. By the time I'd parked in front and made my way up between the topiaries, she had the door open. "Come on in."

I stepped across the threshold and looked around. "Steven isn't here?"

"I haven't looked," Diana said. "But the garage was empty. And his car isn't parked out front."

No, it wasn't.

"I'll run upstairs and change. And see if he's come and gone. The food's on the kitchen counter. Make yourself at home." She waved a hand in the direction of the kitchen. I headed that way while she started up the stairs to the second floor and the master bedroom closet.

The rooms I passed on my way to the kitchen were empty. No surprise there. The house had an empty feel to it, and looked exactly the same as it had when we left it this afternoon. Even the stack of mail on the island didn't look as if anyone had rifled through it. And if Steven had come home while we'd been gone, wouldn't he have been tempted to check what had arrived in the mail today?

I took a quick glance myself, too. It looked like a couple of bills, an insurance statement, something from the state, a request for money for wounded veterans, and some sort of invitation to something. That's judging from the logos up in the corners of the envelopes, and the nice, heavy stationary the invitation came on.

The four food containers were lined up on the counter, and held, in descending order, shrimp and broccoli, chicken lo mein, fried rice, and dumplings. I was opening cabinets looking for plates when Diana walked back into the kitchen, barefoot and in a pair of leggings and a tunic.

"Over here." She opened a cabinet and handed me three plates.

I took them. "Are we expecting company?"

"Jaime Mendoza called while I was on my way home," Diana said. "I ordered enough food for an army, so I figured we'd be all right if I told him to stop by."

Sure. I wasn't planning to eat much. Fried rice and dumplings go straight to my hips.

"Then we'd better talk fast, before he gets here."

I'd realized, after I hung up the phone with Diana earlier, that I couldn't just arbitrarily call Mendoza and tell him about Araminta Tucker and what she'd told me. Diana was my client. My responsibility—and loyalty—was to her. If she told me not to share what I knew with Mendoza, I couldn't share it.

"About what?" Diana wanted to know. She was forking shrimp and broccoli onto her plate.

"I went to see the woman who owns the house next to Mrs. Grimshaw. The house where Steven met with the blonde yesterday."

Was it only yesterday? It felt a lot longer ago.

"Her name is Araminta Tucker. She moved to an assisted living facility in Franklin after her husband died. He was Mrs. Grimshaw's brother. She and Griselda Grimshaw didn't get along, so when Patton died, Araminta moved out of the house next door and started renting it out."

Diana nodded. She had moved onto the dumplings, and was fishing them out of the box with her fork.

"Before she retired, she used to work at the

university."

Diana glanced up. "Where Steven works?"

"The same one. She posts the house for rent on the bulletin boards there. Steven must have seen it, because he contacted her."

"About renting her house?"

"That's what he told her. Or what she said he told her. He wanted to rent the house," I took a breath, "for his daughter."

There was a beat of silence. "Steven doesn't have a daughter," Diana said.

I nodded. "That's what you told me. And what I told her. For what it's worth, Araminta didn't think she was Steven's daughter, either."

Diana arched a brow. "Why not?"

"Different last names, different nationalities." She looked blank, and I added, "Apparently the girl's Russian. Or from somewhere in what used to be the Soviet Union. I'm not up on the various Slavic variations of names. But her last name is Sokolov. First name Anastasia. Araminta Tucker let me see the lease. The girl signed it along with Steven."

"Do you have a copy?"

I shook my head. "I left it with Ms. Tucker. It's hers. I need to know whether you'll agree to let me tell Mendoza about it, so he can go take a look at it."

She looked surprised.

"I work for you," I said. "If you don't want me to share it with him, I won't."

It would be difficult, since I didn't really want to keep anything from him that might help him solve Mrs. Grimshaw's murder. She might not have been a nice woman, but nobody had the right to kill her, no matter how unpleasant she might have been.

Diana nodded. "Of course I want you to share it with him. Any chance the girl did it?"

It was hard to blame her for sounding hopeful. I'd been hoping for the same thing—that I would be able to send Jacquie to prison for the rest of her natural life— after David died. Anastasia Sokolov was even younger than Jacquie. She could look forward to even more years behind bars.

However, I felt I owed it to Diana to point out the truth.

"She might just be a witness. If she was next door last night, she couldn't really have avoided hearing the shot."

Diana made a face.

"Either way, having her name will hopefully help Mendoza find her. Or at least make it easier. And Araminta Tucker saw her, so she can probably help him flesh out the description Zachary gave."

"That's why he's coming here," Diana said. "He set Zachary up with a police artist. They have a sketch. Jaime wants me to look at it, to see if I recognize her."

Good for Zachary.

"Sounds like he's arrived." She tilted her head toward the front of the house.

I sharpened my ears, and heard the sound of a car door slamming. She must have heard the car pull up to the curb outside. "Do you want me to go let him in?" She'd filled her plate; she should probably start eating before the food got cold.

"That's kind of you," Diana said, "but I've got it."

She put her plate down on the counter. "Help yourself."

She nodded to the food on her way out into the hallway. I started picking up and putting down containers while I kept an ear on the proceedings. The soft scuffs of Diana's bare feet on the wood in the hallway. The sound of the front door opening. A soft greeting. The sound of—maybe—a kiss on the cheek?

Whose kiss on whose cheek was harder to determine. But either way, there were no squeals of happiness or cries of recrimination, so it wasn't the wayward husband who had returned. I heard the sound of Mendoza's hard shoes coming down the hallways, and then he appeared in the doorway.

"Evening, Detective," I said.

He arched his brows. "Mrs. Kelly."

"Sorry," Diana said behind him. "I forgot to tell you that Gina would be here." She moved past him toward her plate. "Help yourself to food."

"Don't mind if I do." Mendoza gave me a nod as he faced me across the island. "And how was your afternoon?"

"Busy," I said, and watched as he ladled Lo Mein onto his plate. "Yours?"

"The same. I didn't get any lunch."

Good thing I wasn't that hungry. "Is that an occupational hazard?"

"It happens. Not like you can interrupt a murder investigation to fill your stomach."

I guess not. Or that you'd be very hungry in the middle of what you had to deal with, either. "Diana told me you found Zachary and had him work with a police artist."

He nodded. "Just let me shovel some of this in, and I'll show you the image we came up with."

"I'm not likely to be any help there," I said, "but I'd be happy to take a look. You'll probably have more luck at the university, though. Or with the neighbors. And on that note…"

"After I eat," Mendoza said.

Fine. I made a face, but carried my plate over to the little table in the alcove, where Diana was sitting. She was trying to keep back a smile, somewhat unsuccessfully. I figured she was laughing at me, but since it was the first time I'd seen her smile today, I didn't give her a hard time about it.

Mendoza sat down a few seconds later, and for the next couple of minutes, we all focused on eating. Mendoza wasn't kidding about being hungry. He ate tidily, but fast. Diana mostly picked at her food. I guess it must have sounded good at the time, but when it came to actually chewing and swallowing, she probably felt like there was a big obstacle in her throat. I remembered that feeling. It was only a few months since I'd found out that my husband was cheating on me.

"So how's the dog?" Mendoza asked after a few minutes, and tore me out of my increasingly angry thoughts about cheating spouses.

I looked at him blankly for a second before I hiked my jaw up. "Oh, my God. I forgot the dog!"

I dove into my purse for my phone.

"Dog?" Diana asked while I scrambled.

"Mrs. Grimshaw," Mendoza said, "had a small Boston Terrier."

"The woman who was killed in the house next to the

one where Steven was yesterday?"

He nodded, while I was frantically pushing buttons. "I had to do something with the dog while the CSI crew went over the house, so I gave it to Mrs. Kelly."

Diana turned her attention to me, her eyebrows winging up her forehead. I flapped a hand at her but didn't speak, since Rachel was just picking up. "It's Gina. I'm so sorry. I totally forgot the dog!"

"That's all right," Rachel said. "I left her with Zachary. He said he'd take care of her."

"Will his mother be OK with that?" Zachary lived with his mother. I hadn't met her, and he never said much about her, but there was at least a chance she wouldn't be thrilled about having a dog dumped on her without warning.

"I didn't ask," Rachel said. "Maybe he's planning to sleep on the sofa in the office tonight."

Maybe he was. "I'll swing by on my way home. I'm having dinner with Diana and Detective Mendoza."

"Good for you," Rachel said. "Anything I need to know about?"

Nothing that couldn't wait until tomorrow. "No," I said. "What about me?"

Rachel said there was nothing she hadn't already told me. "I'll see you in the morning."

I told her I'd be there, and hung up. "The dog's fine. Zachary's got it."

"Her," Mendoza said. "I spoke to the lawyer. Next of kin is a sister-in-law in a retirement community in Franklin."

"Araminta Tucker. The widow of Patton Grimshaw, Griselda's younger brother."

Mendoza arched his brows. "Can I ask you how you know this?"

"I was going to tell you," I said, with a glance at Diana. "I had Rachel look up the ownership of the house next door. The one where Steven and the blonde were yesterday. Araminta was listed as owner, with an address in Franklin. I drove down there."

"Of course you did." He sounded resigned but not surprised.

"She already knew what had happened. She saw it on the news. And she was quite disappointed when I showed up and you didn't. She wants to see you."

"Why?" Mendoza asked suspiciously.

"Mostly because she thinks you're nice to look at." I grinned at him across the table. "Partly, I think, because she thinks the whole thing is interesting. She's pretty interesting herself, actually."

Mendoza muttered something. I didn't ask him to repeat it. "She says that Steven contacted her a few days ago, about renting her house."

I explained about the university connection and the girl and the lease and all the rest of it.

"And she showed you a copy of the lease?"

I nodded. "The girl's name is Anastasia Sokolov. Or at least that's what she goes by. Her handwriting looks like she's around twelve, so it was easy to make out the name"

He arched his brows. So did Diana.

"She's not," I said. "Zachary got a good look at her, and he said she was in her early twenties. But I guess she writes like someone who doesn't write a lot. Or maybe it's a Russian thing. The point is, the name was easy to read."

"And it's Anastasia Sokolov?"

I nodded. And spelled it, for good measure, so there'd be no question.

"That's helpful information," Mendoza said.

I smiled sweetly. "You're welcome."

He opened his mouth and closed it again. Not just handsome, but smart. "Anything else?"

I shrugged. "She didn't like her sister-in-law. Didn't make any bones about it. After her husband died—Patton, Griselda's brother—she, Araminta, moved out and into the retirement place in Franklin so she wouldn't have to be next door to Griselda anymore. She says she hasn't seen her sister-in-law in two years. Griselda hasn't visited her and she hasn't visited Griselda. She didn't mention any other family members."

"So bad blood between them," Mendoza said. He didn't write anything down, but I got the distinct feeling he made a mental note.

"That's my impression. Or maybe not bad blood, but not a lot of love lost. She said Griselda was an unpleasant person, and that she was always sticking her nose in other people's business. Araminta didn't seem surprised that Mrs. Grimshaw had been murdered."

Mendoza didn't say anything. His silence said a lot. Or maybe I was just getting better at reading it.

"Surely you're not thinking that Araminta killed Griselda?" I asked. "Why would she? I mean, I know she didn't like her. Or they didn't like each other. But they hadn't seen each other in two years. Why would she kill a woman she hadn't seen in so long? When she could just keep on not seeing her?"

"She's the next of kin," Mendoza said.

"So?"

"So she inherits," Mendoza said. "I checked with the lawyer. There are no other relatives. The elder Grimshaws are gone. Patton Grimshaw died a few years ago. Neither sibling had children. And Griselda didn't make a will in favor of anyone else. Araminta Tucker-Grimshaw is the sole surviving relative. She gets it all."

I blinked. "Is there anything to get? Enough to commit murder over?"

"People have committed murder over a handful of change and a pair of sneakers," Mendoza said. "In this case, there's the house, a few hundred thousand in investments, a life insurance policy of a million dollars, and the dog."

The dog?

"I'm not sure she can keep Edwina where she lives." Are residents in assisted living allowed to have dogs?

"Then she'll have to make other arrangements," Mendoza said. "In either case, depending on her own financial situation, it might be plenty to commit murder over."

I thought about it. And realized he might be right.

Motive aside—and yes, a million dollar life insurance policy, a couple hundred thousand in investments, plus a house, might be plenty of motive for murder—Araminta might have a car. I had no reason to think she didn't. From what I'd seen of her, she would have been capable of driving it. Her eyesight seemed fine, and she had all her faculties. And it's not like it takes a lot of strength to point a gun and pull the trigger. Araminta Tucker was small, sure, but she wasn't too small for that. So motive aside, she might have both means and opportunity.

"I haven't had a chance to check," Mendoza added. Still on the subject of Araminta Tucker's finances, I guess. "But retirement living doesn't come cheap. If she needs cash, that life insurance policy alone will go a long way. And it's not like she liked her sister-in-law."

No. "I guess you'll go see her tomorrow?"

"I think I'd better," Mendoza said. "Both to take a look at that lease and to assess her potential for murderer."

"Will you let me know what you find out?"

He gave me a jaundiced look, and I added, "About Edwina. If she doesn't want Edwina, or can't keep her, maybe she'd let me keep her. I'd be willing to pay for her, if money would make a difference."

Diana looked at me and I said, defensively, "She's nice. A fun, little dog. I like her. And I don't want her to end up at the pound."

Diana didn't say anything. Mendoza said he'd let me know. "I don't suppose you noticed a gun sitting around?"

I hadn't. "But if she'd just used it to shoot her sister-in-law, it isn't likely she'd keep it on the coffee table. Is it?"

It wasn't. Mendoza turned to Diana. "I'm sorry to ask, but I'm sure you understand why I have to. Does Steven own a gun?"

Diana nodded. "We both do."

Mendoza didn't look surprised. I guess maybe I was, a little. It had never crossed my mind that she was packing heat.

And she must have noticed, because she felt compelled to explain. "I get death threats sometimes. Sometimes, one party wants the divorce but the other party doesn't. Some men take it personally when their wives leave them. And sometimes, someone hires me to help them negotiate a fair settlement in the divorce, but the other party doesn't agree on what's fair. And then they blame the fact that they have to pay so much alimony on me. So far it's just been threats. Nobody's tried to hurt me. But I carry a gun just in case."

Mendoza nodded.

"Do I need a gun?" I asked.

They both looked at me. I added, "If I'm going to follow cheating spouses around for a living, maybe one of them will decide it's my fault his wife's leaving him."

Mendoza hesitated. I got the pretty distinct impression that he wasn't in favor of me carrying a gun. It was probably nothing personal. Most cops aren't in favor of civilians being armed. It makes their jobs much harder.

On the other hand, I was sure he could see my point. Especially after what Diana had just said.

Eventually he settled for a bland, "Something to think about." Which I took to mean that it might not be a bad idea, but he wasn't going to be the one to tell me to arm myself. Probably afraid I'd end up shooting myself in the foot. And considering some of the things that came out of my mouth sometimes, he might not be too far off.

"Where are the guns now?" he asked Diana, who told him she kept hers in her purse, and Steven's was upstairs in the bedside table. "Would you go get them, please?"

Diana opened her mouth, and then seemed to think better of it. She nodded and got up from the table. I waited until I heard her footsteps start up the stairs before I said, "Surely you don't think she had anything to do with shooting Mrs. Grimshaw."

"It's procedure," Mendoza said.

"Sure, but Diana had no reason to want Mrs. Grimshaw dead. She didn't even know her."

"Steven did."

True. Steven did. Or it was reasonable to think he must have made Griselda Grimshaw's acquaintance if Anastasia Sokolov had lived next to the old bat, and Steven had visited her. Araminta Tucker had said that Griselda liked to stick her nose in other people's business. It was quite likely she had stuck it in Steven's.

"You think Steven shot Griselda Grimshaw so she wouldn't tell Diana he was cheating on her?"

"I'm not thinking anything," Mendoza said, which had to be a lie. "I just need to see the guns."

"Do you know what kind of gun was used to shoot Mrs. Grimshaw?"

"The ME finished the autopsy this afternoon," Mendoza said. And added, before I could ask, "There was nothing interesting or noteworthy about it. Cause of death was as expected. Two shots point blank to the chest. She was dead before she hit the floor."

"That's good, at least." I wouldn't have wanted her to suffer.

Mendoza nodded. "Both bullets were from the same gun. A 9 millimeter Smith and Wesson M&P." After a second he added, "Military and Police."

My jaw dropped. "The police shot her?" Or the

military? Why?

"No," Mendoza said, with fraught patience. "The Smith and Wesson Military and Police issue is also widely available commercially. It's a popular gun."

"Is that what I should get, if I wanted to get a gun?"

"You should find another job," Mendoza said, "where you won't need a gun. I hear The Bag Shoppe is hiring."

It took a second, then— "The handbag store? You want me to sell accessories for a living?"

"I bet nobody ever stabbed anybody over a designer purse."

"You'd be surprised," I told him. "I've known women who'd kill over a lot less than that. But I don't want to sell purses. I like what I do."

"You have no idea what you're doing," Mendoza pointed out, which was unkind of him, I thought.

"I'm learning. I'm new at this."

"That's why I'm telling you to get out while you still can. Before it's too late."

"You mean, before I realize I'm good at it? Or before I realize I like it?"

"Before someone comes along and shoots you for sticking your nose in where it doesn't belong," Mendoza said and turned to the door as Diana's footsteps came back down the hallway. "Any luck?"

She put her handbag on the table. "My gun's in here. Where it's been all day. Feel free to look."

Mendoza pulled the purse down on his lap and peered in while Diana continued, "But I don't know what happened to Steven's gun. It was upstairs yesterday. Now it isn't."

She tried to sound calm, but I could detect a quaver in her voice, a little ribbon of fear.

"Are you sure you saw it yesterday?" Mendoza had dug her gun out of the purse and was inspecting it. After a few seconds, he put it back and handed Diana the bag. "Can you vouch for Steven's whereabouts last night and this morning?"

Diana nodded. "He came home from work as usual last night. We had dinner. Worked a little. Watched some TV. Went to bed. He didn't get up again until morning."

Neither of us said anything, but she added, defensively, "We slept in the same bed. I would have heard if he'd gotten up."

"I didn't say anything," Mendoza said mildly. "Where does he keep the gun?"

Diana told him it lived in the bedside table drawer on Steven's side of the bed. "He doesn't carry it. Nobody threatens him, and anyway, the university is a gun-free zone. It's just left over from before, when he traveled to some unsavory parts of the world."

Mendoza nodded. "I'll look up the registration. If nothing else, it'll tell me what kind of gun it is. I assume it's probably registered?"

"Of course," Diana said.

"Can you remember the last time you saw it?"

But she couldn't. "Most of the time, I forget it's there. We've never needed it. Steven takes it out and cleans it once in a while, but I can't remember the last time he did that. And I don't go into his bedside drawer, as a rule."

"So the gun could have been gone for a while."

She nodded. "Should I be worried?"

I'd be worried if it were me, although I didn't say so. Mendoza didn't, either. "We'll figure it out," he told her. His voice was reassuring, but I'm sure she noticed, as did I, that he didn't actually tell her she had no reason to worry.

Chapter Nine

By the time I got to the office to check on poor Edwina—and Zachary—it was after eight. Honestly, I expected them both to be gone, but when I pulled into the lot, Zachary's little car was parked in the corner, and the light was on inside.

I unlocked the door and raised my voice. "Hello?"

There was a scramble from the back of the office. Then the sound of nails scrabbling on the floor, and furious, high-pitched barking as Edwina rounded the corner and came for me, bat ears flapping. I took an involuntary step back.

She recognized me, though, and by the time she ran into my calves—because although her feet were no longer moving, she couldn't stop in time—her stubby tail was wagging and her jaws were split in a delighted doggy grin.

"Hello, sweetheart." I bent and gave her a scratch as she danced excitedly in front of me, her hind quarters wiggling in delight. Running my nails through her short fur was a little like scratching a Persian rug.

Zachary burst around the corner a second later, and took several steps down the hallway before he recognized me. "Oh."

He slowed down, and then collapsed against the wall. "It's you."

I nodded. "I have a key. Didn't you hear me let myself in?"

He looked sheepish. "Guess the TV was up too loud."

"We have a TV?"

"I was streaming Jessica Jones on the computer," Zachary said.

Of course he was. I decided not to say anything about it. It was after business hours, and he had stayed behind to take care of my dog. Or the dog Mendoza had given me responsibility for. Who cared if he was using the wifi? He could be watching much worse things than Jessica Jones.

"I came to relieve you," I said instead. "Of the dog. I can't believe I forgot about her. But I went from Franklin directly to Diana's house, and she just slipped my mind. Thanks you for staying to take care of her."

"It was no problem." Zachary looked like he thought about saying something else, but then he thought better of it.

"I saw Detective Mendoza," I said. "He came by to show Diana the drawing you helped him make. Of the Russian girl."

Zachary nodded. "I only saw her for a minute. I'm not sure the drawing is a hundred percent. But it's close. Did Mrs. Morton recognize her?"

Mendoza had shown the image to both us before I

left, and we'd both said we didn't know the girl. I was reasonably sure I'd never seen her before. I'd only followed Steven that one afternoon—yesterday—from the college campus to the house in Crieve Hall. She'd already been there when he arrived, and I hadn't gotten a look at her, and then I'd followed Steven back to the university. Zachary had gone to the door alone with the pizza last night, and this morning she'd been gone. There was no reason for me to have seen her, unless it was in passing, on the street, and if so, I hadn't realized it.

Diana had said the same. She was probably telling the truth.

"Her name seems to be Anastasia Sokolov," I told Zachary, and watched his eyes open wide.

"The detective found her already? That was fast!"

I shook my head. "Sadly, no. I found the name." I told him about my trip to Franklin and Araminta Tucker. "She rented the house to Steven and his 'daughter.'"

I left out the air quotes around the last word. Zachary snorted anyway.

"You're too young to be so cynical," I told him.

He grinned. "You forget. I saw her. And she looked like a stripper."

Had she really? It's hard to tell that from a drawing of a face. Although she'd certainly been very pretty, at least the way Zachary had described her. Blue eyes, long blond hair, Slavic cheekbones, plump lips. If she had the body of an exotic dancer on top of it, it was no wonder he'd been dazzled when he came back to the car last night.

"Did you happen to mention that to Mendoza?" I

asked.

Zachary nodded. "We did a full-body sketch, too. I guess he didn't show you that one?"

He hadn't. Trying to protect Diana's feelings, perhaps.

"She didn't just have the body," Zachary said, and added, pensively, "although boy, did she have that..."

"But?"

His eyes cleared. "She dressed like a stripper. Like she does her shopping at Fredericks of Hollywood or Hustler. Cut down to here and up to there—" He demonstrated, "and like it was painted on. Four inch heels with platform soles. The kind girls use when they hump poles."

Mendoza had definitely been trying to spare Diana's feelings.

"So..." I said. "You're saying she might actually be a stripper?"

He shrugged. "She dressed like one. Or like I figure a stripper might dress. Not like I hang out in those places."

No. He wasn't old enough, was he? And looked younger than he was, with his freckled face and red hair.

"I'm old enough," Zachary said. "They let you in when you're eighteen, as long as they don't serve alcohol."

"Don't those places always serve alcohol?"

He shook his head. "A lot of them don't. Less chance somebody'll try to touch the merchandise, I guess."

Perhaps. "So you're familiar with the Nashville stripping scene?"

He squirmed. "I wouldn't say familiar..."

"Could you take a guess as to where a Russian girl might take her clothes off for money? Is there a Russian, or maybe an East European, part of town?"

"There's a Russian grocery on Thompson Lane," Zachary said, "near Nolensville Road."

"Would they have strippers?"

He shook his head. "Although I've heard the owner's a former ballet dancer."

Really?

"The girl I saw was not a ballet dancer. Too well endowed."

No doubt. I was familiar with the type of girls who appealed to middle-aged, married men, and young, perky breasts seemed a big part of it. "Nolensville Road and Thompson Lane is sort of on your way home, isn't it?"

Zachary shrugged. It wasn't a yes, but it wasn't a no, either.

"Maybe you could drive slowly and take a look around for places the girl might frequent. And if you happen to see a Russian strip club, and they'll let you in, maybe see if anyone knows her?"

His eyes opened wide. "You're asking me to go talk to strippers? On duty?"

"I'll pay you," I said. "I mean, it's part of the job. If we can figure out where the girl is, maybe we'll find Steven, too. Diana's pretty worried."

And she deserved to know something solid one way or the other. Even if it was that Steven was leaving her for a twenty-year-old Russian stripper. It had to be better than this deafening silence from a man who, for all intents and purposes, had just dropped off the face of the earth with no warning.

The least the coward could have done, was tell his wife the truth. After fifteen years of marriage, didn't she deserve that?

"I'll see what I can do," Zachary said.

"Overtime pay," I told him. "Time and half."

He grinned. "I'll go now."

"Take your time." The strip joints, if there were any, probably didn't start kicking until later.

"You'd be surprised," Zachary said. "A lot of husbands like to stop in on their way home from work in the afternoon."

Ewww. "Maybe that's how Steven met the girl."

"Maybe." Zachary hesitated. "If I find a place, I guess I can ask whether anyone's seen him. I can probably find a picture of him on the internet, that I can flash around."

"I'm sure the university website has one," I said. "Just be careful. You don't want anything to happen."

"If I get arrested, Detective Mendoza will get me out of jail," Zachary said. "He owes me."

He did. If Zachary hadn't interceded last month, Mendoza and I would both be dead.

I bent and scooped up Edwina. "I'll take the dog home with me."

"I'll help you carry," Zachary said. He reached for the bag of dog food beside the door.

I shook my head. "Don't worry about it. You fed her tonight, right?"

He nodded.

"Then she can wait until tomorrow morning. We'll see you then."

"I'll go turn off the TV and grab my coat," Zachary said. He headed down the hallway again while I carried Edwina out to the car and put her in the passenger seat. Then I watched as Zachary came back out, shrugging on his jacket, and made sure he locked the door. "I'll see you tomorrow."

"I'll be here," Zachary said, and headed for his car. I reversed out of my spot and drove to the street, where I took off in one direction, down Music Row toward the roundabout and the Gulch, while Zachary went in the other, up Music Row toward Belmont University and the interstate.

When the phone rang, I was pretty sure it was the middle of the night. It felt like the middle of the night. A quick glance told me that it was actually twenty minutes after six, though.

Which isn't exactly the middle of the night, but might as well be.

I fumbled the phone up to my ear. "'lo?"

"Gina!" Diana's voice practically pierced my eardrum. "Gina, you have to come here!"

I guess I ought to say that I assumed it was Diana's voice. It was Diana's phone number. And the voice was female. Pitched so high that Edwina's ears twitched, all the way on the other side of the king size bed.

But I wouldn't have recognized Diana if I hadn't already had her number plugged into my phone. She sounded frantic, hysterical.

"Diana?" I ventured.

"You have to come here!"

I sat up and ran a hand through my hair. It was

almost a month since I'd chopped it off, so it had had time to grow out a little, but I could still pretty much wash it and go. This morning, it looked like I wouldn't even have time to do that.

"What's wrong?"

"Steven!" Diana shrieked.

"Is he back?" Was he dead?

I stopped myself before asking.

"He's been kidnapped!"

Kidnapped? "What do you mean, kidnapped?" How could he be kidnapped? Who'd want to kidnap Steven?

"Just get over here!" Diana told me, her voice so high and shaky I could barely understand the words. "I'm calling the police."

She hung up in my ear. I swung my legs over the edge of the bed and picked up the pair of jeans I had dropped on the floor when I went to bed last night. If I wasn't going to have time for a shower this morning, I might as well wear them again.

I had to bring Edwina, of course. I loaded her in the car, and we took off out of the garage on two wheels—by then it was past six-thirty—and shot up the street. Two minutes later, I squealed to a stop at the sidewalk outside Reservoir Park and let Edwina out. She did her business, I deposited said business in the trash can by the gate, and we got back in the car. And headed for Richland at a more sedate, but still rapid clip.

By the time I got there, Mendoza's sedan was already parked out front. And if he'd been woken from dead sleep earlier than usual, you couldn't see it by looking at him. He looked as fresh as a daisy, well-rested, clear-eyed, and turned out in one of his nice suits, this one a navy blue paired with a pale blue shirt and a striped tie. The knot was perfect. So were his shoes. Just as if he'd been polishing them when Diana called.

"Ugh," I said.

He arched his brows. "Good morning, Mrs. Kelly."

"Nobody should look that good before seven in the morning."

He didn't respond—although his mouth twitched—and I added, "Diana called me. She said Steven's been kidnapped."

Mendoza sighed and stepped out of the doorway. "You might as well come in."

I looked over my shoulder at Edwina, who was eying Mendoza adoringly from the front seat, her doggie tongue lolling out.

"Leave her there," he told me.

"Will you go say hello to her?"

He rolled his eyes. "If I have to."

"I'm sure she'll appreciate it."

He looked less than thrilled, but he nodded.

"Make sure she doesn't pee on the seat," I told him as I ducked past him into the house. "She does that when she gets excited."

"Of course she does."

Of course she did. I hid a smile. "Where's Diana?"

"Kitchen," Mendoza said, on his way down the stairs to say hello to the dog. I watched him walk over to the car and greet Edwina, who looked close to heavenly rapture at his arrival, before I headed down the hallway toward the kitchen.

It was like déjà vu all over again to walk through the

door. Here I was, wearing the same clothes I'd been wearing yesterday. And there was Diana, wearing the same yoga pants and T-shirt she'd changed into yesterday. The only thing missing were the containers of Chinese food. Diana must have put the leftovers away, or maybe Mendoza had taken them with him.

Either way, here we were again.

Diana looked up when I walked through the door, and her face twisted. "Gina."

"I'm so sorry," I said, and walked over to give her a hug. "What happened?"

She took a breath. "I was sleeping. Finally. The first part of the night, I just twisted and turned. Hoping that I'd hear Steven come home."

I nodded. I'd had a few days like that, too, after David moved out. Hoping—and halfway not hoping—that he'd come to his senses and realize that he didn't want to throw away eighteen years of marriage on a girl who'd barely started elementary school when he married me.

Needless to say, he didn't. And then he died.

But we were talking about Steven.

"I guess I fell asleep eventually. And then someone rang the doorbell." She shifted on the barstool. "It took me a second or two to realize it, I guess. I knew I'd heard something, but you know how it is. It takes a moment to realize what it was. And then it happened again."

The master bedroom looked out over the backyard and the garage, not the front. "What did you do?" I asked.

"Ran down the stairs. By the time I got there, whoever had been there was gone. But there was a note on the mat."

It was sitting on the island in front of her. She nudged it toward me. I used the tips of my fingernails to unfold and hold it open, just in case Mendoza planned to have it tested for fingerprints.

If you want your husband back, it said, in spiky block letters, *bring a hundred thousand dollars to the Arena at eleven tonight.*

"And do what with it?"

"Excuse me?" Diana said.

I pointed to the letter. "Bring a hundred thousand dollars to the Arena, and... what? Leave it under your seat? Put it in one of the trash cans in the lobby? Throw it out on the ice? I'm sure whoever wrote the note doesn't plan to come up to you and introduce herself, so you can be sure you give the money to the right person. What are you supposed to do with it?"

Diana shrugged. "Maybe there'll be more instructions there."

Maybe. "This smells weird," I said.

Her nostrils vibrated. "I don't smell anything."

There was nothing to smell. Not even coffee, which—if I'd known about it—I would have stopped on the way to pick up.

I headed for the coffee machine on the counter to remedy the oversight. "Not physically. It feels weird. I mean, what are the chances that Steven takes up with this girl, and suddenly he's kidnapped? And why a hundred thousand dollars? I mean, it's a lot of money. You probably don't have it sitting around. Unless you do?"

"I can come up with it by eleven tonight," Diana

said. "Or eleven this morning. But I don't have it tucked away in my lingerie drawer, if that's what you mean. It'll necessitate a trip to the bank."

So the same type of scenario as if someone had asked me for a hundred thousand dollars. It's not something I keep around in cash, but I could get my hands on it without too much trouble if I had to. David had had money, and I had inherited a third of his estate, so as long as the banks were open, I could liquidate enough cash to fill a small duffel with a hundred thousand dollars pretty easily.

So could Diana, it seemed. And that was part of what smelled. "Why so little? I mean, you're a lawyer. Steven's a tenured professor. You live in an expensive house in a very nice area." Even if perhaps they'd bought the house when it was worth less than it was now. "It stands to reason that you'd have money. A hundred thousand dollars doesn't seem like enough."

So did that tell us something about the kidnapper? He or she was someone to whom a hundred thousand dollars was a lot of money?

Or someone who hadn't thought the consequences all the way through?

Given the penalties for kidnapping, I'd need to get a lot more than that to make it worthwhile, personally. Kidnapping is a felony that carries a sentence of several years on up to a lifetime in prison, depending. Not something I'd want to risk for a measly hundred grand.

"Given what we know," I said delicately—or maybe not that delicately, "is Steven worth a hundred thousand dollars to you?"

"That's a moot point," Mendoza's voice said from

behind me. When I glanced over my shoulder, he was leaning against the door jamb. I had no idea how long he'd been standing there. "We don't ever recommend meeting the kidnapper's demands in cases like this."

"What do you recommend? Filling a backpack with newsprint?" That's what they do in the movies, isn't it?

Mendoza ignored me, just removed himself from the jamb and came into the kitchen. "I'll take the note with me, if you don't mind. And see if I can get any prints from it."

Diana nodded. "What do you want me to do?"

"Not go to the bank and take out a hundred thousand dollars in cash," Mendoza said.

I cleared my throat, and they both turned to me. I smiled apologetically. "Not to butt in where I'm not wanted…"

Mendoza gave me a jaundiced look.

"But maybe that's exactly what you ought to do. What if Steven is watching the account? He probably has online banking, right? What if he's watching, to make sure you take out the money? And if he sees that you're not, he, or she, or they, probably won't show up at all tonight. And you'll miss your chance to catch her. Or him. Or them."

This last was directed at Mendoza, who gave a slow nod. "She has a point."

Diana didn't seem to like this idea. "Are you suggesting that Steven has something to do with this? That he's in on it?"

"I have no idea what's going on," I said. "But he went to the house in Crieve Hall to see the blonde… to see Anastasia Sokolov willingly. Nobody held a gun to his head then. And there's nothing to indicate that he didn't leave the house willingly yesterday morning. Right?"

Diana nodded.

"So maybe he has some reason for wanting a hundred thousand dollars. And a reason for wanting you to believe it's not him who wants it."

"So he can give it to the tramp," Diana said grimly.

Or so they had some seed money for running away together. But I wasn't going to point that out. Instead, I glanced at Mendoza, silently throwing him the ball.

He said, "It's possible. If Steven is part of this, and he's watching the bank accounts, it would probably be best to withdraw the money. He'll see the withdrawal, and believe you're getting the money turned into cash in order to give it to him. Or her. Or them. It will ensure that he'll show up at the drop point tonight."

"Or her," I said. "Or them."

Mendoza nodded. "Safer to make it look like we're complying with the request."

"I'll go to the bank this morning," Diana said. "Is there anything else I can do?"

"I'll take the note in for fingerprinting. While I'm there, I'll send out a BOLO for both Steven and the blonde, using the name we have and the drawing."

A BOLO, for the uninitiated, is a police acronym for Be On the LookOut. Mendoza would make sure every police officer and squad car in Nashville had seen Steven's face and that of the blonde, and would keep an eye out for them.

"It's been twenty-four hours," Mendoza added, "so you can file an official missing person's report on Steven.

Although with the note, it's pretty well moot."

Pretty well. Whether Steven was behind it or not, with a ransom note, Mendoza had to take Steven's disappearance seriously. And I assumed that if it was discovered that Steven was behind it, there would be charges to follow.

I hoped there would be. Part of me was pretty sure he was in on it, and that the whole thing was some sort of convoluted ploy to get a hundred thousand dollars out of the bank without his wife knowing that he was the one who wanted it. But the other part was a little less sure. If he wanted a hundred thousand dollars, he could just get it himself. It was his. There was no reason to scare Diana this way.

"I guess I'll go to the office," I said. "Unless you want me to stay with you? For moral support, or whatever."

Diana shook her head. "Is something going on?"

Not really. At least not yet. I told her, "Last night, Zachary made the suggestion that the Russian girl looked like a stripper. I told him to look for Russian strip clubs."

Diana's eyes widened. "You sent Zachary—sweet, innocent Zachary—out to case strip clubs?"

Mendoza hid a smile.

"He's not that innocent," I protested, although I admit I squirmed a little. "He's over eighteen. He said they'd let him in. And he seemed excited about it."

Mendoza's grin widened.

"Why wouldn't he be?" Diana muttered, and raised her voice. "Let me know what he says. If he finds out anything."

I nodded. Mendoza did the same. And the two of us headed out to let Diana get ready for work and her trip to the bank.

Chapter Ten

Mendoza left us with a last scratch behind the ears for Edwina—nothing but a nod for me—and I climbed into the Lexus next to the dog, and headed for Music Row.

Morning rush hour had started while I was inside Diana's kitchen, so the trip took at least three times longer than it had going the other way earlier. But when I got there, the office itself was still empty and closed. It was too early for Rachel, and since Zachary's car wasn't in the lot, I assumed he'd gone home to his mother's house to sleep last night, after cruising the Russian neighborhood looking for strip clubs.

Given his excitement over the assignment, he'd probably stayed out much too late, and wouldn't be coming in until noon.

Which left me with very little to do.

While Edwina squatted on a patch of dirt, I let myself into the lobby and turned on the lights.

Everything looked the way it had last night when I left. Not that I had expected anything different.

I scooped some food into Edwina's bowl and

refreshed her water, and left her to eat while I headed down the hall to my own office.

The email account yielded little of interest. An offer for free paper with purchase of ink and toner from the office supply store we use, which I forwarded to Rachel. A reminder that I had a doctor's appointment a week hence, along with a—separate—suggestion that an online order of Viagra might seriously change my sex life for the better.

My sex life is non-existent at the moment, and has been since David left me for Jackie-with-a-q. I had a strong suspicion that it would take a lot more than an order of Viagra to fix it.

I didn't expect much from the office phone— everyone who knows me, knows my cell phone number—but when I picked it up, the canned voice told me we had a message. I pushed the button to play it back and leaned back in my chair to listen.

It took a second, and then a male voice came on. "Yeah. Um… Gina. This is… um… Steven."

He said it as if there was a question mark at the end. I sat bolt upright in my chair as he continued.

"Steven Morton?" As if I hadn't already figured out that part. "I know we haven't actually met, but… um… I recognized you yesterday. And the detective. Mendoza. Diana helped him with his divorce a couple of years ago."

Or more accurately, she'd helped Lola, Mendoza's wife. I'm not quite sure how the two of them ended up being friends through it all. It would have made more sense for Mendoza to resent Diana.

"She's probably worried," Steven continued, his

own voice betraying a hint of worry, too. "And I can't call her. So I thought maybe you could tell her—"

At that point, there was a noise in the background. Maybe a door opening? Or someone walking into the room? I heard a female voice, but not what it said.

"Nothing," Steven said, and then the line went dead. I deduced he'd disconnected the call so the woman he was with—Anastasia?—wouldn't realize he was talking to anyone.

If he was on his cell phone, all she had to do was check his calls to see what he'd been doing, of course. But maybe he wasn't.

I thought about dialing *69. That's still a thing, right? But what if the phone rang back there, and Anastasia realized that Steven had called someone last night? If she hadn't realized it already?

So I called Mendoza instead. "Will the telephone company tell me who called me, if they didn't leave a number?"

There was a moment's silence while he must be sorting through my question and figuring out what I wanted. "Who called?"

"Steven," I said.

"From where?"

"That's what I want to know. He left a message on the office machine in the middle of the night. If he wanted to talk to me, I have no idea why he didn't call my cell phone instead…"

"Maybe he didn't want to talk to you," Mendoza said. "Maybe he just wanted to leave a message."

Maybe.

"What did he say?"

"Not much." I repeated the few sentences Steven had said. "Here. It's on the recording. I'll play it back and let you listen to it yourself."

I made sure the recording was ready to go, and then held my cell phone up to the other phone while it ran. When the recording had finished, I put the phone back to my ear. "That's it. I guess the blonde came in at the end. Or someone did. I couldn't make out what she said, but Steven said 'Nothing,' and hung up, so she probably asked what he was doing, or something like that. I have no idea what happened after that."

"And how would you?" Mendoza said. "Did you try dialing *69?"

I told him I hadn't. "I was afraid the phone would ring back there. And that something bad might happen."

"Try it now. You're on your cell phone, right?"

I was. So with that in one hand, I pushed *69 on the desk phone and waited. The phone rang, and rang, and rang. Nobody picked up.

After a minute—or maybe it only felt like a minute but was actually less—I spoke into the cell phone. "Did you hear that?"

Mendoza grunted.

"If I call the phone company, will they be able to tell me where Steven called from? Will they want to? Or is it better if you do it?"

"I'll probably need a subpoena to access phone records," Mendoza said. "It's better if you ask."

"You could just go there in person. As long as the receptionist is female, you'll get all the records you want."

He didn't respond to that. "Let me know what you

find out."

He didn't give me time to say anything. I refrained from sticking my tongue out at the phone screen and went to dig up the number for the telephone company's customer service line.

Getting the information I wanted took much longer than it should have, of course. I spent a long time on hold. And when someone finally answered, she said she couldn't help me. In accented English, so Mendoza probably couldn't have gone to where she was even if he'd wanted to. I was probably talking to India. I was tempted to ask, but instead I asked to speak to a supervisor, and spent more time on hold. When the supervisor came on—if, indeed, it was the supervisor, and not just the customer service rep in the next cubicle pretending to be the supervisor—I was annoyed.

"All I want is to know where a call came from. Someone called me last night. He started to leave a message and got cut off. I tried *69, but no one's answering. All I want to know is where my friend called me from, so I can go there and make sure he's all right."

"If you're concerned about someone's well-being," the supervisor said snottily, "it's a matter for the police."

"I've already spoken to the police. Specifically, Detective Jaime Mendoza with the Nashville PD. Homicide. He told me he could get a subpoena and the information, but that it would be quicker for me to get it myself." And I wasn't even lying. "Of course, if you want to refuse to tell me where the call to my phone originated, while my friend is lying in a pool of blood somewhere..."

An image of Griselda Grimshaw appeared, unbid

and unwanted, and I ground to a halt while I tried not to imagine Steven in that same position, prone on a floor somewhere, with blood soaking his shirt. He hadn't sounded scared last night. He hadn't sounded like he was in danger. But of course that could have changed in the hours since he'd made the call.

And had changed, if the ransom note was real.

The supervisor heaved a long-suffering sigh, but agreed, very clearly against her will, to provide me the information I probably had the right to know. "When did the call come in?"

"Just before one this morning," I said. "To this number." I rattled off the office phone number and waited while she tapped buttons in the background. Eventually she came back with a number. It was local, judging by the prefix, but unfamiliar.

"Any chance you could look it up? Reverse lookup, or whatever? Find out where it belongs?"

It didn't sound like a cell phone. Around here, they mostly start with the same few numbers, which this didn't.

She sighed again, more deeply this time. I heard tapping.

"1843 Blackburn Drive," she said.

"1843…" I stopped in the middle of writing it down. "Are you sure?"

"I'm positive." She sounded irritated that I'd ask. Of course, she'd been sounding irritated about everything else, too.

I finished writing the address on the same piece of paper where I'd scribbled the phone number. "No chance you're mistaken?"

"None." She bit the word off in a way that indicated she'd like to bite me.

"I appreciate it," I said. "Thank you for—" *your time…*

She'd already hung up. This time I did not contain myself, but made the worst face I could manage, right at the phone. And then I called Mendoza back. "It's me."

"I can see that."

This time the background noises indicated that he was driving.

"Where are you going?" I asked.

"I've dropped the note off at the lab and put out the BOLO. I'm in the car, on my way to Franklin to talk to your friend."

She wasn't exactly my friend, and under other circumstances I would have said so. Now I had more important concerns. "You'll have to turn around. I got through to the phone company. The call came from 1843 Blackburn Road."

There was a beat. "That's my crime scene," Mendoza said.

I nodded. And then said, "Yes. Mrs. Grimshaw's house."

"They're messing with my crime scene?"

They probably weren't messing with it. They'd probably gone there to look around. Or maybe because they figured it would be safe, that no one would look for them there.

Or maybe they'd gone back to Araminta Tucker's house, and something had spooked them, so they'd taken refuge in Griselda Grimshaw's house next door. Where there was dried blood on the floor and a murder had taken place.

Maybe that didn't make a whole lot of sense once I started thinking about it.

"Just meet me there," I told Mendoza. I could hear him draw breath—probably to tell me I didn't need to bother coming; he knew where it was—and I hung up before he could get the words out.

He didn't call back to tell me not to come, so I guess he was OK with it. Or at least not so upset about it that he felt he needed to stop me. I left Edwina in the office, with a note for Rachel to let her out when she got there, which ought to be sometime within the next hour. The dog would be OK until then.

"I'll be back," I told her—Edwina—and headed out.

Mendoza had either teleported or been passing the exit when I called him, because when I pulled into Griselda Grimshaw's driveway, his car was already there. He must have just arrived, though, because he was still sitting behind the wheel.

Texting, I realized, when he got out with a grimace. "Sorry. Talking to my wife. Ex-wife."

None of my business. None at all. "Everything all right?"

Another grimace. "Fine. Just figuring out kid stuff."

That can be hard. Not that I have any personal experience with it, but David had two kids when I married him. I spent the first few years of my marriage trying to make friends with Krystal and Kenny, who wanted nothing to do with me—and who could blame them?

"Does your son like his step-father?"

Mendoza muttered something.

"Krystal and Kenny hated me," I said. "Not only did I break up their parents' marriage, but I took David away from them."

"Surely not?"

"That's what they saw. He dumped their mother and married me, and would rather spend time with me than with them. They weren't wrong. Although it wasn't my fault. He just wasn't that interested in what they were doing." And more interested, at that time, in bedding my twenty-two year old self.

Mendoza nodded. "Elias doesn't blame Mitch for anything. Or Lola. He blames me."

"I'm sorry," I said.

Mendoza shook his head. "All Lola did was hire Mitch. And all Mitch did was what Lola hired him to do. I was the one who cheated. And got caught."

"But she didn't have to marry him." And make him Elias's step-father.

Mendoza shrugged. "Water."

Under the bridge, I assumed. And the end of the discussion. Time to change the subject.

I glanced at the house. "Here we are."

Mendoza nodded.

"I guess you're going to ask me to wait outside?"

"No," Mendoza said. "You can come with me. As long as you stay behind me and make sure you don't get shot."

I translated that in my head. "You don't think they're here anymore."

"I think they left here two minutes after Steven hung up the phone last night," Mendoza said. "But just in case

I'm wrong, I'm going in first. And keeping you behind me."

Fine by me.

"Lead the way," I said, and fell in behind him as we made our way to the front door.

Mendoza unlocked it, and reached for his gun. I watched as he pushed the door open and ducked under the crime scene tape, leading with his gun hand. "Metro Police! Stay where you are!"

He hadn't told me I couldn't come inside, so I waited until he'd slithered along the wall to the dining room and turned the corner, still leading with the gun, before I crouched under the crime scene tape and shuffled into Mrs. Grimshaw's house.

I could hear Mendoza moving stealthily down the hallway to the left. Other than his quiet footsteps, everything was silent. If anyone was here, they were being very quiet about it.

The blood was still on the floor in front of the door, and I avoided looking at it as I glanced around. There was nothing I hadn't expected, that I hadn't already seen. The only new addition since yesterday was a lot of fingerprint powder on the doorjambs and flat surfaces.

Mendoza came back, holstering his gun. "Nobody here."

I nodded. I hadn't expected there to be, although part of me had been worried that he'd find Steven dead in one of the bedrooms. It was probably a positive sign that he hadn't. If nothing else, we knew that Steven had been alive, and seemingly unhurt, last night.

"Any clue as to what they were doing here?"

Mendoza shook his head. "I can't see anything that

wasn't here yesterday. Or anything missing. Maybe they just came in to use the phone."

Maybe. Although you wouldn't find me breaking into the home of a murdered woman, with crime scene tape all over the door, to use the telephone. If I didn't want to use my own phone, I'd find a telephone booth—they still do exist here and there—or go to a library or something.

"Hard to do at one in the morning," Mendoza remarked.

The library, at least. Although I might not want to drive around looking for a phone booth at one in the morning, either. Not that I'd be likely to want to call anyone at that time, anyway. "I wonder what Steven wanted."

"Something he didn't want the blonde to overhear," Mendoza said, "since it seems like he waited until she fell asleep before he hoofed it next door to use the phone."

Maybe that's what he'd done. Waited for Anastasia Sokolov to fall asleep, before he braved the elements and the murder house to make a phone call to me, to... what?

"Why didn't he call Diana?"

"You'll have to ask him," Mendoza said, shooing me toward the door, "when we find him."

I ducked under the crime scene tape and back out on the stoop. "Now what?"

Mendoza followed me. I stepped back while he locked the door behind us. "Now we go next door."

I glanced over at Araminta Tucker's house. "You don't think they're still there, do you?"

"Not likely," Mendoza said. "At least not since one

o'clock. But I want to see if they left anything."

If they hadn't left anything the first time—not even the trash in the cans—it wasn't likely that they'd have left anything this time, either. But I wouldn't mind another quick look at Araminta Tucker's house, so I followed him across the grass and up the driveway to the back of the house.

Where he shoved me behind him with one hand while he pulled his gun with the other.

I peered around his shoulder.

Ah. Yes. Unlike yesterday morning, when we'd been here, now the door stood open, the jamb splintered where the lock had been kicked or pushed in.

"Stay here," Mendoza told me, his voice tight. "I mean it."

I nodded. And stayed there while he slid sideways into the kitchen, gun at the ready, and disappeared.

I spent the time while he was gone alternately biting my fingernails and checking the trash and recycling cans, which were still empty. Then Mendoza came back, holstering his gun.

"What?" I demanded.

"Nothing. Aside from the broken lock, it looks exactly the same as yesterday."

So no furniture, no dishes in the cabinets, no empty pizza boxes or Chinese food containers. "No sign they were here?"

He shook his head.

"But we know they were next door."

He nodded.

"Why would they break the lock? They had a key, didn't they?" They must have. The lock hadn't been broken the last time we were here.

"I don't imagine they did," Mendoza said.

"So someone else did? Who?"

He shrugged. "Whoever shot Mrs. Grimshaw?"

"Why would whoever shot Mrs. Grimshaw wait twenty-four hours to break into the house next door? They had plenty of time to do it while Mrs. G was bleeding out on the floor."

"This place was occupied then," Mendoza said.

Yes, but... "If they'd shot Mrs. Grimshaw, it's not like they balk at shooting Anastasia. Or so you'd think."

Mendoza seemed to agree with that. Or at least he didn't argue.

We stood in silence a moment.

"What do we do now?" I asked.

He nodded to the cars in the driveway next door. "I guess we just keep doing what we were doing. I'll go see Araminta Tucker, and tell her that her house was broken into last night. And see if she can tell me anything she didn't tell you yesterday. And if Steven calls again, let me know."

I told him I would, and asked that he return the favor. And then we got into our separate cars and went our separate ways.

Chapter Eleven

I took the time to go home for a shower and a change of clothes before I headed back to the office. The dog had been fed, and by then, Rachel had probably arrived to take care of her. Edwina was covered. So I figured I could safely spend a few minutes getting out of yesterday's clothes.

As a result, it was close to ten by the time I finally made it back to Music Row. Rachel's car was in the lot by then, but Zachary's little compact was still missing.

"Have you heard from Zach?" I asked as I pulled the front door shut behind me.

Edwina looked up from her doggie bed in the corner, her stubby tail wagging.

Rachel shook her head. "Should I have?"

"I gave him a job last night, so I'm waiting to see what he discovered. Although he probably just stayed out too late and is sleeping in this morning."

Rachel arched an inquiring brow, and I told her what I'd done. She clicked her tongue. "Probably sleep until noon. Those places stay open all night. And all day.

He could still be there."

Surely not. "Don't they have to mop the floors sometimes? Like, from eight to ten?"

"Maybe," Rachel said doubtfully. "Do you want me to call him?"

"Let's give him a little more time. And anyway, if he'd discovered anything wildly exciting, he probably would have left a message."

That reminded me of Steven's message, so I told her about that. And then remembered to mention the ransom note that she also hadn't heard about. And the missing gun.

"This doesn't sound like a simple cheating-spouse case," Rachel said.

I shook my head. "We'll have to choose more carefully next time." If there was a next time. "I don't suppose anyone's called?"

"You checked the messages," Rachel said.

"Or emailed?"

She shook her head. "But we've only been in business a week, Gina. We'll get clients once word gets around."

I hoped so, since all the work I was doing now was pro bono, and at some point, I'd have to pay Rachel and Zachary and the electric company again.

With that in mind, I went into my office and drafted a letter which I thought we could send out to all my friends and acquaintances. I don't have a lot, since I've spent the past eighteen years as David's spouse, and most of the women I know are married to his business associates. But that meant that many of them, like me, were trophy wives to older, successful men, and God knows that older, successful men often take up with even younger women than their wives. So for the purpose of marketing my services to women with husbands who might cheat, I was quite well positioned.

With the draft sounding the way I wanted, I gave it to Rachel to proofread, and then we spent the next hour coming up with a mailing list. I told Rachel the names of people I remembered. She looked them up. I wrote down the names and addresses, and when it was all over, we had a list of twenty or so names that Rachel put together into a database.

"You should handwrite the envelopes, though," she told me. "More likely they get opened that way. If they don't look like a business communication."

"And less likely their husbands will realize what the letter is about," I added.

Rachel nodded. "You go start addressing envelopes. Then you can sign the letters, and we'll get them in the mail."

It sounded like a good plan, and the beginning of a mailing list. I retreated to my office and started addressing envelopes. When Rachel brought the letters—printed on nice, heavy stationary—I signed those, and we filled the envelopes. By then, it was past eleven-thirty. "I can take them to the post office," I said. "Or if you want to go to lunch first, you can."

Rachel said she liked the noon to one lunch hour, so I sent her out early, so she could hit the post office on her way. While she drove away, Edwina tinkled on a patch of dirt in the parking lot. When I went back to my office, she followed me in, jumped up on the sofa, and curled in a circle.

It was late enough that I thought it might be time to check on Zachary. He did not, however, answer his cell phone. I left a message—"It's almost noon. Are you planning to come to work today?"—and then dialed Mendoza. Unless Araminta Tucker had had a whole lot to say—or they had bonded over something on the TV— he must be finished talking to her by now. It was irritating how he hadn't called to update me.

I did realize that he didn't owe me an update. He was the police and I was an annoying civilian butting into his case.

But I was sharing what I found out with him. When I got Steven's message, Mendoza had been my first call. It wasn't like I was keeping anything from him. If I hadn't told him about Araminta Tucker—

Well, if I hadn't told him about Araminta Tucker, he would have found his way to her on his own. She owned the house next door to the crime scene, where the Russian girl had been. Mendoza would have made it his business to interview Araminta Tucker sooner or later.

But if I hadn't told him about my visit to her immediately, he hadn't had the girl's name so soon. I'd been helpful, dammit. Couldn't he be a little helpful in return?

Apparently he couldn't. The phone rang, and rang. Finally his voicemail picked up. "This is Detective Jaime Mendoza with the Nashville PD. Please leave a message at the sound of the tone. If this is an emergency, please call 911."

It wasn't an emergency, and I didn't want to be annoying—or any more annoying than I had to be—so I hung up without leaving a message. He'd see that I'd called. When he realized I hadn't left a voicemail, he'd probably figure out that I was just curious and didn't have anything important to say.

Maybe he'd call anyway.

I put the phone down and leaned back in my chair.

Nothing happened.

I twiddled my thumbs.

The phone still didn't ring.

I looked over at Edwina. She was curled into a circle. When she sensed my regard, she opened one eye and looked at me. Her stub of a tail gave a tentative wag. I smiled back. "Hi, sweetheart. I didn't want anything. Go back to sleep."

She closed her eye again. I looked up at the ceiling.

I can't swear to it, but I think I was partially asleep when the phone rang. I'd been hauled out of bed early by Diana's phone call this morning, and the office was quiet and warm. The dog was dozing, and all the various electronics made a soft sort of humming in the air, almost like the white noise you pay a lot of money for. Occasionally, Edwina snuffled. It was a very comforting sort of sound. Almost like sleeping next to David, who had been known to snore.

At any rate, the phone rang. I jerked upright, and the reason I think I may have been asleep, is that there was a thin line of drool on my chin.

I wiped it off with one hand as I reached for the phone with the other. *Jaime Mendoza*, the display said.

I smiled. "Good afternoon, Detec—"

"Save it," Mendoza's voice said. "I need you to come and meet me."

"Sure. Are you still in—" *Franklin?*

"No," Mendoza said. "Southern Hills Hospital. Room 316. Hurry."

He hung up before I could ask any more questions. I grabbed my purse and my jacket and ran.

Southern Hills Hospital sits, as you may have guessed, in the hills on the south side of town. Off Nolensville Road and Harding Place, to be exact. Not too far from Crieve Hall. I took the same exit I'd taken earlier, blew past the turnoff that would have taken me to Blackburn Drive, and barreled down Harding Place at a few miles above the speed limit. I screeched into the parking lot outside the hospital less than fifteen minutes after Mendoza called.

I had spent the whole trip—when I wasn't navigating turns and trying to avoid hitting, or being hit by, the other cars—mulling over what might be wrong.

Maybe Araminta Tucker had had a heart attack? Maybe Mendoza's gorgeousness had been too much for her, and she'd collapsed?

Or maybe he had accused her of having had something to do with her sister-in-law's murder, and a guilty conscience had brought on a medical issue?

She was already in an assisted living facility, though. Surely they had a doctor on staff? And anyway, there were hospitals closer to Franklin, weren't there? It was hard to imagine that they'd drive her all the way to Southern Hills if something was wrong.

Unless she had Southern Hills written down as her hospital of choice. It was the hospital closest to where she'd been living before she went into assisted living.

Or maybe it had nothing to do with Araminta

Tucker. Maybe Mendoza had found Steven. Maybe Steven really had been kidnapped, and had escaped from his kidnappers, and been hurt in the process, and now he was in the hospital. Maybe the blonde had shot him.

Or maybe it was Diana. Maybe she'd had an accident on her way to work. Or on her way to lunch. Or the bank. Or maybe the nutcase who had threatened to hurt her because he had to pay his ex-wife alimony had made good on his threat.

Or Rachel. Maybe Rachel had gotten in a car accident on her way to the post office.

Maybe it was my fault. Maybe I should have taken the damn letters to the mailbox myself...

I slammed the car door behind me and locked it on the run. And hurried through the lobby to the elevator, where I hopped from foot to foot while I waited the hour and a half it took for it to make it down from the fourth floor. When I'd gotten inside, the elevator took its sweet time creaking up to three, and then hung there an eternity before it deigned to open the doors. I turned sideways and slithered through the opening while the doors were still moving.

316 was to the right. I hustled down the hallway—not quite running, since I figured someone would try to stop me if I did, and then I'd have to waste valuable time arguing about why I was running in the hospital—and arrived outside 316 out of breath.

The door was cracked an inch or two. From inside I could hear Mendoza's voice, calm and even, and someone else's croak, too faint for me to make out who it belonged to. There was the whooshing noise of machines, or maybe some of the whooshing was in my head.

I pushed the door open and stuck my head through. And felt that same head go light and sort of fussy when I got a good look at what was going on.

It was a single room with a single bed, with a single occupant in it. He was hooked up to wires and tubes and a machine that looked like it was helping him breathe. That was where most of the whooshing was coming from. And if it hadn't been for the shock of red hair that stuck up—bright as fire against the white of the bandages and sheets—I would have had a hard time recognizing him.

I made an involuntary squeak, and put a hand over my mouth to hide it. But it was too late. Zachary's eyes cut my way, and Mendoza turned his head.

"Oh." He straightened. "You made good time."

"I think I probably broke a couple of traffic rules on the way here." I slipped through the door and into the room. And took a couple of steps closer to the bed. "Zach. That looks painful."

Zachary made a noise that might have been an attempt at laughter, or maybe just agreement.

"I'm so sorry," I said. "Is this because of the job I gave you last night?"

"We were just getting to that," Mendoza said, and turned back to the bed. "You OK for another couple of minutes?"

Zachary nodded. Or moved his head a fraction of an inch on the pillow.

"Would you recognize whoever did this to you?"

Zachary shook his head. His free hand—the other

was hooked up to a variety of tubes and wires—lifted to the top of his head and then moved down to his chin. To me it looked as if he was starting to do the sign of the cross, and I hadn't even realized he was Catholic, which made me feel bad.

Mendoza interpreted it differently. "They put something over your head?"

"M-hm," Zachary said.

"Can you guess where you might have come across them? Or was it random?"

Zach shook his head. "Nuh-uh."

"Not random?"

Apparently not. He said something. I didn't catch it, but Mendoza seemed to. "We'll start there."

That sounded positive. We had somewhere to start. Although I had a feeling when he said 'we,' he didn't mean me.

Zachary said something else. I sharpened my ears. "Tat…"

"Tattoo? Someone had a tattoo?"

Mendoza gave me a look, one that said clearly, "Don't try to help." I arched my brows at him.

"Tati," Zach said. "—ana."

"Tatiana? There was a girl there named Tatiana?"

He nodded. Leaning back, he looked exhausted. And Mendoza must have seen it, too. His voice gentled. "Should I talk to Tatiana? Or avoid her?"

Zachary managed a shrug. The machine must not have liked it, because it whooshed harder for a second before it settled down again.

"Not sure?" Mendoza said. "That's OK. But it's the place where Tatiana is?"

Zachary nodded.

"I'll find it. And find who did this. And arrest him. Or them."

Zachary's lips moved. There wasn't any sound behind the word, and Mendoza had to bend closer to hear it. Under the circumstances, I had no problem keeping my eyes off his posterior—my attention was focused on Zachary—but my peripheral vision noticed, and approved of the movement.

"Them?" Mendoza said. "Two? Three?"

There'd been two. Mendoza nodded and straightened. "We'll let you rest. I'll be back later."

"Me, too," I said, over Mendoza's shoulder. Zach lifted a hand in a weak wave, but I think he was asleep before we'd closed the door behind us.

Outside in the hallway I refrained—barely—from grabbing Mendoza's lapels and pushing him up against the wall so I could shake the answers I wanted out of him. Instead I folded my arms tightly across my midriff, the better to keep from assaulting him. "What happened?"

"I was talking to Araminta Tucker," Mendoza said, "when the hospital called. Zach was brought in earlier this morning. A shopkeeper on Thompson Lane discovered him in the alley behind a discount tobacco store when he came to work."

I opened my mouth, and he added, "He was interviewed. He has nothing to do with anything."

I closed my mouth again. And opened it. "Who interviewed him? You?"

Mendoza shook his head. "He called 911. An ambulance showed up. And a squad car. The officers took a statement."

"And you read it?"

"I spoke to them," Mendoza said. "The shopkeeper is out of it."

Fine. "So Zachary was brought here. What was wrong with him?"

"He'd been given a beating," Mendoza said, something which had been pretty obvious from looking at Zach. Either that, or he'd fallen down a mountainside. But since we don't have many of those around here, I'd assumed it was the second scenario.

"And?"

"It's mostly just scrapes and bruises. I know he looks bad, but most of it'll heal in a week with no after effects."

Mostly... "What's the damage that won't heal in a week?"

"He has a couple of broken ribs," Mendoza said. He sounded reluctant. "I'm guessing someone kicked him. More than once."

My stomach rebelled, and I swallowed. Hard. "And?"

"One of the broken ribs punctured a lung."

"That's why he has the machine that's making the whooshing noise?"

Mendoza nodded. "He'll be breathing on his own by tomorrow, most likely."

"They're keeping him until then, right?"

He nodded. "He'll be here a couple days, yeah. After that, we'll have to figure something else out."

We would? "Won't he be going home to his mother?"

"She kicked him out," Mendoza said. "Last week, when he quit his job at the Apex to go to work for you."

She had? "He didn't say anything about that to me."

"He wouldn't," Mendoza said. "He's been sleeping in your office or his car since then."

That explained the pizza box under the desk and the laundry in the backseat, anyway.

And derailed my train of thought.

"Have you put out a call for Zachary's car? If we find it, maybe we'll figure out where he was when this happened."

"It won't be there anymore," Mendoza said, "but yes, I have a call out for the car."

"Did he tell you anything helpful before I got there?"

He shook his head. "I'd only been there a minute or two. After the ambulance picked him up and took him to the hospital, the doctors knocked him out and worked on him for a while. It wasn't until he woke up this afternoon, and told them to call me, that I realized he was here."

"You didn't get a call this morning?"

"This morning," Mendoza said, "nobody knew who he was. Whoever did this took his wallet with his identification."

"You called his mother, I assume?" She might have kicked him out, but she did deserve to know where he was.

"The hospital did," Mendoza said. "We don't want him going home with her, though. Just in case these guys come back."

I guess we didn't. Although if that was the case, we

didn't want him bunking in the office by himself, either. I might drive up one morning and find him dead. Or the place burned to the ground.

"We have a couple days before we have to worry about it," Mendoza said. "He has insurance, I assume?"

He did. And I dreaded to think of the kind of money I was going to have to spend on this. Hospital stays don't come cheap. But yes, he had insurance. So at least he didn't have medical bills to worry about.

"What happens now?" I asked.

"I work on figuring out where he went last night and who he might have rubbed the wrong way to make them do this," Mendoza said.

I nodded. "I can help you with that. I'll come with you."

"Not a chance," Mendoza said.

I put my hands on his hips. "You realize that this is a free country, right? You can't stop me from going wherever I want to."

"I can put you in jail," Mendoza said. "For interfering with a police officer in the execution of his duties."

"You wouldn't dare."

He arched his brows, and I added, "OK. Fine. You'd dare. But you won't."

"Why not?"

"Because you feel bad for me," I said, and tried to look pitiful. It wasn't very hard at all. "I sent him out last night. It's my fault he got hurt. And I want to help you find who did this to him."

Mendoza hesitated. "I'm going to regret this, aren't I?"

"You'll regret it if you don't let me come along," I said. "And maybe I'll be useful. I can tell people I'm looking for my son. He looks enough like me to be."

"It's the red hair," Mendoza said. "Nothing else."

"It's something. It's more than you can say."

"I can show them my badge and tell them I'm the police."

"And see where that gets you," I said. "We might learn more if people just think I'm a mother looking for my son. The ones who know something might not want to talk to the police."

Mendoza seemed to consider it. Since I had a point, he didn't argue. "So who am I?" he asked instead. "Nobody'd believe that I'm Zach's father."

No. He was too young. And besides, he and Zach looked nothing alike.

"Friend of the family? Or maybe you can just be the cop I roped in to help me with this. You can roll your eyes at appropriate intervals over my insistence that my son would have come home last night, and wouldn't have visited those kinds of establishments."

"You want me to pretend to think you're an annoyance?"

"I'm sure you can handle it," I said. "It won't be too much of a stretch."

When he didn't seem to have an answer to that, or at least didn't have an objection, I set off down the hall. "Let's go."

Mendoza rolled his eyes—I'm sure of it—behind my back, but followed.

Chapter Twelve

We took Mendoza's car. He insisted. I don't know whether he was afraid of having me drive, or whether he just thought it was more appropriate to take the official car, but there it was.

The first place we went was the alley behind the discount tobacco store. There was a couple of them on Thompson Lane, but Mendoza must know the address, because he drove straight to it.

It wasn't anything to look at. Just a paved stretch of blacktop lined by brick buildings on one side and bordered by a chain link fence on the other. On the far side of the fence was a field that at one time must have been host to some sort of building. Part of the foundation still stuck up between the tufts of dry grass and straw.

The alley itself sported the usual array of trash cans and stacks of empty boxes. Behind one of the stores, a swarthy man with large ears was smoking. His eyes followed the path of the car as we rolled past, and I fought back a shiver.

Mendoza glanced over. "Problem?"

I figured, if I told him a random guy with a cigarette had given me a chill, he'd take that as proof that he shouldn't have let me come. So I smiled brightly. "No."

Mendoza grunted and pulled the car to a stop. I opened my door and got out.

There wasn't much to see. The store was a low-slung one story, with a strong steel door on the back, and no windows, most likely to discourage anyone from trying to break in. Tobacco and beer are popular items.

Mendoza nodded when I said so. "Safe spot to dump a body. Even if somebody'd been inside, they wouldn't have been able to see anything."

No. I glanced around. "I don't suppose there are cameras?"

"Not in this part of town," Mendoza said. And added, "I wish."

I wished, too. A camera might have shown us who left Zachary here.

"You said this is a safe spot to dump a body." Not that Zachary was a body. Although he had one. "Do you think the beating happened somewhere else?"

"Most likely," Mendoza said. He was looking around the alley with his hands on his hips. The gorgeous designer suit and polished shoes were in sharp contrast to our less than stellar surroundings. "Not enough blood for it to have happened here."

I suppressed another shiver. "You'd know."

He shot me a quick look. "It's my job."

"That's what I meant," I said. "Although usually your victims are dead. Zachary isn't."

He shook his head. "They weren't trying to kill him. If they were, they'd have made sure he was dead before they dumped him."

"Bar brawl gone wrong?"

"Not likely," Mendoza said. "People who brawl in bars don't generally cover each other's heads with sacks before they whale in."

Perhaps not. I haven't been in enough bar brawls to know. "What, then?"

He shrugged. "They clearly wanted to make sure he couldn't describe them. It looks more like punishment. Or maybe interrogation."

"What would anyone interrogate Zachary over?"

"No idea," Mendoza said. "The Russian girl?"

Anastasia? Maybe. That's the reason he'd been down here, in this part of town.

I took a couple of steps back and looked up and down the alley. The guy with the cigarette was still there, and watching us. "Is there anywhere around here where he might have been? Before he ended up in the alley?"

"Any number of places, I imagine," Mendoza said.

"Let me rephrase my question. When he left last night, it was to see whether he could find a place where the girl, Anastasia, might have worked. We talked about strip clubs, but I suppose there are other possibilities, too. Is there anything like that around here?"

"Nothing I know of," Mendoza said, "but I don't work vice."

"Different department?"

"Special investigations," Mendoza said. "Narcotics, gangs, gambling, and organized prostitution. In criminal investigations, we mostly deal with homicides and missing persons."

"Like Steven."

"More like missing persons we don't assume are in bed with someone other than their spouses."

Right. "What about kidnapping and ransom notes? Who handles that?"

"In this case," Mendoza said, "me. Usually, that's a federal crime. The FBI takes over. But since it's connected to the homicide I'm working on, it's mine."

Lucky him. "And Zachary?"

"Is mine, too," Mendoza said, "by virtue of being connected to the homicide I'm working on."

"So for you, does it all come back to Mrs. Grimshaw?"

He hesitated. "Not necessarily. I have a feeling it'll turn out to come back to the girl. But I can't be sure."

"Did Araminta Tucker give you the impression that she'd be capable of driving to Crieve Hall to shoot her sister-in-law?"

Mendoza's lips quirked, and a dimple made a quick appearance in one cheek. My stomach swooped. "Araminta Tucker gave me the impression that she'd be capable of pretty much anything. She propositioned me."

That didn't even surprise me. And not only because it was Araminta Tucker. "That probably happens to you a lot. Doesn't it? The blonde news reporter yesterday…"

"Not in old folks' homes," Mendoza said. "Can we get this conversation back on track?"

I wasn't aware that it had left the track, but if he wanted to talk about Zachary, I'd talk about Zachary. "I think we should talk to the guy down there, with the cigarette."

"Why?" Mendoza said.

"Because he's been watching us since we drove into this alley. And because he's a couple doors down from where the... from where Zachary was dumped. He might know something."

"Knock yourself out," Mendoza said.

"Me?" He wanted me to go talk to the guy? When I'd said that I thought we should talk to him, I'd really meant that I thought Mendoza should.

"You're the one who said that people might not want to talk to a cop," Mendoza said. "And you're the one with the PI license. If you're going to investigate crimes, you're going to have to get used to talking to people."

"I wasn't planning to investigate crimes," I said. "I was planning to investigate cheating spouses."

"Surprise," Mendoza answered.

Right. I glanced down the alley and took a breath. "Wish me luck."

He didn't, but he nodded. I could feel his eyes at my back as I headed down the alley toward the rear of the store where the guy was hanging out, smoking.

He watched me approach with dark, expressionless eyes. I smiled brightly. "Good afternoon."

He didn't answer. "My name is... um... Nancy." Probably better not to give him my real name, come to think of it. "Do you work here?"

He sat just to the left of a steel door. There was no sign on or above the door to indicate what kind of business it was. The only ornamentation was a small buzzer next to the door. I guess if you were back here, and you pushed the button, it was because you knew what kind of establishment you wanted to get into.

I also deduced that it probably wasn't the kind of business that took deliveries of any kind. If they did, the back door would have been more clearly marked. The discount tobacco store proclaimed, in big letters, what it was, even here in the rear.

The man didn't answer. He just kept looking at me with unblinking, dark eyes.

"I'm looking for information about what happened last night," I said. "My son," the lie came more smoothly this time, "was beaten up and left outside the back of the tobacco store."

He didn't say anything.

"Were you here last night?"

He shook his head. So at least he understood what I was saying. I guess that was something. "What about this morning?"

He shook his head.

"You're here now."

He stared at me. I gave up. "Thanks for your time." I turned on my heel. *Thanks for nothing.*

He watched me trudge back up the alley. Unlike Mendoza, I was pretty sure this guy was looking at my butt.

The detective was waiting where I'd left him. He arched his brows at me. "Anything?"

"No. I don't know whether he can't speak, or just didn't want to speak to me. But he said—or I asked and he shook his head—that he wasn't here last night. Or this morning."

Mendoza glanced down the alley. "So he knows nothing."

"Or won't share what he knows." If he did know

anything. "I told him Zachary's my son. So if you decide to go talk to him, or you come across him again, keep that in mind."

"If he wouldn't talk to you," Mendoza said, "he isn't going to talk to me. Let's go." He headed for the car. I followed.

We drove down the rest of the alley, and around to the front of the building. In case I haven't mentioned it, it was a strip mall. A long row of stores stuck together. The discount tobacco store was toward one end. The storefront the guy had been sitting outside turned out to belong to a dry cleaner. There was also a Radio Shack, a Chinese restaurant, and the ubiquitous Great Clips hairdresser.

"Did you say there's a Russian grocery around here?" Mendoza asked.

I nodded. "That's what Zachary said."

"Any idea where?"

I didn't. "But if you'll hold on a few seconds, I'll look it up."

Mendoza held on while I accessed Google on my phone. "A quarter of a mile that way." I pointed right. Mendoza turned the car in that direction.

Two minutes later, we pulled to a stop outside the Russian market. Mendoza cut the car engine. "Let's go."

"You're coming in?"

"I'm going to talk to whoever's here," Mendoza said, "and ask whether they were open late enough last night that Zachary might have stopped by. And if he did, if he said anything. You can look around. You probably think more like he does."

I wouldn't be too sure about that. I was twenty years

older than Zach, and female. Mendoza was only thirteen or fourteen years older, and male. Chances were that he thought more like Zach.

But he was the detective, and he had the badge and gun. I had neither. So when we walked into the store, he headed for the cashier and I started wandering, trying to see the store through Zachary's eyes.

It was pretty interesting. I've been in ethnic grocery stores before. Mexican and Asian, mostly. The more mainstream ones. This one carried some things I didn't expect to see. Like caviar in tubes. The kind you squeeze. Like a tube of toothpaste. And they had several kinds of caviar, both red and black. Until I saw it, I hadn't had any idea that red caviar was even available. Or for that matter, tubed caviar.

There was also a healthy selection of Eastern European beers, and an even healthier selection of herring in jars and tins. By itself, in tomato sauce, in mustard sauce, in wine sauce or cream sauce. Pickled herring. Fermented herring. Herring in aspic.

Then there was the canned beef. Including meatballs in sauce. Made from reindeer.

Up near the checkout registers, there was the usual assortment of candy. Russian candy. There was also a bulletin board, with some pieces of paper stuck to it. I wandered in that direction. A few yards away, Mendoza was busy charming the woman behind the register.

In addition to the usual fliers for lawn care and moving services, there was a schedule for the Nashville Ballet pinned to the corkboard. Maybe not so surprising, as Zachary had told me the owner of the grocery store was a former ballet dancer. There was also a calendar turned to the current month. (October, in case you wondered.) The picture above the calendar showed a building topped by several onion domes. The Kremlin? Or maybe they're more like our church spires, and occur mostly on places of worship?

I'll be the first to admit I don't know much about Russian culture. I know that the domes are uniquely Russian, or at least Americans associate them with Russia, but I don't know enough to know whether they only occur on certain types of buildings.

It was a pretty photograph, anyway: a brick building topped by a tower (with a tiny, golden onion dome on top), and several, much bigger onion domes. A white and blue stripe, a yellow and green swirl, a red and green checkered *and* swirled pattern, a red and white zigzag…

St. Basil's Cathedral, Moscow, the tiny script below the picture said.

I stared at it, rapt, for a full minute—how did they do that?—before I remembered what I was doing here, and turned my attention to the rest of the services on offer.

A business card for a local vet was tucked into the corkboard frame, along with a couple others. A seamstress or tailor with an Eastern European name. A liquor store; maybe they specialized in vodka.

Or maybe not.

A club. Stella's.

Music. Dancing. Girls.

"Hey," I said.

Nobody answered. I looked over my shoulder. Mendoza had his elbow on the counter and was dimpling at the girl behind it. He seemed to have settled in for the duration. She looked dazzled, as well she should.

"Hey!"

He straightened. The girl gave me a look of concerted dislike.

"Never mind," I said, since I had realized that what I was doing was stupid. Much better to leave Mendoza to be charming—he did it so well, and if there was anything to get out of the girl, he'd get it. Meanwhile, I'd just take the business card out of the frame of the corkboard and stick it in my pocket.

I did just that, and headed for the front door. "I'll wait for you outside," I told Mendoza on my way past. I think he nodded, but I didn't look over my shoulder to be sure.

It was another five or ten minutes before he finally sauntered out. By then, I'd had time to inspect the business card in detail—there was nothing on it that I hadn't already seen—and look up the address of the club on Google maps. It was within a mile of here, not too far from the funeral home where I'd held the services for David last month.

"What?" Mendoza wanted to know when he came out the door.

I gestured to the car, and he opened it. When we were both inside, I told him. "I found something. What about you?"

He turned the key in the ignition. The sedan purred to life. It wasn't much to look at—incognito police vehicles rarely are—but it drove well. As he reversed out of the parking space, he said, "She worked last night. She remembers Zachary. He looked around for a minute, and then he asked her if she knew a girl named Anastasia."

"Not very diplomatic." Or smart.

Mendoza shook his head. He was watching the traffic on Thompson Lane, and when he spotted a gap, he punched the gas. We shot across four lanes of traffic and into the far lane that would be going south at the intersection with Nolensville Road. I swallowed a shriek as we came close to being creamed by an oversized SUV coming up behind us. The driver lay on the horn. Mendoza flipped a switch on his dashboard, and blue lights flickered in the sedan's rear window. The SUV fell back, and Mendoza flipped the switch off. "Works every time."

I hid a smile. "So what else did the girl say? Her name wasn't Tatiana, was it?"

He shook his head. "Susan."

"And did she know Anastasia?"

"She said she didn't," Mendoza said, and took the turn onto Nolensville Road without slowing down. "To me and to Zachary."

"And?"

"He asked her if there were any other Russian or Eastern European businesses where Anastasia might work. Or where they might know her. She referred him to the bulletin board."

I pulled out the business card I had appropriated. "Ta-dah!"

Mendoza squinted at it.

"Eyes on the road," I told him. "It's a club called Stella's. They're advertising the old cliché: women, wine, and song."

Mendoza arched his brows and I added, "Music, dancing, girls. I'll let you see the card, but not while you're driving. I want to get there in one piece."

"Tell me where to go, then."

I did. "It's just below the entrance to the zoo. On the other side of the street."

The car zoomed down Nolensville Road, past Boling & Howard Funeral Home. We were already almost back to Southern Hills Hospital. The entrance to the zoo was coming up on the right.

"You said you talked to Araminta Tucker earlier," I said.

Mendoza nodded.

"Did you happen to bring the conversation around to Edwina?" If Araminta was Griselda Grimshaw's nearest relative and heir, chances were Edwina's fate was in her hands.

I tried to imagine Edwina living in the fussy living room with the big screen TV. Those big bat ears would probably take a beating from the volume. The poor thing would go deaf in no time.

"She doesn't want Edwina," Mendoza said.

"Are you sure?"

"It's a pet free zone. And she wouldn't want Griselda's animal, anyway. She said to take her to the pound."

My jaw dropped. "Surely not?"

"That's what she said."

"You aren't going to, are you?"

He shot me a look. "I planned to tell her that the dog's taken care of. If she chooses to believe that I took her to the pound, then she can believe that."

"Thank you."

After a second I added, "So you'll let me keep her?"

"I thought I'd give you first refusal. If you don't want her, I'll find someone else. But I'm not taking that sweet little dog to the pound."

Good. "I'll keep her," I said. "I didn't realize I wanted a dog. Or... I didn't want a dog. But I kind of like having a dog."

It was nice to share my bed with another warm body, even if this one was around twenty pounds and not good for much except licking my feet.

Mendoza nodded. "If you change your mind, let me know."

"I won't change my mind," I said. "And if something happens to me, I'm sure Rachel will step up. Or Zachary. Once he gets out of the hospital."

The nightclub was coming up on the left, and I pointed it out to Mendoza.

He flipped on his turn signal. "It might be a while until he's ready for active duty again. You'll have to go easy on him."

"No undercover assignments for a while?"

Mendoza's lips quirked. "Better not. And don't expect him to walk the dog for you. It'll be some time until his lung is healed and he can breathe as well as he did."

He slotted the car into a parking space outside Stella's.

"I feel terrible about what happened," I admitted.

Mendoza put the car in park, twisted the key in the ignition, and turned to me. "You didn't do anything wrong."

"I sent him out to look for information."

"He's an adult," Mendoza said. "And if I know him, he was probably excited about it."

He had been. But— "If I'd realized what would happen…"

Mendoza nodded. "You wouldn't have done it. That goes without saying. But you couldn't have known. It isn't logical that someone would do that to him just for asking questions."

"So maybe he did something else. Hit on someone's girlfriend or something."

"Zachary?" Mendoza said. "I don't see that happening. Do you?"

I didn't, now that he mentioned it. Zachary is cute and freckled, and a nice kid, and smart and funny with a lot of other good qualities—plus, he'd saved my life—but I didn't see him as any kind of a Don Juan.

"Maybe there's something about the girl we don't realize."

"That's what I'm thinking," Mendoza said. He pushed his door open. "Are you coming in, or staying here?"

I looked at the building. It was large, and looked like it might be an old mattress warehouse or something, that someone had morphed into something else. The exterior was painted black with purple trim, and next to the steel door was a mural of three scantily clad women dancing among shooting stars. It looked weirdly familiar, but it took me a full minute to place it. Then it clicked.

"*Xanadu!*"

"Bless you," Mendoza said.

"No, no. *Xanadu*. The movie. It looks like the mural

from the movie." Somewhat. Enough that the comparison had struck me.

Mendoza looked at it. His face stayed blank.

"You're too young," I said, disgusted. "It probably came out a decade before you were born."

He shrugged. "Coming?"

I opened my door. "Yes."

From the outside, at least, it didn't look like a strip club. The women in the mural were scantily clad, perhaps, but they wore more than pasties. And there wasn't a pole in sight. At least not in the picture.

Mendoza led the way to the door and twisted the knob. Nothing happened.

"I guess it's before business hours," I said.

Zachary and Rachel had both said strip clubs stayed open twenty-four/seven, but this one was clearly locked up tight.

"Let's check the back." Mendoza was already moving. I trailed behind him around the corner of the building, looking left and right. The parking lot was pretty much empty aside from Mendoza's sedan. Zachary's car was nowhere to be seen, but of course that didn't mean he hadn't been here last night.

"There's the back door."

Mendoza headed for it. I followed.

It looked a lot like the service entrance to the dry cleaners on Thompson Lane. Another steel door with a buzzer next to it, and nothing else. Mendoza put a finger on the buzzer and leaned.

Nothing happened. We couldn't hear anything through the steel door and the cinderblock walls, but I assumed that somewhere, a bell was ringing. Or a light was flashing, or something was happening. Something to indicate that there were people out here.

Nobody answered, though. The door remained stubbornly shut.

"I don't suppose this would fall under the same criteria as Araminta Tucker's house," I said.

He glanced over. "Excuse me?"

"You went into Araminta Tucker's house to look around yesterday."

"It was next door to a crime scene," Mendoza said.

I looked around. "This might actually be a crime scene. If Zachary was attacked here."

"We don't even know that Zachary was here," Mendoza said.

"We may not be able to prove it. But I'm pretty sure he was. I told him to check out any clubs he found where a Russian girl might work, or might have worked. It makes perfect sense that he'd check out this one. But we can ask him."

"Later," Mendoza said. He had his head tilted back, and was looking up under the eaves of the building. After a second, he pulled out his badge and opened it up. "Police. Open the door."

I tilted my head back, too, and squinted up into the darkness under the overhanging eaves. After a second I could make something out. "Camera?"

Mendoza nodded.

We waited a little longer. Nothing happened this time, either. Either no one was inside—most likely—or Mendoza's badge did nothing to convince them that they should open the door for him.

"Guess we'll have to come back later," I said.

He shot me a look. "I might be a little busy. I have an operation to set up at the Arena tonight."

Oh. Right. I'd forgotten about that in the excitement. "Thanks for reminding me. What do you want me to do?"

"Go home," Mendoza said, moving away from the door and around the building. Since he was still talking, I was forced to follow. "Take your little dog with you. Don't come back here alone. If they beat up Zachary, they won't be happy about you coming around asking questions."

I trotted behind him toward the car. "I meant about the Arena thing. The money drop. Or the newspaper drop, I guess. What do you want me to do?"

He stopped next to the sedan. "Go home. Take your little dog—"

"Thank you." *Sheesh.* "I heard you the first time. You mean, I'm not supposed to be at the Arena tonight?"

"No," Mendoza said. "I've got it."

"Don't you think Diana might want some moral support?"

He sighed. And then he unlocked the car doors and opened mine. Instead of getting in, I watched as he walked around the front of the car to his own side. "We'll stay out of your way."

"Sure you will." He opened his own door and slid behind the wheel. The door closed with a decisive *thump*. I was just about to follow suit when a car took the turn into the parking lot and bumped to a stop next to us.

Chapter Thirteen

The driver was a man around Mendoza's age, but a lot less good-looking, with a prominent nose and lank, brown hair that fell across his forehead. "Help you?"

Mendoza must have decided to let me handle it, because he didn't get back out of the car. I turned to the man. He was looking me up and down in a rather unpleasant way, and then he addressed a comment, in a language I didn't know, into the car. I guess he had a buddy in the passenger seat. While I couldn't understand the words, the gist was crystal clear. It was a comment on some part of my anatomy, or maybe the overall package, and something about it seemed to amuse the gentlemen. If I can use the term loosely.

I ignored it. As one has to. "I'm looking for someone."

He gestured to the building. "We're closed."

"I can see that. I'm looking for information about my son. He might have been here yesterday. Hold on."

I fumbled my phone out of my purse and flicked through the photographs until I came to a selfie we had taken last week, on our first day in the office. Me in the middle holding the phone, with Rachel on one side of me, and Zachary on the other. I showed it to the man. "There he is."

He looked at it. "Don't know him."

"Are you sure? Someone told me he might have come here last night."

He didn't answer, and I added, "Would you mind if I ask your friend?"

I didn't wait for an answer, just took a step past him and leaned into the open doorway. The man in the passenger seat might have been the first guy's brother, and maybe cousin. Same big nose, same deep-set eyes, same brown hair.

I shoved the phone in his face. "See? My son. With the red hair and freckles." I was perhaps emphasizing the resemblance a little too much, since I was afraid there wasn't enough of one. So I moved on quickly. "Have you seen him? Maybe yesterday?"

He shook his head. "No." And pushed my hand back, and me out of the car. But not before I had seen three other people in the backseat.

Girls. Or young women.

It was just a quick impression, but they were all pretty and blond. And stewed together in the rear of the car like three herring in a can. Behind some sort of divider between the front and back seats.

I pretended I hadn't noticed them, and straightened. "Are you sure you haven't seen him?" I shoved the phone back at the first guy. He took a step back.

"Listen, lady..."

"I'm sorry," I said, and tried my best to channel

motherhood, "I'm just worried, you know? He didn't come home last night."

He said something else I didn't understand—was it Russian?—but the gist of this, too, was all too obvious. Maybe he'd gone home with a girl, and what kind of mother was I, anyway, who didn't let my little boy grow up and be a man?

"That reminds me," I said. "Do you have a girl working here called Anastasia?"

He shook his head, but I think I saw something flicker in his eyes for a second. Although I admit it was hard to tell. They were dark and very deep-set, under prominent brows.

I wondered whether I should ask about Tatiana, but if she was one of the girls in the backseat, it might be better not to.

I dropped my phone back in my purse. "Thank you for your time."

He grunted.

"I'll get out of your way and let you open up your establishment."

He didn't say anything else. I moved past him toward Mendoza's car. And I admit the back of my neck was crawling a little. The whole situation was creepy. The two men were creepy. The fact that they had three young women stuffed into their back seat was a bit creepy. And the fact that I believed Zachary had been here last night, and had gotten beat up for his trouble, made the whole thing more than creepy.

Until I was actually inside the car with the door closed, part of me was worried that they wouldn't let me leave.

"Go," I told Mendoza as soon as the door was shut behind me.

He went. "You OK?"

"More or less." I watched in the mirror until we were out of sight of the nightclub, and told him, "Turn around. And go back the other way."

He shot me a look.

"Just do it," I said. "I'll explain in a minute."

I'm not sure what he thought, but he did it. On the next block, he waited for a gap in traffic and made a U-turn that put us on the other side of the road, going back toward the nightclub.

"Here." I pointed to the parking lot of a fast food restaurant. "Pull in."

"You have a craving for a Big Mac?"

Yuck. No. A Big Mac would add a good half hour to my workout tomorrow morning. And that was in addition to the half hour I had to add from not working out today.

"I want to see," I said. "They had three girls in the backseat of that car. Young women. Late teens, early twenties. Blond. Pretty. I want to see what they do with them."

Mendoza didn't say anything. There wasn't much to say, I guess. The implications were pretty clear to both of us.

Unfortunately, what we could see wasn't much. By now, the car—a black sedan; why are they always black sedans?—was on its way around the corner of the building.

"Taking them in through the back," Mendoza muttered.

So it seemed. And much smarter of them. The parking lot ended in a retaining wall. There was nothing behind the building but a hillside, and on top of that, maybe an apartment complex. A couple of two-story brick buildings with blank walls facing us. Barely visible behind a scraggly line of trees.

"If we were on top of that hill," I began.

Mendoza nodded. "No way to get there before they're inside, though."

No. They had probably moved their cargo through the back door already. By the time we could figure out how to get up to the apartment complex and make our way into the trees, there'd be nothing to see.

"Do you want to go ring the bell again?"

"It won't do any good," Mendoza said. "But I think I might want to have a talk with this guy I know in Special Investigations. And maybe ICE."

"Immigration and Customs?"

He nodded.

"Trafficking?"

"We're not immune from it," Mendoza said. "A lot of what goes on is interstate trafficking. Young American girls selling themselves—or being sold by their pimps—at truck stops up and down the interstates. But we see our share of foreign trafficking, too. It isn't all that long ago that Special Investigations shut down a string of Asian massage parlors that were a front for prostitution."

I hadn't heard anything about that, but I'd take his word for it.

"It happened in the spring," Mendoza said. "You weren't interested in crime then."

I guess I hadn't been. I'd been the happily married trophy wife of David Kelly, with no idea that my husband had already taken a mistress and was juggling both of us until he could see his way clear to divorce me.

I scowled. "It's not that I'm particularly interested in crime, you know. All I was supposed to do, was figure out whether Steven Morton was cheating on Diana."

Mendoza nodded.

"It wasn't my fault that somebody got killed next door."

He shook his head.

"And if it hadn't been for Edwina walking around loose, I wouldn't even have known about it."

He shook his head. His lips were twitching.

"Things have gotten a little out of hand. But it's not like I can leave Diana to figure this out on her own at this point. She asked me for help."

"Of course," Mendoza said, and sounded like he meant something else entirely.

I folded my arms across my chest and stuck my lower lip out.

Across the street, nothing happened.

"We might as well go," Mendoza said. "I'm guessing they're in there for the rest of the night."

I guessed the same thing. "Are there any other places we should look at while we're down here?"

There was the Russian-sounding seamstress and the vet who'd had their business cards next to the card for Stella's. But it wasn't likely that either of them had been open when Zachary set out on his errand last night.

Mendoza shook his head. "I'll take you back to your car."

He put his own into gear and reversed out of the parking spot. We headed back up Nolensville Road toward Southern Hills, where Mendoza found my car and slotted his into the empty space next to it. "There you go."

"You're not coming up?"

His brows drew down. "You're going up to see Zach?"

"I thought I might," I said, with a glance at the dashboard clock. I still had almost an hour before Rachel left the office. Enough time to check on Zachary and see whether I could get confirmation that he'd actually been at Stella's last night. There wasn't any doubt in my mind, but independent corroboration would be nice. "Unless you'd prefer that I don't?"

He would clearly prefer that I didn't. However, before I could remind him that it was a free country and that I would be paying for Zach's hospital stay, he turned off the car. "I'll come with you."

"I was going to tell you what happened," I said, but I got out of the car, too. We walked toward the entrance side by side.

Upstairs, Zachary was dozing in the same hospital bed as earlier. He was alone. If he'd been my son, or rather, if I'd been his mother, I would have been by his side. Zachary's mother was nowhere to be seen.

I'd never met her, but I found myself developing quite a dislike for the woman.

Zachary blinked at us when we stepped into the room. It seemed to take a few seconds before he recognized us. "Oh," he said eventually, his voice scratchy. "'s you."

I smiled brightly. Maybe it was just my imagination, but the bruises on his face looked even worse than they had just two hours ago. "We're back."

Zachary looked blank.

"We were here a couple hours ago," Mendoza told him, and moved closer to the bed. "How are you feeling?"

Zachary shrugged.

I stepped up next to Mendoza. "We had a look around, trying to figure out what happened to you. Or who did this."

Mendoza added, "Susan at the Russian grocery store says hello."

Zachary looked nonplussed for a second, before he nodded.

I pulled the business card for Stella's out of my bag. "Do you remember seeing this? Did you go there?"

Zachary looked at it. It seemed to be hard for him to concentrate. Or maybe his memory was shot.

It was even possible he might have a concussion. Mendoza hadn't mentioned it, but maybe he didn't know, either.

"I think," Zachary whispered, "maybe…?"

"Don't worry about it." Mendoza gave me a look and I dropped the card back into my purse. "You mentioned Tatiana. Who's she?"

Zachary's eyes got that vague look again, that indicated he was trying to remember. His pupils were tiny, probably a result of whatever was going into his arm from the clear bag hanging above his bed.

"A girl. I met her…" He trailed off.

"At the club? Stella's?"

"Yeah..." After a second he added, "Maybe."

"OK." Mendoza must have realized, as I had, that this wasn't getting us any forwarder. "Have some rest. I'll be back tomorrow."

"Me, too," I said. "Everything at the office is fine. Rachel is taking care of the dog. I'll take her home with me. Edwina, not Rachel."

The corners of Zachary's lips turned up. At least I'd made him smile.

"You've missed some things while you've been laid up here," I added. "Tonight Diana's supposed to bring a hundred thousand dollars to the Arena downtown, in exchange for Steven. The ransom note came this morning."

Zachary's mouth dropped open.

"I'll stop by in the morning and tell you all about it."

He nodded.

"Get some rest," Mendoza told him. "We'll be back."

Zachary nodded and closed his eyes obediently. We tiptoed toward the door and out.

Back in the parking lot, Mendoza said, "I'll go see to the arrangements for tonight."

"I'll go pick up the dog and check in with Diana," I said. "And if she wants my company, I guess I'll see you later."

"Hopefully that won't happen," Mendoza said, dashing all my hopes, "but if you're there and you see me, pretend you don't know who I am."

Seriously? Was I that much of an embarrassment? "Why?"

He looked at me as if the answer was obvious.

"Because I don't want to be made for a cop. Just another hockey fan."

Ah. Yes, that made sense.

"If I see you, I won't bat so much as an eyelash," I said. "You'll be dead to me. I promise."

His lips twitched. "You don't have to go that far. Just ignore me. And tell Diana to do the same."

I promised I would, and we went our separate ways. He headed for downtown to make arrangements, and I headed for the office to update Rachel and rescue Edwina.

Rachel was shocked and appalled, of course, when she heard what had happened to Zachary, and stated her intention to stop by the hospital later to spend some time with him. "I can't believe his own mother wouldn't be there with him. Why, if he was my baby…!"

I nodded. "It's horrible. Did you know that his mother kicked him out? Did he tell you?"

"I wondered," Rachel said. "I saw all the clothes in the back of his car. And his computer. And some other belongings. It looked like he was carrying most of his life around in that car. But I didn't want to ask and make him feel bad."

I nodded. I'd noticed the clothes, too—I had assumed he was planning to do laundry, so I hadn't even been as quick on the uptake as Rachel—as well as the pizza box in the office: the same pizza box he'd taken home for dinner two nights ago. I should have figured it out sooner than I did. "We're going to have to work something out. He'll be in the hospital for another day or two, but when he gets out—with cuts and bruises and a punctured lung—we can't have him sleeping in his car."

Rachel agreed. "That wouldn't be good for him."

"He can stay here, I guess. Once we figure out what's going on with Steven and the Russian girl, and there's no danger in it. Although I'd prefer for him to be somewhere safer. And more comfortable." More comfortable than both the car and the office couch.

Rachel nodded.

"I can't take him to the Apex with me," I said. "If his mother had a problem with him working for me, she definitely wouldn't appreciate it if he moved in with me. And anyway, I only have the one bedroom."

"I have two," Rachel said. "I could take him in, if he wanted. But he's a grown man. He'd probably prefer his own place."

He probably would. "We'll have to talk to him about it, I guess. Once he's out of the hospital and he can think straight again. Right now, he's too out of it to string more than a couple of words together."

Rachel tsked.

"We did find the place where we think he was last night. We went to the Russian grocery store he told me about, and the clerk said he'd been there. And there was this business card on the bulletin board." I pulled it out of my purse and put it on Rachel's desk. "We went there, but it was closed up tight. But just as we were about to leave, this car drove up."

I told Rachel about the two men and the three young women. Her lips pursed as she listened, and after a second she started clacking on the computer keyboard. "The place belongs to someone called Stella Ivanov. Hence the name, I guess."

I nodded.

"She's owned it a couple of years. Bought it off a corporation called BGH. Got a good deal on it, too."

Good for her.

Rachel leaned back on the office chair. It creaked. "Let me guess. You're going there tonight, when they close, to see if you can get a better look at the girls."

The thought had crossed my mind. However— "I'm not sure I'll be able to. It depends on how long this operation at the Arena takes. I have to call Diana next, and see if she wants moral support."

Rachel refrained from rolling her eyes, but I could see that she wanted to. "Just tell her you don't want to miss the excitement, Gina. You don't have to fib to the person who hired you."

I guess I didn't. But it still seemed more polite to couch the request as me doing her a favor rather than her doing me one.

"At any rate, I don't know how long I'll be there. I guess it depends on what happens. Mendoza is making arrangements, so I guess they're hoping to catch someone in the act of picking up the money. It could take some time. And I don't know how late the club stays open."

"Later than the Arena," Rachel said. "My guess is you'll have time to do both. Unless you plan to get some sleep at some point tonight."

I hadn't really thought about that part of it. I'd been up early this morning. If I went to the Arena, and then to Stella's to lie in wait and watch when the two Russian men and the three girls left, and then perhaps follow them home, I might be looking at tomorrow night before I got any sleep.

On the other hand, if I didn't do it tonight, there was no guarantee I'd get to do it at all. They were there tonight. They might not be there tomorrow. The fact that I'd been there asking questions, on top of Zachary having been there last night, might mean that they'd suspend operations for a while.

By the time I got there later, they may have closed up shop and left, if it came to that.

"I think I'd better try," I told Rachel, and explained my reasoning.

She nodded. "Would you like me to come along? For company? Or moral support?"

I blinked. I hadn't expected her to offer to do that, but it was nice of her. "Are you sure you want to? I'm not paying you to do field work." Just office administration.

"You're not paying me at all right now," Rachel pointed out. "The only one of us who's getting paid is Zachary, and he's in the hospital. If I can help figure out who put him there, I'd like to."

"That's really nice of you," I said. "Bring binoculars."

"Anything else?"

"Dark clothes. Something you don't mind getting dirty, or getting ripped. We might be crawling around in the trees."

She looked at me. If I haven't mentioned it, Rachel is about fifteen years older than me, in her mid-fifties, and not skinny.

"Not in them," I clarified. "We're not climbing. Just hanging out under them. Where we can see the back door of the club when theye take the girls out."

Rachel nodded. "Give me a call when you're ready to go. I'll meet you there."

I warned her that it could be late. "Maybe we'll open late tomorrow. It's not like anyone's beating down our doors."

"We'll talk about it later," Rachel said, and pushed her chair back. "Take the dog with you."

I planned to. She was looking at me expectantly, and wagged her tail hopefully when I turned her way. "Time to go. Car ride."

She jumped up, grinning happily, her doggie tongue lolling. "Mendoza gave her to me," I told Rachel as we all headed for the door.

"I know. Yesterday morning."

"Permanently. Araminta Tucker doesn't want her. She wanted Edwina taken to the pound. Can you imagine? So Mendoza told me I could keep her."

We both watched as Edwina pranced out the door and over to the bare ground under the small tree where she liked to do her business.

"Better you than me," Rachel said, and headed for her car. "Call me."

I assured her I would, and then I scooped Edwina up and put her in the car so Rachel wouldn't run over her—or she wouldn't get spooked by the car coming at her and take off out of the parking lot and down the street. That done, I locked up the office and drove the two of us to the nearest pet store, where I bought food and snacks and another couple of bowls so Edwina could have a set at the office and a set at home.

"Welcome home," I told her when I put her down in the foyer of the penthouse. "I know you've been here before." Last night, and yesterday morning after Griselda Grimshaw's murder. "You might remember. Or maybe you were too distraught at the death of your human. But this is your permanent home now. Griselda's gone, and Araminta doesn't want you. And I'm not giving you to the pound. So it's going to be you and me. Here. And at the office. I'll take good care of you, I promise."

Or the best care I knew how, anyway. She was my first dog. She'd just have to deal with any mistakes I made.

I looked around. "I'm sorry there's no yard." Maybe I needed to rethink this penthouse business. I liked living here. It was a nice change from the house in Hillwood, which had so much space I didn't need, now that there was just me. And besides, it had been nice to take over David's love nest, snubbing my nose at him, even if he was dead and probably didn't have any idea what I was doing. But if Edwina needed a yard...

"We'll take a walk after I feed you," I said. "Get some exercise. It'll be good for both of us."

Edwina wagged her little stub of a tail and headed for the living room. In the doorway, she turned and looked at me over her shoulder.

I lifted the bag of dog food and bowls more securely and followed.

Chapter Fourteen

The Gulch, where the penthouse is located, isn't more than half a dozen blocks from the Arena. Diana rang my doorbell at ten-thirty, and I headed downstairs and got into her car. "Is that it?"

There was a bag in the backseat. Your standard duffel, with a shoulder strap and a zipper.

She nodded, her jaw set.

"A hundred thousand dollars doesn't take up a lot of space, does it?"

She glanced at me. "It's newspaper."

Right. "But that's what a hundred thousand dollars in cash would look like, if it was stuffed into a bag. Right?"

Diana shrugged. "If we don't know, I don't think whoever's picking it up will."

She had a point. "Did Mendoza give it to you?"

"A uniformed officer dropped it off, with Jaime's compliments. And the suggestion that I should leave you home tonight."

"I hate him," I said.

Diana smirked. "Sure you do. Anyway, it was too late. I had already agreed to take you with me."

"You could have changed your mind."

She shrugged. "I wanted the company. This is weird. And a little scary."

It *was* weird. And a little scary. "Are you worried that Steven's actually in danger?"

"Not so much," Diana admitted, as we took the turn from Twelfth Avenue onto Charlotte, into downtown proper. "There's no reason to think he's in danger. Right? He was with the girl willingly."

He had been. At least as far as I'd been able to tell.

"Did Mendoza happen to mention that I got a phone call from Steven in the middle of the night?"

"No," Diana said, with a sharp glance at me. "How come you didn't mention it yourself?"

"When I saw you this morning, I didn't know about it."

She looked confused, and I added, "It came in on the office phone. I didn't get it until I got to the office this morning. After I left your house."

Outside the window, the State Capitol building went by on the left. Diana signaled to turn right on Fifth. "And you didn't think to call and tell me?"

"I called Mendoza," I said.

"Mendoza isn't married to Steven!"

Again, she had a point. "I'm sorry. After we're done here, we can go up there and I'll let you listen to it. It isn't very long. Just a few sentences. He said he'd recognized me yesterday—two days ago now—and that you must be worried. And that he wanted me to tell you something. But before he could get it out, someone came in and caught him. The girl, I guess. He said 'Nothing,' and hung up. I assume she asked him what he was doing."

Diana's knuckles were white on the steering wheel. "Did she hurt him?"

"Not that I could hear," I said. "He didn't sound scared of her. Just like he didn't want her to know that he'd been trying to get a message to you."

"Why didn't he just call me? Instead of you?"

"I have no idea," I said. "He didn't want to deal with you directly? You'd ask questions he didn't want to answer? Or maybe he just didn't want to talk to anyone in person. I wondered why he'd called the office in the middle of the night—it was around one in the morning when the call came in. He had to know nobody would be there. And Mendoza said that maybe that was the point. He wanted to leave a message, not talk to a real person. If he'd called either of us on our cell phones, we would have picked up. Even if it was the middle of the night. Especially you."

Diana nodded. Her hands had relaxed on the wheel again. Up ahead, we could see the plaza in front of the Arena, and the barricades blocking Fifth Avenue to vehicular traffic south of Broadway.

"Maybe we should have called a cab," I said. "It's going to be hard to find somewhere to park."

"Jaime said to pull behind the barricade." She drove across the intersection and straight up to it.

The uniformed cop on duty took a couple of steps toward the car, his mouth opening. He was getting ready to tell us to beat it, I'm sure. Diana rolled down her window. She didn't even have to speak. The young man took one look at her and nodded. "Just a second, ma'am." He hustled to pull the barricade out of the way so Diana could drive through and up to the curb. A car that tried to sneak in behind us was summarily waved off, and left with an irritated blast of the horn.

Diana cut the engine and sat for a second without speaking or moving. The dashboard clock showed that we still had some time to spare before eleven, so I didn't push her to move more quickly. We'd still get inside by the deadline. As for what happened after that…

"Have you gotten any further instructions about this?" I asked. If she had, she hadn't told me about them. And the note this morning had been vague. Just 'bring the money to the Arena,' but nothing about what to do with it once it got there.

She shook her head. "I guess we just walk in with the bag and see what happens."

I guessed so. "Are you ready?"

"No," Diana said. "But I don't think I'll be any more ready if we sit here for another five minutes. Let's just get it over with."

My feelings exactly. I opened my door and got out. Diana did the same, and reached into the back seat for the duffel bag. The young cop had stepped back to guard the barricade again, but he gave us a nod as we headed inside.

The guard on the door didn't ask us if we had tickets, he just swung the door open and let us into the building. With my newfound PI skills, I deduced that he was probably another cop—this one undercover in a Bridgestone Arena uniform—and he was expecting us. Diana gave him a pleasant smile, and we headed across the lobby just as the doors to the interior opened.

It was like opening the flood gates on Percy Priest Lake and letting the water burst over the dam. They frothed out, a mass of people in team colors. Hundreds of them. Thousands. A surging mass of humanity aiming for the doors to the outside.

I moved a little closer to Diana and looped my arm through hers, keeping the duffel bag between us. In this kind of crush, it would be only too easy to snatch it out of her hand and melt into the crowd before she even realized the bag was gone. And I was damned if I'd let whoever was behind this get away without giving us a good look at his or her face. Even if there was nothing but newspaper in the bag.

Mendoza's face floated out of the crowd. He was scanning, and for a second, he met my eyes straight on. I almost forgot that I wasn't supposed to know him; it was only at the last second that I remembered that he didn't want me to give any indication that I knew who he was. But he was close to us. Maybe he'd realized, as I had, that snatching the bag in the melee as everyone was fighting their way to the exits, had been the plan all along.

Another familiar face floated out of the crowd, just in front of me. It took a second of frowning concentration before I was able to put a name with it. "Ms. Tucker? What are you doing here?"

She looked up at me. Standing, she was even smaller than she'd appeared yesterday, sitting cross-legged on her couch. Hardly more than five feet, if that. Both Diana and I towered over her.

She must have had the same problem I had, in

placing a familiar face in unfamiliar surroundings, because she looked from me to Diana and back to me for a second before she said, "I like hockey."

I knew that. Or I guess I'd known it. She'd been watching a hockey game on TV yesterday, when I'd knocked on her door. If I hadn't been so distracted by all the people, and the noise, and the seriousness of the situation, I would have remembered that.

Araminta Tucker glanced over her shoulder. "I thought I saw that handsome Detective Mendoza earlier."

She probably had. "Maybe he likes hockey too," I said lightly. "Ms. Tucker, this is my friend Diana Morton. Diana, Araminta Tucker."

"A pleasure to meet you," Diana said automatically, her eyes still scanning the crowd, and then the name seemed to register. "I'm sorry… Araminta Tucker? You own the house my husband rented in Crieve Hall?"

Araminta nodded. "Yes, dear. He called me off a notice I posted at the university. Said he was looking for a place for his daughter."

"Steven doesn't have a daughter," Diana said.

Araminta looked at her, bright bird eyes shining. "So your friend told me."

"Mendoza said he stopped by earlier today to show you the drawing of the girl," I said. "What did you think of the likeness?"

She smiled. "Oh, very good. That's just what she looked like."

Good to know. At least we had that going for us. A good likeness. If she was here, and came close enough to us that we could see her, we'd recognize her.

Probably.

"We should let you go," I said. "It's late, and you have a long drive home." Had she driven here herself? Or maybe the retirement community had a shuttle that took the old people to where they needed to go when they needed to go there? "Oh, and if you happen to see Mendoza again, just pretend you don't know him."

Her eyes danced. "How exciting! Is this a sting?"

"Between you and me," I said, "we're hoping that the Russian girl will be here, and we can catch her."

"Oh, dear!" She looked around, her brows furrowed. "I'd better get home, so I won't be detained."

Since there was no way on earth anyone—especially Mendoza—would mistake her for a tall, blond, twenty-year-old Russian stripper, I didn't think she was in any danger. But if anything happened, I wanted her out of the way, too. So I nodded. "Good luck, Ms. Tucker. Drive carefully."

She scurried off toward the exit, her yellow and navy team jersey blending with the crowd.

It was starting to thin out a little by now. Or at least the crush wasn't such that I was afraid of being knocked to the ground and trampled underfoot if I lost my balance. It was also easier to see each individual face, now that there weren't so many of them. Diana and I both scanned the lobby. The duffel bag still hung between us. I could feel it knocking against my leg occasionally, as someone bumped into it.

A minute passed. The lobby emptied out some more. I loosened my death grip on Diana's arm and took a step to the side, to give us both some breathing room.

"I'm still holding the bag," Diana said.

I nodded. "I don't know what happened. I didn't see her, did you?"

She shook her head. "I'd have told you if I had."

And I hadn't seen Steven, either. Not that I'd really thought he was behind this, but there had been the possibility. More likely that it was the girl, but not impossible that it was Steven.

"What do we do now?"

I looked around. "Wait for the lobby to clear out all the way, I guess. And wait for Mendoza to show up and tell us what to do."

Diana nodded. We remained in place while the remnants of the crowd filed past on both sides. A few people gave us curious sideways looks, but nobody said anything. And nobody made a move toward the bag.

Finally Mendoza appeared in front of us. "Nothing?"

We both shook our heads. "I still have the bag," Diana said, lifting it.

"Nobody tried to grab it," I added. "Nobody slipped either of us a note telling us to put it down somewhere. And we didn't see the girl. Or Steven."

Mendoza put his hands on his hips. Like most of the crowd, he looked like a fan of our local hockey team. Yellow and blue jersey, faded jeans, sneakers.

It was only the second time in my life I'd seen him in anything but a suit—the other time was when he'd shown up in the middle of the night because the house in Hillwood was on fire—and he was just as appealing in casual civvies as in his usual designer suits. Maybe even a tiny bit more appealing. There's something very nice about a good-looking man in a pair of faded jeans.

However, at the moment, this good-looking man was scowling.

"This might have been a diversionary tactic." He glanced at Diana. "Maybe someone wanted you out of your house for a while."

"But I was at work all day," Diana protested.

"They may not have realized that," Mendoza said. "With the note, maybe they thought you'd be home. Maybe they figured this would take you out of the house at a predetermined time, and they could get in."

"Why?"

"I have no idea," Mendoza said. "But I think I should come home with you and check things out. Just in case."

Diana nodded. Obviously she was just fine with that. I would have been fine with it, too, if it had been my house under possible attack.

"You can drop me off at the Apex on your way past," I told Diana, since that suited me just fine. "And if you still want to hear that recording, you can stop by the office any time tomorrow. Someone's there from nine to five, pretty much. Rachel, if not me."

She nodded. Mendoza gave me a suspicious look. "I'd have thought you'd want to come with us. To see for yourself."

Was that a subtle—or not so subtle—insinuation that I was nosy?

I gave him a sweet smile. "I have other plans. I left Edwina in the penthouse alone, and I don't want to be gone that long. She isn't that used to the place yet. And the floor-to-ceiling windows are a little scary."

Not to mention that the rugs were white. But

probably better not to actually mention that.

Mendoza still looked suspicious, but he nodded. "Let me take that for you." He reached for the bag. Diana handed it over, and we all headed for the exit.

"I'll meet you there," he told Diana when we were outside. "Don't go inside until I get there."

She promised she wouldn't. He turned to me. "Good night, Mrs. Kelly."

There was something pointed about the words. Something along the lines of, '*I want you to go home and stay there, and not give me any more trouble tonight.*'

"Good night, Detective," I said politely. "Be careful."

He grunted. I hid a smile as I watched him walk across the plaza with the duffel hanging from his hand.

"Come on," Diana said, tugging on my arm. "I want to get home to see if Steven's there."

He probably wasn't, although I didn't want to say that. So I went obediently to the car, and got into the passenger seat.

The trip back to the Apex was just as uneventful, but took longer than the trip to the Arena. The streets were filled with people and cars going home after the hockey game, so it took us more than twice as long to make the short drive.

As we crept along the city streets, I had the idea that someone might run up to us from one of the sidewalks and yank the door open and demand the bag of money.

But of course the car doors lock automatically, so there'd be no yanking. Anyone yanking on the door would meet resistance. I did scan the crowds on my side of the street as we drove, though. A couple of women with long, blond hair merited a second look, but other than that, I didn't see anyone of interest. And of course no one actually ran up to the car and asked for the duffel. A good thing, too, since Mendoza had taken the bag when he left.

Diana pulled up in front of the Apex and I slipped out of the car. "Call me when you get home. Let me know if you find anything."

"Are you sure I shouldn't wait until tomorrow? I don't want to wake you."

"I'm not going to bed for a while yet," I said. "But if you'd rather, you can send a text. I just want to know if anyone's there. Or has been there."

She nodded. "I'll do that. Sleep well, Gina."

"You, too," I said, while I reflected that it would be a while before I saw my bed.

What I'd told Mendoza was actually valid. Edwina was new to the condo, not used to it, and I probably shouldn't leave her alone any longer than I had to. So I went upstairs and got her, before I called Rachel to tell her that the Arena Sting was over, and I was on my way to Stella's to meet her.

"How did it go?"

"Nothing happened," I said, while I put Edwina in the passenger seat and shut the door. "Nobody came for the money. We stood there for thirty minutes while the Arena emptied out. Then Mendoza took the duffel bag with the newspaper in it and left."

I opened my own door and slid behind the wheel. "He had this idea that maybe the whole thing was a setup to get Diana out of her house for an hour or two. If they wanted access, they could have gone there at any time during the day, but maybe they didn't realize that. Anyway, he went home with her to see whether anyone had been inside while she was gone."

I reversed out of the parking space and drove through the garage toward the exit. "At this point I'm in the car and on my way south on Granny White Pike. I guess I'll get to the nightclub in about twenty minutes or so."

"I checked how to get up to the apartment complex behind the nightclub," Rachel said in my ear. "Here's what you do."

She gave me directions for how to end up on top of the little bluff behind Stella's. I memorized it all as best I could and told her I'd call her back if I got lost. Then I hung up the phone and concentrated on getting to where I was going.

Because it was late and the roads were mostly clear of traffic, it took less time than I'd thought. I drove into the apartment complex just as the dashboard clock clicked over to midnight, and made my way past the buildings, between the rows of cars parked tail ends out. Most everything was dark, but here and there was the glow of a window or the blue flicker of a TV. A woman with a small dog scurried in front of us and disappeared between two cars, over to a lighted staircase. Edwina pressed her snub nose against the inside of the passenger window and rumbled deep in her throat, but she didn't bark.

"Good girl," I told her.

She wagged her stubby tail and turned her attention toward the front as the car rolled slowly forward.

At the very end of the development, where the

parking lot ended in a grassy lawn and then a line of scrubby trees, I found Rachel's white car. She had found a parking space that wasn't marked with a number for a unit, and had pulled into it. The space next to her wasn't marked either, and I slotted the Lexus in there and turned off the engine. Silence descended.

Nothing moved. The lady with the dog had gone inside. The branches of the trees rustled a little as they scraped together. And there was the far-away hum of cars down below us, on Nolensville Road.

"Stay here," I told Edwina and opened my door. "I'll be back."

She wagged and watched me get out. As soon as I'd shut the door, she jumped across the middle console into my seat and pressed her nose against that window while her pop eyes watched me walk the few feet to Rachel's car and try the door handle.

The car was locked. I bent and peered through the window.

Empty, too.

I straightened again, and peered into the trees. She must have gone off already.

Nothing for me to do but follow, I guess.

I made my way across the grass, and straightened my shoulders before I plunged into the darkness between the trees. "Rachel?"

"Over here." Her voice came from the right of me, and I changed direction and headed that way. After a few steps, I could see her huddled against the trunk of a tree near the edge of the bluff.

I picked my way over to her, careful to put my feet on solid ground. "How long have you been here?"

"Just a few minutes," Rachel said. She gestured. "There's nothing going on down there. People coming and going—mostly going—but nothing to see."

I peered over the edge of the bluff down into the parking lot behind Stella's.

As I'd surmised, we had a perfect view of the back door from up here. The only issue was the distance. Hard to get a good look at anything when you're a football field's width away and thirty feet above.

Luckily Rachel had remembered her binoculars, and I had transferred mine from the glove box in the turquoise convertible I used to drive to the glove box in the Lexus when I bought it. Those binoculars had come in handy when I was skulking around behind David and Jackie-with-a-q. Now they had a chance to be useful again.

I put them to my eyes and fiddled with the knob in the middle. The back door at Stella's sprang into view as sharply as if I'd stood ten feet away.

There was nothing going on. The door was shut, and I didn't see anyone moving around. The parking lot was about half full. The black sedan from earlier—at least I figured it had to be the same black sedan; it looked similar—was parked a few feet away. The rest of the cars were parked mostly around the front and sides of the building.

I counted. There were seventeen cars in the lot, including the sedan. I knew that one had had five people in it when it arrived. If the others had brought between one and four people each, we were looking at a crowd of sixty or so inside the club.

Time passed slowly. Cars went by down on the

road, fewer and fewer of them the later it got. Slowly, the parking lot below us emptied out. We'd hear a burst of sound as the front door opened, and a second or two later, a person—or two or three—would scurry across the parking lot to a car, get in, and drive away. From where I was sitting, it looked like they were all male.

Rachel nodded when I said so. "Looks that way."

"Makes me worry what those poor girls are doing in there."

"I could tell you what I think," Rachel said, "but I'd rather not."

I'd rather she didn't, either.

We sat in silence as the lot emptied out. When the last car but the black sedan had driven away, Rachel got to her feet and stretched. "If I go now, I can probably get down there before they leave."

She probably could. It wasn't a long drive. "Don't you want to watch them come out?"

"I assumed you wanted to know where they're going," Rachel said. "That means one of us has to follow them. And I figured that would be me, since you wanted to be up here with the binoculars."

"And since they've already seen me. If they catch you, you can make up some story about what you're doing. If they catch me, they'll know I'm following them."

"Exactly what I was thinking," Rachel said, dusting off her posterior. She was dressed in yoga pants and an oversized sweater: one of the very few times I'd seen her in anything but a frumpy but perfectly appropriate business suit. "I have my phone. We'll keep in touch that way."

That sounded good to me. "Don't get too close to them."

"I'll do my best," Rachel said, "but it isn't the best time of day to follow someone, you know. There's not much traffic. I can stay back, but I'll still probably be the only car behind them."

Until I joined the hunt, and then there would be two of us.

"Just do your best," I said. "Once you've driven a few minutes, as long as I've caught up, you can peel off down a side street, and I'll stay behind them for a while, and then, when you get behind me again, I'll peel off and you can follow. It's known as a two-vehicle leapfrog."

Rachel didn't say anything, but she looked impressed. At least as far as I could tell in the dark.

"You'd better go," I reminded her. "Before they come out."

She nodded. "I'll text you when I get there."

She crunched off through the dry leaves and twigs. To anyone nearby, she probably sounded like a buffalo, but since we weren't really worried about anyone up here noticing us, I didn't say anything about it.

Half a minute later, I heard her car drive off, and I devoted myself to the surveillance of Stella's while I hoped that Rachel would get down there in time.

Chapter Fifteen

I didn't see her arrive down below. But a few minutes after she'd driven off, my phone alerted that I had a text. *I'm in the McDonald's parking lot. They're open 24 hrs.*

Good, I texted back. And it was. An excellent place to be. Nobody—specifically the two Russian men—would think twice about anyone being there. Not if the store was open around the clock. *I'll let you know when they move.*

We went back to our surveillance. To tell the truth, I was starting to get tired. It was getting close to two in the morning. I'd been up since just after six. And it had been an eventful day. The only things that kept me awake were the chill in the air, and the moisture that was slowly seeping through the knees of my jeans from their contact with the ground.

I was about ready to give up when something finally happened. A rectangle of light opened in the darkness and then was extinguished quickly. It stayed on my retinas for a while, as such things do, as I reached for the binoculars and lifted them to my eyes.

Yes, there they were. One man in the lead, with… was that a gun in his hand?

Surely not. I mean, normal people don't walk around with guns, do they?

Or maybe, if they're operating successful nightclubs and transporting the night's take, they do.

He had a bag in his other hand, that might be full of money. It didn't quite have the dimensions of Diana's duffel, but there'd be room enough for a fair amount of newspaper in there.

Or maybe there was another—or additional—reason for the gun.

He opened the passenger door of the black sedan, and put the bag on the seat. Then he closed the door again. And opened the door into the back. And walked back to the door into the nightclub.

The girls filed out and over to the car, where they scrunched together in the back seat. He slammed the door after them and went around the car and got behind the wheel. Meanwhile, his associate locked up before getting into the passenger seat. I saw the movement when he transferred the money bag from the seat to the floor before he sat down.

The lights came on. I grabbed my phone and texted Rachel. *Get ready. They're moving.*

She didn't respond. I hoped that meant that she was getting ready, and not that anything had gone wrong.

Down below, the black sedan pulled around the building and out of sight. I refocused the binoculars on the opposite side of the street, and saw Rachel's car pull into traffic.

Time to go.

I jumped to my feet—not as quickly as when I'd been twenty—and made my way toward the Lexus. And while I'd like to think I didn't sound like a buffalo moving through the brush, I wasn't anywhere close to quiet, either.

Edwina was thrilled to see me, of course, and I had to nudge her over into the passenger seat before I could get in. Then she kept insisting on sitting on my lap, and I had to keep pushing her over into her side of the car. It wasn't until I was down on Nolensville Road, that I was able to dig my phone back out of my pocket and dial Rachel.

"Where are you?"

They were well out of sight by now, of course. It had taken me several minutes to get down here. By now, both cars might be several miles away in several different directions.

"Going east on Harding," Rachel's voice said in my ear. "Probably headed for the interstate."

This was good news, in a way. It was bound to be easier to follow them there, undetected, than on the smaller, mostly empty roads.

On the other hand, it would be easier to lose them there, too.

"Just keep the phone on," I told her. "Put it on speaker and leave it in the console or somewhere, so we can stay in touch. I'll try to catch up."

I dropped the phone in my lap, where Edwina wouldn't be likely to trample it, and stepped on the gas. The SUV shot off up Nolensville Road toward the intersection at Harding.

When Rachel announced that they were passing the

interstate—without turning onto the ramp—I was still two blocks behind. "Where are you going, then?"

"Looks like straight ahead," Rachel said. "Toward the airport."

Hopefully they weren't headed there. Hopefully they were just going toward the airport, not actually to it.

"Any other cars around?"

Rachel said there weren't.

"I think I can see your taillights up ahead. Turn off somewhere, so they think you aren't following them. I'll take over for a while."

"Roger," Rachel said.

"Excuse me?"

"I'm turning."

She was. I could see the car ahead of me start to signal and then go off to the right. Much farther ahead, the taillights of the sedan were winking in and out as it navigated through the industrial area on the other side of the interstate. Up above us, a plane was coming in for landing, so close I could almost see faces in the lighted windows. I pushed down on the gas and sped up.

By the time I had the sedan more reliably in my sights, Rachel reported that she'd turned around and was behind me. "I can't see you, but I'm coming."

"I'm probably good for another couple of minutes," I said. "We're getting close to Murfreesboro Pike, though. More traffic, but they may notice if I turn the same way they do. It might be best if you're ready to take over then."

Rachel said she'd speed up and be ready. "Just don't lose them."

I promised I wouldn't and we carried on.

On Murfreesboro Road, I let the sedan go right while I went straight. Then I spent a couple of minutes finding a place to turn around—it wasn't easy, since I had strayed onto airport property, and they like you to follow the road in a big circle around the terminal instead of turning around. As a result, both the sedan and Rachel were way ahead of me by the time I got back to Murfreesboro Road.

"They're turning east on Bell Road," Rachel reported.

"I'm nowhere near Bell Road," I told her. "You're just going to have to turn, too, so we don't lose them. I'll try to catch up."

"I'll do my best to be inconspicuous," Rachel said.

"Please. These are the guys I think beat up Zachary. We don't want them to notice us." Just in case they beat us up, too.

Rachel agreed that we didn't. She followed them onto Bell Road toward the lake while I scrambled to catch up.

By the time I took a left on Bell, Rachel had followed the sedan onto smaller roads. She read them off to me as she wound her way through the neighborhoods southeast of the lake behind the sedan.

"They're stopping!" she said finally, in an excited whisper.

"Pull over and stay where you are. Don't go any closer. I'm almost there."

I was almost there. It took a couple of minutes, during which Rachel gave me the exact address and reported that the car had driven straight into a basement garage, and she wasn't able to see anything that happened after that.

"We'll figure it out," I said. "I'm coming around the corner now. With my lights off."

I switched them off just as I swung onto the street where Rachel was parked. I could see her car halfway up. And I was reminded of what Mendoza had told me a lifetime ago, the day before yesterday. This wasn't the kind of neighborhood where cars were parked on the street. Rachel's little white compact stood out like a beacon.

I picked up the phone again. "Drive off down the road. You're too conspicuous sitting there. There aren't any other cars parked on the street."

I imagined her taking the same look around as I'd taken when Mendoza told me the same thing two days ago. "What do you want me to do?"

"I'm going to pull into this driveway," I said, and did. The house was dark and silent, and the inhabitants were probably dead asleep at this time of night. "Go around the block, park out of sight, and come back and join me."

A second passed, and then Rachel's car rolled off down the street. With the lights on. I rolled my eyes, but refrained from comment. Chances were nobody around here was awake to notice, and if the Russians happened to be looking out the window, then all they'd be concerned about, was the fact that she was leaving.

I stayed where I was, in the driveway of a house two doors down and across the street. The view of the house where Rachel had said the Russians went in, was pretty good.

It looked like your standard mid-century split-level, one of four or five I could see on the block. A rectangular shoe box, it had pale brick on the bottom half and what looked like vinyl siding on the top half. One door, a little offset from the middle, sat halfway between the top and bottom floor, with a double picture window to the left and two single windows to the right.

My right.

The driveway led directly to a two-car garage on the bottom floor, below the two single windows. On the opposite side from the garage, past the front steps, was another double window, only half as tall as the one above.

I figured the bigger picture window was probably the living room, while the two single windows were bedrooms with a window each. The basement room could be anything from another bedroom to a den or a workout room or something like that.

There were no lights on anywhere. Not even a sliver where the curtains didn't quite meet. The inhabitants were either werewolves, who could see in the dark, or they'd boarded up all their windows.

A shadow suddenly appeared next to the car, and I swallowed a scream. Edwina, who had curled up to take a nap now that the car was finally still, raised her head and gave a short, sharp bark.

"Shhhh!" I told her. "It's Rachel. You know Rachel. You like her."

I unlocked the door and snagged the dog so Rachel wouldn't sit on her. "That was fast."

"I've been working out," Rachel said and slid into the passenger seat. Edwina growled, but once she recognized Rachel—one of the two people who gave her treats and took her outside when I wasn't there—she subsided.

"You didn't tell me you were bringing the dog," Rachel added.

"I was afraid she'd pee on David's white shag rug. She isn't used to the apartment yet. Plus I like the company."

Rachel nodded. "What do we do now?"

I wasn't entirely sure, to tell the truth. I'd wanted to find out where the Russians took the girls after the nightclub closed. And we'd done that. I wasn't sure why we were still here. I could have just told Rachel to go home, and then tomorrow, I could have called Mendoza and told him where to go. I wasn't really sure why I hadn't done that.

"I guess we could have a look around." Although we probably couldn't expect to find much. Especially since I wasn't sure what we were looking for.

Unless… Was there a chance that Anastasia was working with this group, and they had Steven inside? Was that why they'd beaten up Zachary when he came around asking questions? Because they didn't want anyone to realize what was going on?

"That's possible," Rachel agreed when I said so. "They're clearly up to something. And after what happened to Zachary, it's pretty obvious that Anastasia has something to do with it. One way or the other."

It was.

"I'm not sure whether we shouldn't just let Mendoza know what we've found out and let him deal with it, though."

"What if they kill Steven?" Rachel said.

"Why'd they do that? It wasn't Steven's fault that they didn't get the money this evening." Or what they thought was the money. "Diana was there with a big bag. Nobody came to pick it up."

"Maybe they recognized you," Rachel said. "Or Mendoza."

Maybe. I thought back to the crush of bodies at the Arena as the game let out. Had I seen either of the Russian men in the crowd? Even just in passing, without really realizing it?

I didn't think I had. And I didn't think they'd gotten a look at Mendoza this afternoon, so they wouldn't have recognized him.

Although they could have picked up on the police presence without actually recognizing Mendoza. And I didn't have to have seen them for them to have seen me. There'd been so many people there that someone I knew could have passed within a few feet of me and I might not have noticed.

"We should go take a look," Rachel said, with a glance at the house in the rearview mirror.

I didn't really want to take a look, but she was right: we probably should. They might have Steven tied to a chair in the basement, and if they did, we owed it to him to find him as soon as possible.

"Fine. But I'm leaving Edwina in the car."

"I wasn't suggesting that we bring her," Rachel said and opened her door. "Come on."

I put Edwina back in the passenger seat and told her to be a good girl. "I'll be right back. Ten minutes, tops. Much better than last time."

She sighed, but made a circle on the seat and settled into a curve with her nose on her back legs. I closed the door softly and followed Rachel down the driveway and across the street.

We approached the split level through the yard next door. Less chance we'd be seen that way, if we skulked along the shrubbery. There was the risk that the neighbors might notice us, or that they had an alarm system with flood lights that would come on if someone tried to sneak across their property. Hillwood, where I'd lived with David, was full of such things.

Not here. This was more of a working class neighborhood. The houses were closer together and people weren't worried about intruders. We made it across the neighboring property without attracting the attention of people or guard dogs, and without setting off alarms or flashing lights.

The split level was dark and silent. We approached from the side opposite the garage, so the first thing we got to was the double-wide, half-height window on the lower level, just above the ground.

I signaled Rachel to stop while I squatted for a closer look.

There was nothing to see. The window was covered by blinds, shut in such a way that it was impossible to see between the slats, and there might even have been curtains or something else on the inside of the window, since not even a sliver of light peeked through.

Then again, at past two in the morning, there were probably no lights on, so maybe it wasn't so surprising.

We moved on, around the back of the house.

There was less to see there. No windows on the

lower level, which was built into the bank in the rear. The ground sloped up, so once we reached the back of the house, we were standing just below the top level windows.

They were dark, too. Again, not surprising, since it was the middle of the night.

I saw a crack in the curtains, and went up on tippy-toes to press my nose to the glass. A forest of dark shapes met me. It took a few seconds for my eyes to adjust enough that I could make out a dining room table and chairs, with a living room beyond. And a kitchen off to the left. I could see the glow of the digital clock on either the stove or microwave. Or perhaps it was the ice dispenser on the fridge. We humans have a lot of small lights in the kitchen.

There was a tall window, likely a bathroom, beyond the kitchen, too high up the wall for me to see through.

"You can stand on my shoulders," Rachel offered, her voice soft.

It was tempting, but— "I don't really think there's going to be anything interesting in the bathroom. Do you? If they have Steven at all, they wouldn't lock him in there. They'd have to move him every time someone needed to use the bathroom."

"Unless there are two," Rachel said.

I supposed there could be two. A lot of these older homes—and this one was from the early nineteen-sixties—only have one bathroom to share. But there might be a second bath downstairs. Or maybe one of the bedrooms was a master, with an attached bath of its own.

I was still contemplating the bathroom situation

when hell broke lose. Two dark shapes hurtled toward us, one from each end of the house. I had enough time to squeal, but not enough to run, before they were on us. A fist connected with the side of my head, and that was all she wrote.

I wasn't knocked out. I was pretty woozy for the next few minutes, though. Woozy enough that there was nothing I could do to avoid what happened.

The shorter Russian—the one who had sat inside the car earlier today—hauled me up over his shoulder. It was uncomfortable to hang like that, with my head and arms dangling and his hand in the vicinity of my butt, keeping me in place, but it wasn't as uncomfortable as the pain radiating from my head.

Behind us, the second guy, the one who'd been driving the car, the one I'd been talking to, grabbed Rachel under the arms and began dragging her around the house.

They took us up to the top floor and into the living room, where they pretty much dropped us onto the sofa. And sat there, with guns in their laps, while they waited for us to wake up.

Or I should say that they waited for Rachel to wake up. The second guy must have hit her harder than the first guy had hit me. I was conscious, and pretty much alert. Rachel was out cold.

"That wasn't necessary," I told them, as I looked around surreptitiously.

The living room was furnished in late twentieth century castoff: a fairly ugly sofa they might have picked up second hand at a thrift store, with two mismatched chairs opposite and a chipped coffee table in the middle. No pictures on the wall, or other decorations to speak of. A big screen TV opposite the sofa. An ash tray on the table, filled to overflowing with ashes and cigarette butts. An open pack of Marlboro's and a lighter next to it.

And two men with guns staring at me.

The three girls had to be here somewhere, but there was no sign of them.

"You're the lady with the son," the first guy said, as if he'd just now realized that.

I nodded. Best to just let them believe I was still looking for Zachary. "I followed you from the nightclub. To see if you were going to where my son is."

I looked around, like I expected to see him materialize out of thin air.

"Your son's not here," the second guy said.

"Would you mind if I took a look around?"

He hesitated. Then he opened a hand as if to say, "Knock yourself out."

I got up from the sofa and headed off down the hallway. My knees were a bit weak, so I had to brace myself against the wall at regular intervals. And my head really pounded.

Of course I knew that Zachary wasn't there—he was safe at Southern Hills hospital—but they weren't trying to stop me from looking around, so I figured I might as well take advantage of it. I thought maybe I could find Steven, or see the bloodstains from where they'd beaten Zachary, or something.

In that I was disappointed. There were three bedrooms at one end of the house. Two in the front, one in the back of the house. All three were empty. Of people if not furniture. So was the bathroom.

One of the men with the guns followed me anyway, and watched me look into each room. "Where are the girls?" I asked when we got back to the living room. Rachel was still out cold, or maybe just pretending to be out cold. But if she was pretending, she didn't give me a sign to let me know.

The two Russians looked at one another. "Girls?"

"The three young women you had in the car with you when you arrived at the nightclub this afternoon. The three young women you marched back out to the car when you left tonight. You didn't stop anywhere on the way, so they were still in the car when you drove it into the garage twenty minutes ago. They have to be here somewhere."

"They're downstairs," Russian guy number one said. "Would you like to see?"

I wouldn't mind. I had no real illusions that they'd let me walk out of here, but if by some miracle I made it out in one piece, at least I'd have some information I could give to Mendoza. And if I didn't... well, I'd just left my hand prints all over the upstairs. Hopefully Mendoza could make something of that, if I didn't survive the night.

"Sure," I said. "I'd love to see the downstairs."

"We should bring your friend along," the Russian said, and nodded to his friend, who grabbed Rachel under the arms. "Why don't you take her feet?"

I didn't want to take her feet. I'd prefer to have both hands free, just in case I had a chance to knock either or both of them cold with a handy fire poker or something.

Or if nothing else, so I could leave more handprints for Mendoza to find. Like bread crumbs down the basement stairs.

But I didn't think the objection would go over well. "Shouldn't we just leave her here?"

"I think we should take her." He gestured with the gun. I picked up Rachel's feet and moved toward the stairs to the lower level.

If it hadn't been for Rachel, I might have tried to get out the front door when we passed it. If the two goons had been carrying her, I might have had just enough time to get the door open and get through it before they put her down and pulled one or both of their guns. Although even then I would have thought twice about running away and leaving her behind.

As it was, there was nothing I could do. I glanced longingly at the door as we staggered past—a regular lock, a deadbolt, and a chain; something to remember if I got the chance to get back up here—but there was nothing I could do, not with that gun pointed at me.

So I continued down to the lower level, and ended up in a sort of den or man cave between the garage to the right and another door on the left, that must go into the room with the short double windows that I hadn't been able to look into.

There was a key in the lock. On the outside. The Russian with the gun—the one who wasn't carrying Rachel—turned the key. "In."

"It's dark," I protested. "I can't see where I'm going."

He clearly didn't care, just gestured to me to proceed. With the gun. "In."

I went in. Rachel was shoved in after me, and the door slammed. The key turned in the lock, and we were left in what the poets are pleased to call stygian blackness.

Chapter Sixteen

Something rustled. In the first moment of panic, I was sure it was a mouse. Or maybe a rat. Something big.

It didn't take much more than another second before I realized that I was hearing bed clothes. Blankets. Sheets. Something like that.

Then a light came on.

My eyes had gotten so used to the dark that for several seconds I wasn't able to see anything. Finally, as my pupils adjusted, I could squint around at my surroundings.

A room, roughly twelve by twelve feet or so. Maybe a little less. Institutional green. Plain to the point of looking like a prison cell. Two bunk beds, one on each side of the room, with a chest of drawers between. Four drawers. And three Russian girls, long blond hair falling over their scantily clad charms, sitting up. The top bunk on the left was empty, and I had a pretty good idea who used to sleep there.

I tried a smile. "Hello."

They stared at me. And stared at Rachel, slumped

on the floor. Finally, one of them said, in accented English, "What happened?"

To Rachel, I assumed. "They hit her."

She glanced at the other two. All three of them slithered out of their beds and gathered around Rachel. A second later, they had dragged her to the nearest bunk and laid her out. One of them checked her pulse and said a couple of words in Russian. Or Ukrainian or Belarusian or wherever they were from.

The spokesperson had hair that was a little more honey than the others', and while they were all pretty, her face was heart-shaped and sweet. "Her pulse is strong," she told me. "She'll wake up soon."

Good. At least we wouldn't be stuck in here with a corpse.

"My name is Gina," I said. "I came here to find out what happened to my… um… son."

My purse was in the car, with my cell phone in it. *Smart move, Gina.* Not only didn't I have a picture of Zachary to show them, I had no way of calling for help, either.

Next time I was going sleuthing in the dark, I'd definitely stick my phone in my pocket.

Although, given the circumstances, I probably wouldn't have gotten to keep it anyway. The bad guys would have taken it before they shoved me in here. So it was a moot point.

"His name is Zachary," I added. "He came to Stella's last night. Not tonight. Yesterday night. He has red hair, like mine."

I put a hand to it. I wasn't sure how much they understood, so it was best to keep things simple. Only one of them seemed to be comfortable communicating with me. Perhaps the others didn't speak English well enough. Or at all.

If they were in the US doing what I thought they were in the US doing, that probably didn't matter.

"I spoke to him," the girl with the honey-colored hair said.

"You're Tatiana?"

She nodded. "It was only a few words. He didn't... he wasn't..." She flushed. "Yuri took me away for a customer."

Right. I could read between the lines on that one. Zachary wasn't there to buy sex, and other men were, and she was expected to take care of them.

"He wanted to know about Anastasia," she added.

I wandered over to sit down on the bunk next to Rachel's feet. "Anastasia used to be one of you?"

She nodded, and sat down opposite. The two other girls swarmed up to the bunk above her head, and curled up, listening. It was possible they understood more than they could communicate, so I kept my questions simple. "How did you end up here?"

A shadow crossed her face. "Newspaper ad. Modeling."

I glanced up at the top bunk. "You two, as well?"

They both nodded, so at least they'd understood that much.

"And Anastasia?"

"Anastasia is smart," Tatiana said. "She knew it wasn't modeling. But she wanted to come to America." After a second she shrugged, "Everyone wants to come to America."

The land of opportunity. Or at least the land of more opportunity than Russia.

"But when you got here, it wasn't modeling?"

They shook their heads. "Stella's," Tatiana said. "Dancing. And taking care of the customers."

She glanced up at the other two and back at me. "They told us after three years, we can stop working. But we don't think we believe them."

I wouldn't believe them, either. "What happened to Anastasia?"

One of the girls on the top bunk said something, and Tatiana nodded. "She said she would get away," she told me. "That she would escape, and then she'd come back and help us. But she hasn't."

"How long ago did she escape?"

They conferred for a moment. "Three days," Tatiana said.

So probably the night before I'd seen her in Crieve Hall. "How?"

The glanced at each other again. "Her father helped her," Tatiana said.

"Excuse me?"

It probably wasn't a smart thing to say, because it made Tatiana think she'd pronounced something wrong. She said it again, more slowly and clearly. "Her father helped her."

"I heard you," I said. "She had a father? Here?"

She nodded. "She sent a letter to him. We distracted Yuri and Konstantin and she pretended to run away, but all she really wanted was to put a letter in the mailbox." Her face darkened. "They hit her when they got her back, but they didn't realize the letter was there."

"And Anastasia's father got it? And came to the club?"

"Two times," Tatiana said. "First to meet her. To make sure she was..." She trailed off, searching for the words.

I nodded. "To make sure she was who she said she was."

She lit up. "Yes."

"And he believed her?" This had to be Steven. I had no idea how he'd ended up with a Russian daughter that it seemed neither he nor Diana had known about. Or maybe he hadn't. Maybe he'd helped her just because she needed help, whether she was his daughter or not. But we had to be talking about Steven.

"He helped her," Tatiana said. "He came back. He paid for thirty minutes with Anastasia. Olga," she glanced up above her head at the two girls perched there, "broke the fire alarm in the club. There was water pouring down, and people screaming and running. Anastasia and her father got away."

Good for Steven. Although it might have done more good if he'd gone to the police when he first met Anastasia and heard her story. That might have saved all the girls, and not just one.

But it explained a lot of what was going on. "I guess when Zachary—my... um... son—came to the club asking about Anastasia, the two goons—" What had she called them? "—Yuri and Konstantin probably thought he knew more than he did?"

"He had seen Anastasia," Tatiana said. "They wanted to know where she was."

Of course they did. Having her on the loose would

be a threat to them.

And Zachary had probably told them what they wanted to know. Given that they were beating him up, I wouldn't blame him.

Had they then gone back to Araminta's house, where Zachary had seen Anastasia, and found her and Steven there?

If they had, they had stashed them somewhere else. Anastasia and Steven were nowhere in this house. Unless there was a part of it I hadn't seen yet. And I didn't think there was.

Of course, they could both be dead. But then Yuri and Konstantin would be looking at a much bigger mess than they were looking at now. They hadn't killed anyone yet. Not as far as I knew.

Next to me, Rachel groaned, and I turned to her. "Finally."

She blinked, her eyes unfocused. It took several seconds for her to recognize me. Or put my name with my face. Or process that I was there. Something. "Gina?"

I nodded. "We're in the basement of the split level. Yuri and Konstantin knocked you out and dragged you inside."

She looked blank, and I added, "Do you remember following the sedan from the nightclub?"

She tried to nod, and winced. "Yes. We went to check out the house." She lifted a hand to check the back of her head, and her face twisted. "Ow."

"Sorry," I said.

She tried to raise herself on one elbow and seemed to think better of it. "How come you're not flat on your back?"

"I don't think they hit me as hard as they hit you," I said. "Or one guy didn't hit as hard as the other guy. I got lucky. I've been awake for most of it."

If you could call it lucky. My head still hurt, and had been hurting since they hit me. Rachel had only woken up to the pain now.

She looked around, moving mostly just her eyes. They lingered on the low window high on the wall. "Basement room?"

I nodded. "Looks like they boarded up the window." That was why we hadn't been able to see even a strip of light when we were outside. A thick sheet of plywood was nailed to the window frame all the way around. With a lot of nails.

"What are we going to do?" She decided to try to sit up again. I gave her a hand, and managed to haul her upright. She slumped against the wall, but at least she was awake and mostly aware.

"We hadn't gotten to that part yet," I said. "Turns out the Russian girl really was Steven's daughter. Or so it seems. He helped her get away from the guys who run the club. They brought her and these other three girls—" I gestured to them, "here from Russia to work at Stella's."

Rachel nodded.

"They beat up Zachary because he'd seen Anastasia and they wanted to know what he knew about her. But we don't know whether they have found Anastasia and Steven or not."

One of the girls said something, and Tatiana nodded. "They would have told us if they found Anastasia. They would want us to know that we can't get away. That they'll find us."

Good point. "They probably don't have them, then," I told Rachel.

"But they have us," she responded.

And of course they did.

She added, "What are they going to do with us?"

I had no idea. It wasn't as if they could make us work in the club, the way the girls did. And I didn't like to consider any of the alternatives.

"We probably won't be here long," I said, trying to inject some optimism I wasn't feeling into my voice.

"We've been here more than a month," Tatiana told me.

"Yes, but nobody knew you were here." Other than the patrons at the club, and the kinds of men who went to a nightclub to purchase sex from young women couldn't really be expected to care about those girls' wellbeing. "My car is parked in the driveway across the street. With my dog in it. Once your neighbors wake up and find it, I'm sure they'll call the police."

"Unless Yuri moved it already," Tatiana said.

I dug in my pocket. "I have the key."

"My car is parked around the corner," Rachel added. "Someone will probably notice that, too."

And chances were, when Diana tried to get in touch with me tomorrow morning, which I hoped she'd do, to hear that recording of Steven, and when she found the office empty, and she couldn't raise me on the phone, she'd call Mendoza and tell him I was missing. I had to trust that she'd do that, and that he'd take action. He might know me well enough by now that he'd realize I would have taken an interest in the nightclub and the girls.

Although that put our rescue out another day, since Mendoza couldn't very well follow Konstantin and Yuri home from the club until they'd actually been to the club for another night.

And that was if they wanted to take the risk of bringing the girls there tomorrow night. After tonight, they might think things had gotten a little too hot for that. And they wouldn't be wrong. But that meant Mendoza had no way of finding them—or us—at all.

If that happened, we could be here a while. Unless we found a way out on our own.

"I suppose you've tried to take the plywood off the window?"

Tatiana nodded. "The first day we were here. We can never get enough of the nails out in one night to get out, and the next day they always nail them back in."

Understandable. It isn't easy to pry nails out of plywood without any tools, and of course the bad guys would check for something like that.

"I guess we'll just have to wait until they come back, and overpower them." There were twice as many of us as there were of them. We ought to be able to figure something out.

All three girls looked at me in disbelief. "They have guns," Tatiana pointed out, as if I could have missed that.

"I know. But they can't shoot all of us. At least not at the same time."

There was a pause. "Are you volunteering?" Rachel wanted to know.

I guess I would, if it came to that. If there was no

other choice. But we weren't there quite yet. "What about the door? Any way out of that?"

They shook their heads. "There's no lock on this side," Tatiana said. "No knob, either."

There wasn't. But there was both outside. And when we came down here, the key had been in the lock.

Offhand, I couldn't think of any way of getting it out of the lock, though. And anyway, without a lock to unlock on this side of the door, having the key wouldn't do us any good. Although I supposed it would keep the bad guys out...

"They feed you, right?"

All three girls nodded.

So all they'd have to do would be to withhold food, and starve us into giving them the key back. And we'd be right back where we started.

"Can we take apart one of the beds and brain them with a piece of wood when they come down with breakfast in the morning?"

One of them would be carrying the tray, I assumed. If there was a tray. And the other one would be standing by with a gun, to make sure none of the girls made a break for it.

If I could knock the gun out of the second guy's hand, while the first guy was still holding the tray, we might have a chance.

"We tried to take the beds apart," Tatiana said.

And presumably they didn't come apart, since they were in one piece at this point. A pity. Now that I looked at them more closely, they were made of metal. A nice metal pipe would be handy.

"Is there a bathroom?"

"They let us use it before we went to bed," Tatiana said. "They take us, one by one, to shower in the morning."

If there was a lid on the toilet tank, that might offer opportunities. Or the shower curtain rod, if there was one.

At any rate, it seemed that we'd get the chance to attack our captors. If only we had something to attack them with.

I looked around. There was nothing here but the two bunk beds and the dresser. The beds were a no-go, according to the girls. And they were probably right. It's not easy to take apart metal without tools.

The dresser was made of wood, though. (Hard to find a dresser that isn't, I guess.) Each drawer would be a little too unwieldy to lift, but perhaps we could take it apart...

I got to my feet and wandered over to the it.

It was tallish, but sort of squat and solid. Nothing elegant about it. The legs were fat little stubs of wood, to short to do any good. I wanted to be able to hit the Russians from at least a foot away. Once I got close enough to grab, I wouldn't give much for my chances of success. But if I could hit the arm with the gun, and the gun went flying...

The three girls and Rachel watched me as I pulled out the top drawer and examined it.

It was full of clothes. Mostly skimpy underwear, plus some oversized T-shirts, like the girls were sleeping in.

I dumped the contents on the bed next to Tatiana and took a closer look at the drawer itself.

Like all drawers, it was made of four pieces of wood put together in a rectangle, with a bigger, thinner piece of wood nailed to the bottom.

If we could take it apart, there'd be a piece of wood for each of us. We'd give the big piece to Rachel, since I didn't expect much help from her. I had a feeling she had a concussion. She'd been out cold a long time, and her pupils weren't quite the same size.

"If I start throwing this around," I asked Tatiana, "will they hear me? Do they go to sleep, or does one of them stay awake on guard?"

One of them stayed awake and on guard. Of course. "But this," she glanced around the room, "is sound proof. If the landlord sends someone here—for the bugs, maybe—they can't hear us if we scream."

That was disturbing. Yuri and Konstantin seemed to have thought of everything.

However, now that attention to detail benefited us. If I started tearing at the drawer, they shouldn't be able to hear me.

I lifted it, experimentally.

It was well made. Old enough that the joints were dovetails, and the two pieces of wood were not just nailed together. Although the dovetails were neat enough that they'd probably been cut by a machine, not by hand.

I decided that the bureau was old, but not so old that destroying it would be a crime. And between you and me, I would have taken a Sheraton apart if I thought it would get me out of here in one piece.

It took time and some hard work. At first we tried to pull the drawer apart. It didn't work. We either weren't strong enough, or the glue between the dovetails was too strong. But after Tatiana and I hung off one side, and the other two girls (still up on the top bunk) held onto the other, and the drawer still didn't budge, we gave up on that idea.

"You're sure they can't hear us?" I panted.

Tatiana nodded.

"Even if they can, I guess it won't be a big deal. We want them to come down here. And if it's just one of them, to see what's going on, maybe that would actually be better."

"They can't hear us," Tatiana said.

Fine. I took a better grip on the drawer and swung it, straight at the upper corner of the bunk bed.

The girls shrieked. The drawer held.

And nothing else seemed to happen. Nobody came running down from upstairs to see what was going on.

So I did it again. And again. And one more time, for good measure.

By the time the drawer splintered into pieces, I was out of breath and sweaty, and it's possible I may have strained a muscle in my upper back. But I had four dangerous-looking, jagged pieces of wood. Nothing I personally would want to run afoul of. The splinters alone would be enough to take out someone's eye.

I distributed them among the girls. "When the door opens, be ready."

They looked dubious, but nodded. Rachel was dozing, and I left her alone, although I made sure to poke her every now and then, just in case she did have a concussion. The last thing I wanted was for her to slip into a coma. If we had to fight our way out of here, I wanted her alert and able to move under her own steam.

The girls drifted off to sleep one by one. They'd probably had a long and hard night, no pun intended. I should have been worn out myself too, after the day I'd had, but by now I'd gone beyond tired and was as wired and twitchy as if I'd downed a gallon of cappuccino. Instead of getting drowsy from the dark and the closed-in room and the regular breathing of everyone in it, all the little noises made me hyper alert.

And so it was that, an hour or three later, I was the first to hear the tiny scrape of the key turning in the lock.

A slight miscalculation on my part. I'd thought I'd be able to hear someone coming down the stairs. But if the room was sound proof—and it seemed as if it was—of course I wouldn't be able to hear anyone moving around outside any more than they'd be able to hear me screaming my head off in here.

By now it was too late to try to wake the girls. By the time they woke up and got ready, the door would be open and our chance gone. I had to deal with this myself. So I took a better grip on my part of the bureau drawer and raised it above my head as I moved into position next to the door.

The knob turned.

On the outside, I mean. We didn't have a knob in here. But the door started inching open. I held my breath as I prepared to bring the piece of oak down on a Russian head.

The door swung back, and a figure stepped into the doorway. I braced myself for attack.

"Gina?" a voice said.

I brought the drawer front down in a whistling arc,

half an inch from Mendoza's perfect nose.

Chapter Seventeen

He was not pleased. I wouldn't have been, either, had it been my nose.

"I didn't actually hit you," I pointed out, not for the first time, later. "And it wouldn't have happened if you'd given me some warning."

He scowled. "I did give you warning."

"And that's why you don't have a broken nose right now. If you hadn't said my name, I would have cracked your skull open."

He glanced at the jagged piece of drawer front, lying next to me on the front steps of the house. "I believe you."

I was sitting outside, getting debriefed, while a lot of things were going on around us. Mendoza had suggested doing the honors inside, in the living room where Konstantin and Yuri had talked to Rachel and me last night, but I'd told him I'd rather be outside. I'd only been locked in for a few hours, but it had been enough to make me appreciate not being locked in.

Mendoza had rescued Edwina from the Lexus and brought her to me, and I was holding on to her. It was very calming, having her warm weight on my lap while I ran my hand over her short fur.

Konstantin and Yuri had been taken off by immigration officials. So had the girls. I didn't know what would happen to them after this, but I figured, even if they were returned to Russia, they'd probably be relieved to be out of the life they'd lived for the past several weeks.

An ambulance had shown up, and had taken Rachel to the hospital. She had a spongy lump on the back of her head that they wanted to X-ray, to make sure the skull wasn't cracked. I asked them to please take her to Southern Hills, so I could visit her and Zachary together once this was over.

At the moment, it was just Mendoza and me out here on the stoop, and half a dozen cops and immigration enforcement types crawling all over the house, looking for information.

"We put a tracer on the car," Mendoza explained. "Last night, before the whole Arena fiasco, I talked to the folks in vice about Stella's. They were interested in what we'd seen, and called in ICE. At one point during the evening, an agent went into the parking lot and put a tracer on the black sedan, so we could follow it home."

"That must have been before Rachel and I got up on the bluff."

Mendoza's lips twitched. "The two of you were up there?"

"We talked about what a good vantage point it would be, remember? So after what you call the fiasco at the Arena, when you went home with Diana... did you find anything there, by the way?"

He shook his head.

"When Diana dropped me off at the Apex, I picked up Edwina and met Rachel on the bluff. We kept watch until the last car was gone from the parking lot, except the sedan. Then Rachel took her car down to the McDonald's parking lot, and waited. I let her know when the sedan began moving, and we took turns following them here."

"And somewhere along the way, they must have made you." His lips didn't twitch this time, but his eyes were dancing.

I made a face. "I guess so. Probably when Rachel stopped in front of the house. Or maybe when I pulled into the driveway down the street. They didn't actually catch us until we were snooping around in their yard, though."

Mendoza nodded. "How's the head?"

"Fine," I said. "Yuri didn't hit me as hard as Konstantin hit Rachel. I have a lump and a headache—" I reached up to feel it; the lump, not the headache, like a small bird egg under my fingertips, "but it's no big deal. Nothing like what Rachel has."

"How many fingers am I holding up?"

He held up two.

"Four," I said. "I'm fine. If I needed medical attention, I'd get medical attention."

His eyebrows drew down. "If you see four fingers..."

"I see two. Index and middle. A nice victory sign. Or are you too young to know what a victory sign is?"

"I'll be thirty-four in February," Mendoza said. "I know what a victory sign is."

And I'd turned forty last July. "Great."

"It's not like you're old enough to remember World War Two yourself, you know, Mrs. Kelly."

No. Far from it. But hearing that he wasn't even thirty-four yet, made me feel very old. I petted Edwina some more. At the rate I was going, I'd end up like Mrs.—excuse me, Miss—Grimshaw. Alone, with a pet dog. "If you want me to feel younger, you could stop calling me Mrs. Kelly. Mr. Kelly is dead. I'm not Mrs. Kelly anymore."

And wouldn't have been, even if David hadn't gotten himself murdered.

Maybe I should drop Kelly and just go by my maiden name from now on.

"I'm not sure that's a good idea," Mendoza said.

"You called me Gina earlier." Unless I'd imagined it.

He didn't answer. "To continue. While the two of you were playing leapfrog behind the sedan, we were also tracking the sedan by GPS. We weren't planning to make a move until morning, but once we saw the two of you being captured, we thought we'd better step up the schedule."

"And we appreciate it," I said.

This time he smiled. "You looked like you didn't need much help."

"I would have brained Yuri or Konstantin. But that doesn't mean we would have gotten out. I might not have brained him hard enough. And then he might have killed me. So I'm grateful you showed up when you did. I have no need to be a hero."

After a second, I added, "I'm sorry I almost hit you."

He shrugged. "You didn't, so don't worry about it."

"It would have been a shame to break that perfect nose, though."

"I snore," Mendoza said.

Well, it looked perfect from the outside. As for the snoring, I doubted I'd ever get to experience that for myself. "So what happens now?"

"ICE and vice fight over Yuri and Konstantin," Mendoza said. "I'll have to sit in on some of the interviews, to see whether they had anything to do with Griselda Grimshaw's murder, but my gut feeling is they didn't."

I shook my head. "I'm wondering whether Anastasia didn't shoot her. Steven probably gave her his gun so she could protect herself. Under the circumstances, it's hard to blame him. She must have been terrified that Yuri and Konstantin would find her again. Maybe, when I showed up, and you showed up, and Zachary showed up, she got scared."

"Maybe," Mendoza said.

"I don't know why that would make her kill Mrs. Grimshaw, but maybe she misunderstood something. Or maybe she didn't mean to."

Mendoza grunted. I have to admit I didn't make a very convincing case for leniency. But there was no reason I could think of why Anastasia might have deliberately killed Mrs. Grimshaw. There'd be no reason for that.

Unless Griselda had threatened her somehow, I guess.

"She might actually be Steven's daughter," I said.

"That's what she told the other girls. And apparently what she told Steven."

He nodded. "Doesn't mean she actually is."

No. "But Steven may have believed it."

"And Griselda might have believed otherwise."

So Anastasia shot her. That didn't make any more sense, but was equally possible. "No way to know until we find them, I guess."

Mendoza shook his head. "I don't think these goons can help us with that."

I didn't, either. "If they knew where Anastasia was, I'm sure they'd have dragged her back here by now. In pieces if they had to. Just to show the other girls what would happen if any of them tried to get away."

"That'd be my guess, too," Mendoza said.

We sat—and in Mendoza's case, stood—in silence a moment.

"You should go," Mendoza said.

"Can I?"

"You haven't been charged with anything. You're the victim here."

Hardly. "The girls are the victims. I just stumbled into this due to my own stupidity, and got a crack on the head for my trouble. But I wouldn't mind going home."

I tucked Edwina under one arm and extended the other hand. "It's been a long night. Would you mind?"

He hauled me upright. "You look pretty good for not having slept for twenty-four hours."

"So do you," I said.

He smiled. "Occupational hazard."

"Will you let me know what happens?"

He said he would. "Would you like me to walk you

to your car?"

"I can find it," I said. "And I'm not so tired that I'll pass out on the way there. Just go inside and see what's going on."

He nodded. But he stood there and watched while I carried Edwina across the lawn, all the way until I was in my car and on my way down the street.

I was still too wired to sleep, so after taking a shower and getting into fresh clothes, I loaded Edwina back into the car and drove to the office. I had told Diana someone would be there most of the day, and with Rachel and Zachary both laid up at Southern Hills, it looked like that someone would have to be me.

Good thing, too, because she did show up just a few minutes after I arrived. "I'll let you listen to the message," I told her, "but a whole lot has happened since we left the Arena last night, and we'll have to talk about some of it."

She was pale and looked like she hadn't slept well, with dark circles under her eyes. She didn't have that jittery, over-tired edge I sensed in myself, though. I probably looked like a monkey on speed, all twitchy and jumpy.

"What happened?"

"Message first. Then I'll tell you."

She listened to the message. Then I told her everything that had happened in the less than twelve hours since I'd seen her last. Ending with, "I don't know whether it's true or not. She could be lying to everyone, including her friends. But this girl took a big risk getting here to find her father, if he isn't really her father."

Diana didn't say anything.

"Did Steven spend any time in Russia, between twenty and twenty-five years ago?"

"That was before I knew him," Diana said, "but yes. Steven spent time in a lot of places back then. He was a photo journalist. He was in Berlin when the wall fell. And he was all over Europe and the Middle East for the decade after that. I'm sure he didn't stay celibate all that time. If he had a child with someone he slept with over there, she never told him, though."

"Or maybe he just didn't tell you?" I suggested.

She shook her head. "He would have told me. He would have wanted to help. To send money, or to bring them here. If she really is his daughter."

"So you think it's possible that she might be?"

"Anything's possible," Diana said. "But I guess we won't really know until we find them."

No. And maybe not even then. "Any more thoughts on where they could be?"

"I'll call the family again," Diana said. "Maybe one of them has heard from him by now. But no. Other than that, I can't think of anywhere they might have gone. Although if they were hoping to get a hundred thousand dollars yesterday, and they didn't, they're probably still around Nashville somewhere."

Probably. "Did you freeze your accounts? Or Steven's accounts?"

"Jaime did," Diana said. "Yesterday. And they aren't frozen. But they're flagged, so that if Steven shows up, they'll call 911 and delay him long enough for the police to show up."

"But so far, he hasn't tried to get any money?"

Diana shook her head. "I'll guess we'll just wait. Sooner or later he'll need money."

Sooner rather than later, probably. There are only so many places someone can stay for free. "I don't suppose you guys own camping gear?"

"No," Diana said. "My idea of roughing it is a cabin in the Smoky Mountains. With a hot tub."

There'd been a photograph like that in their house the other day, of the two of them at a mountain cabin. "Do you own something like that? Could he have gone there?"

Diana shook her head. "Not without spending money. And his credit card is flagged, too."

So probably not. "Let me know if you hear anything," I said.

She nodded. "Thanks for all your help, Gina."

Oh, sure. Big help I'd been. "This wasn't what you signed up for when you gave me this job. It got really complicated really fast." Kidnapping and human trafficking and murder…

"No," Diana agreed. "But at least it doesn't look as if he's cheating."

It didn't. And probably a positive sign that she could see the silver lining.

I let her out and waved her off, and went back inside to Edwina. And no sooner had I sat down at the desk, than my phone rang.

"It's me," Rachel's voice said. "Get me out of here."

I blinked. "The hospital? Are you in the hospital?"

"Yes! And I want to go home."

"I'm not sure that's a good idea…" Especially if she had a concussion. She lived alone, didn't she? "Will they let you leave?"

"If I have someone who'll stay with me," Rachel said. "I'll come to the office. We can stay together."

Oh, sure. Like I'd let her sit here all day, when she should probably be in bed.

On the other hand, if I didn't go there and pick her up, she'd probably just get someone else to do it. She must have other friends. I guess I should be flattered that she'd called me first. "Just hang on. Don't go anywhere. I'll be there."

We could update Zachary, too, while we were at it.

So I loaded Edwina back into the car, and took her with me. She wasn't allowed inside the hospital, of course, but the weather was cool enough even in the middle of the day that she'd be OK in the car for a bit. I cracked a window to make sure she had enough air, and trusted that she'd bite anyone who stuck a hand in. "I'll be right back. I promise."

This situation was untenable. I didn't dare leave the dog alone in David's penthouse—my penthouse now, but with all his fancy purchases in it; fancy purchases she could poop on and chew to bits—but I couldn't keep dragging her around with me, either. She hardly ever felt grass under her paws, poor thing. She just went from car to office to car to apartment. It wasn't fair to her.

And then there was Rachel. And Zachary, who couldn't stay with Rachel if Rachel had a concussion. She'd offered to take him, but now that she was injured too, she was in no position to take care of him as well as herself. And there wasn't enough room in the penthouse for even one of them (in addition to me and Edwina), let alone both.

"Here's what we'll do," I told Rachel when I'd found her. "We'll go see Zachary and update him on what happened yesterday. And see when they'll let him leave the hospital."

It probably wouldn't be today, but maybe tomorrow.

"Then I'll take you home so you can pack a bag. And then we'll all move into the house in Hillwood together."

There was plenty of room there, as well as grass for the dog. And I should probably check up on the renovations, anyway, and put some pressure on the construction crew to finish the job. I hadn't made it out there much while I'd been cramming for my PI license, and of course the past few days had been full of Steven and all his doings.

"I thought your house in Hillwood was under construction," Rachel said.

"Yes and no. The fire last month took out the ceiling in the family room and the floor in the master bedroom, and part of the exterior wall in both. That's all been fixed, even if the drywall hasn't been painted and the new wood floors aren't in." At least those details hadn't been done the last time I was out there to check on progress. "The master bedroom isn't habitable. But there are plenty of other bedrooms. Enough for all of us."

Rachel looked unconvinced.

"It'll be good for Edwina, too," I added. "I can't leave her alone in David's penthouse. And I'm sure she'd like a yard. She used to have one." And the house in Hillwood had a yard that put Griselda Grimshaw's to shame.

"You don't have to stay long," I added. "But it makes more sense than anything else. As soon as you feel well enough, you can go home to your own house."

"I feel well enough now," Rachel grumbled.

Her pupils were the same size again. That was probably a good sign. But a bit smaller than they ought to be. I deduced she was probably riding high on some sort of heavy duty pain killer, and once it wore off she'd feel a lot worse than she did right now. "Just give it a day or two. Zachary will probably be more likely to agree if you're there, and it isn't just me."

Rachel sighed. "Fine. If you're sure it isn't an imposition."

I said I was sure. And I was. I enjoyed the penthouse, but taking on the responsibility for Edwina had made things more difficult. Not that apartment-dwellers can't have dogs. But if the last couple of days were any indication of what life together would be like, she might be happier in Hillwood.

Or with someone other than me. But we weren't going to go there.

The discharge nurse insisted on getting Rachel into a wheelchair. "Procedure," she explained while she expertly hefted Rachel from the bed into the chair.

"We're going to visit someone in another room," I explained.

"Take the chair."

Fine. We took the chair. I pushed it into the elevator, and pushed it down the hall to Zachary's room.

He was alone, and awake, watching something on TV. It had lots of explosions and people running. When we walked—and rolled—in, he turned the sound down.

"What happened to you?"

"Concussion," Rachel said.

"One of the Russian guys who beat you up hit her over the head," I added.

Zachary's eyes widened.

He actually looked worse today than yesterday, if that was possible. The cuts and bruises had reached maximum color by now, and his face looked like a boxer's after a title match. But he seemed more alert, and more able to follow what we were saying. He also talked more. And the whooshing machine that had been helping him breathe yesterday was gone, and he was managing on his own.

I went over the whole thing, the way I'd done with Diana earlier, and with Mendoza before that. By now, I was really getting the telling of it down to a science. It made for an exciting narrative.

When I finished, the first words out of Zachary's mouth were, "What'll happen to the girls?"

I told him I had no idea. "ICE took them. For debriefing, I'm sure. I don't know whether they'll be sent back to Russia or what will happen."

They were here on some sort of student visa, Mendoza had said, so maybe they'd actually be allowed to stay if they wanted to. "You should ask him," I told Zachary. "He's down there with the detectives from vice, who were also part of the sting. Mendoza's everybody's hero at the moment."

Zachary nodded.

"He'll probably stop by later, to talk to you about it." In fact, I'd give him a call and make sure he did. "Meanwhile, I'm taking Rachel back to the house in

Hillwood for a day or two. Until she's OK to be on her own again. We thought maybe, when you're released, you'd like to join us."

The parts of Zachary's face that weren't scabby or bruised, flushed red. "I guess Detective Mendoza told you about my mother, huh?"

"Just that you're not living with her anymore," I said. "It's none of my business."

He pleated a corner of the sheet between his thumb and forefinger. "She got angry when I quit my job at the Apex to work for you. She said I shouldn't quit a real job to play detective."

"You're not playing detective," I said. "You were instrumental in stopping a human trafficking operation and saving three Russian women from a life of prostitution. You put your own life and health at risk for someone else. That makes you a hero."

He flushed again, but shook his head. "I don't think my mom's gonna see it that way. And anyway, you were the one who told me what to do."

"But you were the one who did it. You're the one who got beat up for it. But you don't have to take my word for it. When Mendoza stops by, he'll tell you the same thing. So would the guys from ICE and vice, I'm sure."

He didn't answer, but he looked a little more cheerful.

"So would you like to come stay in the house in Hillwood until we can figure something else out? At least until you feel better physically?"

Zachary allowed as how he might see his way clear to doing that.

"Good." I got to my feet. "I'll go get Rachel settled. Any idea when they're likely to let you out of here?"

"They said tomorrow morning," Zachary said.

"Then I'll be back later today to see you. And tomorrow we'll get you out of here."

He nodded. "Thanks, Gina."

"No problem," I said and wheeled Rachel out of there. You lose a husband; you gain a whole, makeshift family, dog included.

Chapter Eighteen

The house I had shared with David for the past eighteen years of my life squatted like a malignant toad on top of a little rise. I had expected—or let's say hoped—to see construction vehicles on the parking pad, and maybe hear some banging or sawing from inside.

There was nothing. The driveway—twice as long as Griselda Grimshaw's—was empty, and so was the parking area at the end of it.

There was no sense in pulling into the garage—I'd have to leave again later, to go see Zachary—so I just pulled the car to a stop outside the house and turned the key in the ignition. "Here we are."

Rachel nodded. She'd been here before, of course. Both before and after the fire. "It doesn't look too bad."

It didn't. Most of the exterior damage had been repaired, to keep out the elements. We were into fall, and going into winter, which in the South means a lot of rain and maybe some snow. I'd been insistent that the roof and exterior wall be done first, so at least the rest of the interior wouldn't take any more damage than it already had.

I reached into the back and grabbed Edwina. "Here you go, sweetheart. Check it out."

I put her down on the concrete. She started sniffing, and eventually made it off the edge of the parking pad and into the grass, where she squatted.

Meanwhile, I hauled Rachel's suitcase out of the back and headed for the front door. "Come on inside. Let's get you situated."

She followed me up the walkway, and after some more sniffing, so did Edwina.

I unlocked the door and turned to the alarm system, only to find that, for some reason, it was turned off.

That figured. The construction crew was supposed to turn it back on when they left at night, so the house wouldn't be unprotected during the time they weren't here, but God only knew when they'd last been by. The house could have been sitting like this for a week or more.

Guess I'd have to call them and cause a stink. And see if I could light a fire under someone, to get the work finished.

I picked up the suitcase again. "The bedrooms are upstairs. Let's go find you one. Come on, Edwina."

The terrier pranced across the floor of the foyer. When Rachel and I started up the stairs to the second floor, she stood for a second at the bottom, head cocked to one side, contemplating the staircase. She might not have seen one before. Griselda Grimshaw's ranch had been all on one level, and of course the penthouse was a flat, too. As well as the office.

I stopped halfway up. "Do you need help?"

"No," Rachel said, holding onto the railing. "I can make it."

I hadn't been talking to her, but it turned out to be moot. Edwina backed up to get a couple of steps' running start, and bounded up, past us and all the way to the second floor, where she stood grinning down, pleased with herself.

"We can take a breather," I told Rachel, since she clearly wasn't feeling great. Her face was pale, and there were beads of sweat along her hairline. "You probably should have let them keep you another few hours, at least."

"I hate hospitals," Rachel said. "I'll be all right once I get to the top."

She kept going. I did the same.

Once we got to the second floor, we did take a breather before I led Rachel down the hallway. "There are four bedrooms up here in addition to the master. Two on each side of the hallway." With the master (still under reconstruction) at the end. I'd probably end up in one of the guest rooms too, while we were here. "You might like this one."

I turned the knob and pushed open the door to what I knew was a feminine, lacey sort of room, with floating curtains and ice blue walls.

Only to stop with my mouth open. "What the hell…!"

It was all I got out before I found myself staring down the barrel of what was most likely a Smith and Wesson M&P 9 millimeter pistol.

And no, I won't pretend I can distinguish one handgun from another. I based the assumption on the woman who was holding it. Blond, with Russian cheekbones, big, blue eyes, and a terrified expression on her face.

I dropped the suitcase and lifted my hands. Next to me, Rachel did the same. Edwina made to prance inside, and I shifted my foot to try to keep her out.

"It's all right."

The girl—Anastasia—looked at me. I have no idea whether she even understood what I said, but she didn't shoot, so we were doing fine.

"Is Steven here?"

Her eyes flickered. I didn't need the nod to figure out that he was.

"My name is Gina. This is my house." I let that sink in for a second before I added, "I'm going to call for Steven, OK?"

She didn't nod, but she didn't shoot me, either. I put my head back. "Steven!"

At first there was nothing. Then a scramble from the next room, and Steven's voice. "Anastasia?!"

The door opened and slammed against the wall next door. The fake impressionist painting that David's decorator had insisted on hanging on the wall in here quivered. Steven thundered down the hall and skidded into the room, straight into Rachel, whom he knocked several steps forward. The two of them clung to one another to stay upright.

There was a beat.

"Oh," Steven said. "Gina. I can explain."

"I'd like to hear that," I said, "but perhaps a little later? Could you tell your daughter to put the gun down first?"

"Oh." This time he flushed, and looked, for a second, ridiculously like Zachary. "Anastasia…" He went off into Russian. Apparently he spoke it well enough that they could communicate.

It took a minute or so, and then the gun disappeared into the sheets. I don't think Anastasia was entirely comfortable, though, and I was pretty sure she kept a hand on it out of sight. But it was nice to be able to lower my hands again.

"I should let you know," I said, slowly and clearly, to both of them, "that Konstantin and Yuri were arrested last night. ICE and Metro police ran a joint sting operation that ended with Konstantin and Yuri in the prison and the other three Russian girls getting rescued."

Anastasia said something. Steven nodded. "We were getting around to that. I just wanted to make sure that Anastasia was safe first."

"I guess she really is your daughter?"

"We haven't done any testing," Steven said, "but she seems to be. I knew her mother back when. And she has my eyes."

She did. A dark slate blue, tilted up at the corners.

"Diana will be relieved."

Steven looked confused. "What…?" And then he looked disgusted. "Oh, for God's sake!"

"You might have told her what was going on," I said mildly. "I mean, what was she supposed to think?"

"Not that I'd cheat on her with someone young enough to be my daughter!"

"In justice to her, she didn't think that. When she first asked me to look into it, it was just because she thought you were acting weird."

Steven admitted that he probably had been acting weird. "It isn't every day a man gets a letter from a grown daughter he never knew he had, saying she needs help escaping from human traffickers."

No, it isn't. "Tatiana told me how you got her out of there. That one of the other girls hit the fire alarm and the two of you got away in the confusion. And Araminta Tucker said that you contacted her about her house for rent."

Steven nodded. "There was a notice on the bulletin board at the university. I figured we'd be safe trying to find a place for Anastasia that way. I couldn't take her home with me. I didn't want to put Diana in danger, and anyway, I wanted to be sure…"

He trailed off. I nodded.

"Would you like to explain what happened the other day?" I glanced from Steven to Anastasia and back. "I followed you from the university to Araminta's house. And then the neighbor, Mrs. Grimshaw, got worried because I was parked on the street, so she called the police, and Mendoza showed up…"

"She guessed the truth," Anastasia said from the bed. She spoke English about as well as Tatiana, it turned out. Maybe even a bit better. "She asked me to come to her house for tea. And she asked a lot of questions. I told her a little bit, and she guessed the rest."

So when Griselda Grimshaw had been muttering darkly about the X-files—unless Mendoza had been joking about that—she hadn't been talking about space aliens, but illegal aliens. That made a lot more sense.

"What happened?" Had Griselda threatened to betray Anastasia, and so Anastasia shot her?

The girl took a breath. "Your car was there. Big and black."

Like the sedan, I guessed. It might make sense that she'd be a little worried about that.

"And then the police came. Yuri and Konstantin told us we wouldn't get any help from the police. That the police knew about us and wouldn't do anything. Russian police is... how you say... corrupt?"

"Mendoza isn't corrupt," I said. "He just came to reassure Mrs. Grimshaw that I wasn't dangerous."

Anastasia didn't respond to that. "And then, later, the boy came. With the pizza. When I hadn't ordered a pizza."

"That was Zachary," I told Steven. "We wanted to get a look at Anastasia. You know, for Diana."

He nodded. "You can understand why Anastasia would be worried, though."

I could, I guess. Although it still didn't make it all right to shoot Mrs. Grimshaw and leave Edwina an orphan.

"Go on," I said.

By now, Rachel had sat down in the chair over in the corner, and put Edwina on her lap. She and the dog both looked close to being asleep.

"I was scared," Anastasia said. "I stayed by the window, and I kept watch. But it was late, and I got tired. And I fell asleep. Right there, on the floor. And then I heard a loud noise. And someone was outside, trying to get into the house. Into my house. The back door opened. And I opened the front door and ran."

Her eyes had widened, and so had her pupils. If she wasn't genuinely reliving a very scary experience, she was an Oscar-worthy actress.

"Where did you go?" I asked.

She forked the fingers of one hand through her long, straight hair, pushing it back off her face. "I ran and ran. And then I asked the way to the university. And I went there."

"On foot?"

She nodded. "I walked all night. I had no money for the bus or a cab, and I was afraid to..." She stuck her thumb out in the universal gesture for hitchhiking.

I choked. "Yes, that was probably a good idea." God knows what could have happened to a girl like that, hitchhiking through Nashville at night. "Did you see who shot Mrs. Grimshaw? It must have been the shot that woke you, right?"

Anastasia shook her head. "I didn't see anything. I ran."

"What about a car? Did you see that?"

But she hadn't.

"So you didn't shoot Mrs. Grimshaw?"

She looked sincerely shocked that I'd ask. "No! She was nice to me. A nosy old woman, but she gave me tea. And she told me she'd keep watch for anyone bad. I wouldn't want to hurt her."

Another Oscar-worthy performance.

"That's your gun, right?" I asked Steven, gesturing to it. "Diana said you had one, and that it was gone from the bedside table."

He nodded. "I usually keep it in the drawer. Nobody bothers a university professor. Diana keeps hers in her purse."

"Mendoza will probably want a look at it. If it

wasn't used on Mrs. Grimshaw, it'll be a formality."

"Of course," Steven said, with a glance at Anastasia. "Are you going to call him?"

I guessed I would, eventually. However— "I think you should probably do that yourself. I'll give you the number. And then you'll have to explain everything to Diana."

He swallowed.

"But it's safe to leave. Konstantin and Yuri are in prison. They can't hurt you. Her. Either of you."

It was a not so subtle hint that I'd like them to vacate my house.

"By the way," I added, as they started to do just that, "how did you end up here?"

"Oh." Steven stopped halfway down the hall to the room where he'd been staying. "Did you get that message I left on your machine the other night?"

I nodded.

"So you know I recognized you. And I remembered that Diana had told me what happened with you and your husband. And that you'd had a fire here, and you'd moved into your husband's penthouse downtown. I figured, if you weren't here, maybe we could use the house to lie low for a couple of days."

"Smart," I said. Steven inclined his head. "I don't suppose you've seen my contractors in the time you've been here?"

But he hadn't. I let him disappear into his room—or the room he'd claimed for himself while he was here—to get ready to go.

When he came back out two minutes later, he was properly dressed and groomed. "Sorry for the trouble," he told me.

"It's no trouble. The house was just sitting here. I'm glad you could make use of it. But you might have told me you were coming."

"When I made the phone call, I didn't know," Steven said. "We'd gone next door to use the phone, and then the black sedan drove up…"

Konstantin and Yuri acting on the information they'd beaten out of Zachary, I guessed. "What happened?"

"They busted the back door into Anastasia's house," Steven said. "And spent some time looking through it. They didn't realize we were next door. But we were afraid they'd come back, so we left. And that's when I remembered about your house."

Made sense. "One more thing before you go. The ransom note."

"What ransom note?" Steven said.

Since he sounded sincere, and not like he was pulling my leg, I explained about the ransom note. "It arrived at your house yesterday morning. Early. A demand for a hundred thousand dollars in exchange for you."

"That's crazy," Steven said. "I wasn't kidnapped. And if I wanted a hundred thousand dollars, I'd go to the bank. I have a hundred thousand dollars in my account." His face changed, and he added, "At least I used to."

"You still do. I don't suppose she…?" I glanced at the door to the other room, where Anastasia was still getting ready, and let the question trail off suggestively.

Steven shook his head. "We were together yesterday

morning. If someone dropped off a ransom note then, it wasn't either of us."

Someone had definitely dropped off a ransom note then. Unless Diana had been lying, but I couldn't think of any reason why she would.

"I appreciate it," I said. "Do you want me to call Diana and let her know you're coming?"

He shook his head. "I'll take care of it. Thanks, Gina."

"No problem," I said. "Good luck."

They went on their way, down to the garage and into Steven's brown sedan, which was parked there. If I'd only decided to put my own car into the garage when we arrived, I'd have had some warning that they were here.

But it had all turned out as well as it could have, I guessed. Nobody'd gotten shot. I'd gotten rid of them. They knew they didn't have to worry about Konstantin and Yuri anymore. If Anastasia really was Steven's daughter, the ICE couldn't send her back to Russia, no matter how much they might want to—and that was assuming they wanted to, which I didn't know.

The only thing left to do was get Rachel situated.

I went back upstairs and plucked Edwina from her lap before hauling Rachel to her feet. "Come on. Just a few more steps."

I took her into the bedroom across the hall, where the sheets were fresh and where nobody had been sleeping. "Is this OK?"

"Anywhere's OK," Rachel said, and made a beeline for the bed. "I'm just going to lie down for a bit."

She was slurring her words, and was practically

cross-eyed.

"Good idea." I got in front of her and yanked the comforter down just before she tumbled onto the mattress. "Get some rest. You'll feel better."

She was already out cold. I closed the door behind me and got busy stripping and washing the sheets and towels my uninvited guests had used. If I had to stay here, and Zachary was coming, we'd need clean sheets on   every   bed.

Chapter Nineteen

With Rachel settled and the sheets in the dryer, I finally found time to call Mendoza to tell him what had happened. And, of course, got his voice mail. He was probably still sitting in on the interviews with Konstantin and Yuri and the Russian girls.

Boy, was he in for a surprise when he picked up his messages.

"It's Gina," I said. "You'll never guess what happened. I picked up Rachel from the hospital and took her to the house in Hillwood to recuperate, since they wouldn't let her leave unless she had someone to stay with. I'll get Zachary, too, when they let him out— probably tomorrow morning—and we'll all camp out here for a few days. And speaking of camping out... you'll never guess who we found when we got here."

I took a breath, both because I needed one, and to prolong the suspense.

"Steven and Anastasia! Set up, as pretty as you please, in two of my guest rooms. She pulled a gun on me when I walked through the door, although we got that part of it straightened out. And she says—they both say—that they didn't shoot Mrs. Grimshaw. I can't think of a reason why they would have shot Mrs. Grimshaw, but I told them you'd need to test the gun, and if they hadn't shot Mrs. Grimshaw, then they had nothing to worry about. Anastasia said that someone else shot her, and then that someone tried to get into her house. Anastasia's house. Or Araminta Tucker's house, I guess, but the house where Anastasia was staying. She said they were coming through the back door, and she ran out the front and walked all the way to the university, where she intercepted Steven the next morning. And the two of them went on the run."

I took another breath.

"Steven seems pretty certain Anastasia is his daughter. He said he knew her mother back when—'back when' being the time before the girl was born, I assume—and that she has his eyes. And she does, sort of. But I'm sure they'll have a paternity test done, to make sure. Anyway, I told them what happened last night, and that Yuri and Konstantin are no longer a threat, so they decided to venture back into the world. I told them to talk to Diana first. If you contact her, she can probably tell you where to find them."

I took another breath. Had I left anything out?

"I think that's all. Except for who actually shot Griselda, I guess. I don't think it was Anastasia. She seemed sincere when she said she didn't. And it couldn't have been Konstantin and Yuri. They didn't know about Araminta Tucker's house until the next night, after they beat the information out of Zachary. So while I'm sure vice and ICE are happy with you for putting them on the trail of Konstantin and Yuri, you still have a murder to solve. Let me know if there's anything I can do to help. If not, I guess I'll see you around."

I paused another second. I'm not sure why. It wasn't like I expected him to answer. And of course he didn't.

"Bye, Detective," I said, and disconnected the call. And sat down at the kitchen table to wait for the sheets to make it through the wash cycle so I could throw them in the dryer.

Had I left anything out?

I didn't think so. Nothing important, anyway. Except maybe the ransom note. Someone had sent it, or put it on Diana's doormat. And it hadn't been Steven and Anastasia. As Steven had said, it was his money. And if Anastasia really was his daughter, she had no reason to want to steal his cash. Even if she were mercenary, and I had no reason to think she was, she'd be better off keeping on his good side. And that was aside from the fact that Steven had sworn they were together the other morning.

So it wasn't Steven and Anastasia.

And it couldn't have been Konstantin and Yuri. There was no reason to think they even knew who Steven was, let alone where he lived.

Although Zachary might have told them that, too. Assuming they'd asked. I'd have to find out if they had. But even if they knew who Steven was, and where he lived, was a ransom note something that would have crossed their minds?

Somehow I didn't think so. And the Russian girls wouldn't have been able to get out of their room and over to Richland, where Diana and Steven lived.

Diana herself?

It would have been easy for her to set it up, anyway. Just unlock the front door and drop the note on the mat, and then call me, frantic.

So Diana had had means and opportunity. But maybe not so much in the way of motive. Like Steven, it was her money. If she wanted it, she could just take it out of the bank.

Would it benefit her somehow for us to think that Steven had been kidnapped instead of running off with his young mistress, which is what we'd been thinking then?

I couldn't see how.

So who did that leave? If Diana was out, and Steven and Anastasia were out, and Konstantin and Yuri were out, and the Russian girls were out... who was left?

Anybody?

The only other person I could think of was Araminta Tucker. She'd known about Steven and the girl. She'd known who Steven was, and that he was a professor at the university, so she might have figured out where he lived. A quick computer search or even checking the phone directory might get her that information. And she did get around. I didn't know how, but she'd made it to the ice hockey game the other night, so she had access to some form of transportation. She might have made it to Diana's house in the early hours of yesterday morning.

The other shoe dropped, and in retrospect, I can only marvel that it took as long as it did.

Araminta Tucker knew all about Steven and Anastasia. She'd rented them her house. Right next to her sister-in-law. The sister-in-law with the million dollar insurance policy.

Anastasia had said that she'd been woken up by a loud noise. The shot that killed Griselda, I assumed. And then someone had been at the back door to her house. Araminta's house.

Someone who had been on their way in through the back door when Anastasia ran out the front.

That's what she'd said, wasn't it? That someone had been on their way in?

There'd been no sign of forced entry the next morning. That's when I'd been skulking around Araminta's house, and also when Mendoza had taken me inside, a little later in the afternoon. If someone had tried to force the back door then, the way they had the following night, one of us would have noticed. The way we'd noticed the following day, after Konstantin and Yuri had made their visit.

So had the person who shot Griselda had a key?

Who'd have a key to Araminta's house other than Anastasia? Steven, presumably, but he'd been home with Diana.

Griselda might have. Araminta's sister-in-law and neighbor. Patton's sister. The one who stuck her nose into everything. Yes, Griselda had surely had a key to her brother's house next door. And it was possible that whoever shot Griselda had gotten the key to Araminta's house from Griselda's house. But that still left me with an unknown murderer.

And of course Araminta would have a key to her own house. All landlords do, just in case.

So maybe Araminta killed Griselda.

I turned that thought over a couple of times.

Mendoza had said it once, that she was the obvious suspect. I'd laughed at the idea, but he was right, of course. She lived next door, or used to. She was Griselda's sister-in-law. They didn't like each other. And she inherited the money.

Assisted living isn't cheap. That nice million dollar life insurance policy would probably come in very handy.

The hundred thousand dollars from Diana would be helpful, too.

Araminta had been at the Arena last night. She was the only person involved in the case—that I knew about—who had been.

As Sherlock Holmes used to say—I think it was Sherlock Holmes—when you've eliminated all the other possibilities, the only suspect that's left is the murderer, even if it doesn't make any sense.

Or something like that.

Maybe I'd just go pay her a friendly little visit. Make sure she made it home from the Arena in one piece last night. Tell her that Konstantin and Yuri were in prison and that we'd found Anastasia and Steven. And see what she said.

I grabbed the phone again, and dialed Mendoza back. And got his voicemail again. "I'm going to see Araminta," I told him, and laid out the reasons why. "I'll be careful. It won't be like last time. I won't be taken by surprise. I won't eat or drink anything. And I'm sure she's not going to pull out a gun and blow me away right in the middle of the assisted living facility. I'll just see what she says—if she lets anything slip—and then get back to you."

Maybe I'd tell her I'd like to keep Edwina, and that I'd be happy to pay for her. If Araminta accepted money, that might be a clue that she was guilty.

I hung up the phone and tiptoed up to the second floor to check on Rachel. She was sound asleep, so I left a note next to the bed telling her where I'd gone and why. After hesitating, I added a post-script: *If I'm not back in three hours, call Mendoza.*

I tiptoed back down. Edwina lifted her head to look at me, but seemed pretty content to be stretched out on the rug in the kitchen. "I'll be back," I told her. "Rachel's here. I don't want to bring you, just in case Araminta takes one look at you and changes her mind about wanting to keep you."

Of course, if she had killed her sister-in-law and was going to prison, she couldn't take Edwina with her. But I wasn't willing to take any chances. So I left the dog on the kitchen rug and headed back out.

I spent the drive going over the case in my head, fitting the pieces together in different ways. Had I overlooked anything? Was there another solution? Another suspect I hadn't thought of? Was it possible that Anastasia was lying and she actually had shot Griselda, and the story about someone trying to get into the house was just that: a story?

Yes, of course it was possible. I only had Anastasia's word for what had happened. So it could be a lie.

But what would be her reason for wanting Griselda dead?

The only person who had a solid motive for that was Araminta. And the only person who had showed up for the money drop at the Arena was Araminta.

Everything pointed to Araminta. No matter how I turned the pieces of evidence around and tried to put them together in different ways, I came back to Araminta.

The first thing I saw when I drove into the parking lot of the assisted living facility was Mendoza's car.

Or not the first thing. I saw a lot of other cars first, along with several spindly trees and dry grass.

But I did see a car that looked like Mendoza's, parked in one of the visitor slots. It was the right color, with Davidson County government plates, and the extra antennae and mirrors that differentiate plain police cars from regular cars.

I pulled the Lexus into the slot next to it and got out. And peered through the window of the sedan.

It was empty. If it was Mendoza's, there was no way to tell for sure.

I headed into the lobby and over to the desk. "I'd like to see Araminta Tucker, please."

The nurse behind the desk squinted at me. "Weren't you here the other day?"

I nodded.

She began tapping on her computer, and soon spat out another sticker with my face on it. She handed it across the counter. "She already has someone in with her."

I had suspected as much. "Good looking cop named Mendoza?"

She nodded.

"He won't mind," I said glibly. "I'm meeting him here."

She looked doubtful, but I guess there wasn't much she could do to stop me. I headed down the hallway to the elevators.

Between you and me, I didn't know whether Mendoza would mind me showing up or not. It depended entirely on what he was doing here, and whether he'd gotten my voicemails.

If he had, he was probably expecting me. If he hadn't, he might not be happy to see me.

Did he know that Araminta was suspect number one in Griselda's murder?

I had to assume he did, whether he'd gotten my voicemails or not. I mean, he wasn't stupid. Solving murders was his profession. He was the one who had pointed out her motive in the first place. And if I could figure out that Konstantin and Yuri hadn't shot Griselda, and that Anastasia might not have, Mendoza certainly could figure out the same thing.

So was he here to arrest her? To look for a confession?

The elevator stopped on Araminta's floor, and the doors slid open. I stepped out into the hallway and headed for her room. Like last time, I could hear the TV from yards away, but this time, the connotation was more sinister. What if the TV was on so loudly to drown out any noises Mendoza might be making as he choked to death on a cookie?

The door was open a crack. I peered through the opening. Araminta was sitting, pretty as you please, on the sofa facing the TV. Mendoza had his back to me, but I could see his head above the back of the wingback chair I'd occupied the last time—and first time—I was here.

Between them on the coffee table was a plate of what looked like scones, and two dainty cups of tea on saucers. As I watched, Mendoza grabbed a scone and lifted it to his mouth.

"Nooooo!"

I pushed the door open and launched myself through the air, knocking the scone out of his hand and taking him down to the floor while I was at it. His head grazed the corner of the coffee table going down, and when I ended up on top of him on the floor, he blinked up at me, confused.

He has very pretty eyes, in case I neglected to mention that.

"Tsk, tsk."

Araminta clicked her tongue, and I tore my attention away from Mendoza's face—with a touch of difficulty—to look at her. "Sorry. I thought there might be something wrong with the scone."

Mendoza closed his eyes in what looked like pain. I wasn't sure whether it was because of the head wound or what I said.

Probably the latter.

"Dear me," Araminta said, clucking. She unwound herself from the sofa and bent to peer down at Mendoza. "Is he all right? Do you need help?"

"I think we're all right." I removed myself from on top of Mendoza. It wasn't easy, in the confined space between the chair and the coffee table. "He hit his head. I think he could use a Band-Aid."

"I'll get one." Araminta bustled out, through the doorway into the rest of the apartment. I extended a hand to Mendoza, who eyed it without favor and proceeded to right himself without my help.

"Sorry," I said.

He sighed. "What are you doing here, Mrs. Kelly?"

I sat down on the chair he'd been forced to vacate and watched as he pulled himself up on the now-empty sofa. "Did you get my messages?"

"Yes," Mendoza said. He looked like he wanted to roll his eyes but thought better of it. The little trickle of blood at his temple made him look very rakish, although I was sorry to see that he was a touch paler than usual.

I grabbed a napkin and extended it across the table. "I'm sorry I knocked you down. But I was afraid the scone might be poisoned."

"The scones are fine," Mendoza said. "I've already had one."

"And you feel all right?" In that case, I wouldn't mind one myself. They looked good.

I reached for the one Mendoza had dropped—might as well pick it up off the floor—as Mendoza said, "I did. Until you showed up."

"I said I was sorry." I took a bite of the scone. It tasted great. Almond and raspberry, unless I was mistaken.

It crossed my mind that there was some old poison that tasted like almonds—arsenic, maybe? Or strychnine? The kind you read about in old murder mysteries—but if Mendoza said the scones were all right, I'd take his word for it. "This is good."

He nodded. "So what are you doing here?"

"I couldn't get you on the phone," I said, around the bite of scone. "I figured you were still sitting in on the interviews with the Russians. So I thought I'd come down here and… um…"

I swallowed, since I didn't exactly know how to end the sentence. I mean, I had told him what I thought on the phone. It wasn't hard to figure out that I was here to see if I could discover whether Araminta was guilty.

"Uh-huh," Mendoza said dryly.

"I was just trying to help."

"And I'm grateful."

He didn't sound grateful. I took another bite of the scone so I wouldn't say so. "Anything new on the Russian front?"

"No," Mendoza said. "Anything new on your end?"

"Nothing I didn't already tell you by voicemail." I popped the rest of the scone in my mouth and chewed. "That was really good."

"Thank you, dear," Araminta said from the doorway. "Have some tea."

I wouldn't mind if I did. Except Mendoza shook his head.

"No?"

"Remember what happened last time?"

I did remember what happened last time. There'd been something in the iced tea. "Maybe some other time," I told Araminta over my shoulder. "Thanks, though."

She made a face. "Then I'm afraid I'll just have to shoot you." She glanced at Mendoza. "And you."

He made himself more comfortable on the sofa. "No Band-Aid?"

"I'm afraid I forgot to look," Araminta said. "About the gun…"

It was in her hand, where it looked very big and

scary, although that might have been because she had very small hands.

"It's the one you used to kill Griselda," I said, "right?"

The words hitched a little, I admit it. I was scared, and it was hard to breathe. It isn't every day a girl is faced with a gun, and a woman with nothing much left to lose.

Then again, I'd been faced with a gun less than twelve hours ago, too, and had lived to tell the tale. And Mendoza didn't seem worried.

Araminta nodded. "Yes, dear. It was Patton's gun. It came to me when he passed."

Of course it had. "And you decided that now would be a good time to kill your sister-in-law?"

"I'd been thinking about it for a while," Araminta said calmly. "For the money, you know. Places like this don't come cheap."

She waved a hand at her surroundings. It was the hand with the gun, and I think both Mendoza and I held our breath until she'd lowered it again.

"Patton didn't leave me much, you understand. Griselda was the one with the money. And she was happy to share it with Patton, but when he died and it was just me... well, it was a very different story."

"So you decided to get rid of her. And inherit."

She nodded. "I've thought about it for years. But the time never seemed right. I couldn't make it too obvious, you understand."

I nodded. "Of course not. You didn't want it to look like you were behind it. It had to look like someone else did it."

She beamed. "Exactly, dear. I knew you'd understand."

Oh, sure. I smiled back. "So when Steven called and wanted to rent the house for Anastasia, you saw your chance."

"They made it so obvious, they might as well have come straight out and talked about the Russian mafia." She shook her head, clucking. "There was no way they'd go to the police. And she was probably illegal, anyway. Nobody would believe that she didn't do it. It made perfect sense."

"So you drove over there, and… you have a car, I assume?"

She smiled sweetly. "Of course, dear. This isn't prison, you know. I come and go as I please. And I'm not so old yet that they've taken away my driver's license."

No, physically there didn't seem to be much wrong with her. Her eyesight was obviously good, and so was her mind. Even if it was a little unhinged.

"So you went there, and you knocked on the door, and when Griselda opened it—which she would do, even late at night, seeing as you were her sister-in-law and someone she trusted—you shot her."

Araminta nodded. "And went next door to spook the Russian girl into taking off. It wouldn't do for her to be there the next morning, or whenever the body was found."

Of course not. "And then, when I showed up and told you Steven was missing, too, I guess you got the idea for the ransom note?"

She looked very pleased, with me for catching on, or with herself for thinking of it. Or both. "It seemed like such a golden opportunity. It might take a while for the insurance company to pay out under the circumstances—not that anyone in their right mind would suspect *me* of having had anything to do with it!—and I could use a little cash to tide me over until I got the insurance money. And you did say your friend is an attorney. I thought she must be able to afford it."

"You know," I said, "when I saw you at the Arena last night, I didn't suspect you at all. I thought it was a coincidence."

Mendoza arched his brows at me, and I added, "That's why I didn't tell you. I didn't think it was important. Sorry."

He didn't say anything, just rolled his eyes. Araminta snickered. "I saw you both, of course. And realized I wouldn't be getting the money. But at least I could get away clean. Nobody ever suspects a little old lady of anything bad."

"How do you plan to get away now?" I asked, curiously. "I mean, you just confessed."

She smiled sweetly. "I'm just waiting for the poison in the scones to kick in, dear."

There was poison in the scones?

I turned to Mendoza. "You said the scones were fine."

He shrugged. "Guess I was wrong."

Guess so. "What kind of poison?" I asked Araminta.

She waved her hand vaguely. The one with the gun. "Something from Griselda's medicine cabinet. Heart medicine, maybe? She always had a rotten heart."

It sounded like that particular affliction was going around. "So what kind of symptoms are you waiting for?"

"I'm not sure, dear. I thought you might get woozy, but you don't seem to be." She furrowed her brows. "Perhaps another scone?"

"I'm not really hungry anymore," I said. "How about you just tie us to the furniture instead, and take off while you can? You don't have to wait. And with the TV on so loudly, nobody's likely to hear us scream even if you don't get the gags just right."

She nodded pensively. "That's a good idea."

"You can use my scarf." I pulled it from around my neck and held it out to her.

"Thank you, dear." She took a step forward and reached for it. I kicked the gun out her other hand.

It went flying through the air and hit the floor with a loud noise. It wasn't until I heard an electric sizzle, and then a crack before everything went silent, that I realized the gun had gone off on impact and shot the big screen TV.

The bullet must have passed within a few inches of the top of my head.

Not that I had much time to think about it. Like me earlier, Mendoza had launched himself across the coffee table, and had landed on top of Araminta. Unlike me earlier, she didn't seem to enjoy the proximity. She was shrieking like a banshee, and beating at him with her fists. And he was handicapped by the fact that while he had her by ten inches and probably seventy pounds, she was a little old lady with fragile bones, and if he broke any, she'd probably holler about police brutality.

He got her turned around, though, and her screams muffled in the Persian rug, so he could fit handcuffs around her skinny wrists. They had to be adjusted to their smallest circumference, or she'd be able to just slip her hands right out through them.

He hauled her upright and onto the sofa while she was still wailing. "You have the right to remain silent…"

"So now what?" I asked when he had gone through the appropriate motions.

He glanced at me. "I'll call the Williamson County sheriff and have her picked up. We're in his jurisdiction. Then we'll have her transferred to Nashville, since most of her crimes were committed there."

"I'm more concerned about me and you," I said. "And dying from ingesting Griselda's heart medicine."

"I feel fine," Mendoza told me, "but the bathroom's down the hall, if you want to go stick a finger down your throat."

I felt fine, too, now that it was over. But I thought maybe I'd make a short trip to the bathroom anyway. If nothing else, I could make sure I hadn't accidentally wet myself when the gun went off. And maybe I could find a Band-Aid for Mendoza, while I was at it. "I'll be right back."

He nodded and reached for his phone. "I'll be here."

Chapter Twenty

"So that's what happened," I told Diana that evening. We were all sitting around the kitchen table in the house in Hillwood. And by 'all,' I mean Diana, Rachel, Zachary, and I, with Edwina curled up on the rug in front of the sink. "Araminta killed Griselda and tried to put the blame on Anastasia. She also tried to shake you down for money. And she's charged with attempted murder of me and Mendoza, even though the pills she ground up and put in the scones expired several years ago. I guess she didn't notice."

"So no ill effects from the experience?" Diana sipped from her glass of wine.

The rest of us were all strictly alcohol-free this evening. Zachary and Rachel because they were taking pain pills—and Zachary was technically too young to drink, anyway—and I because the doctor who had examined me had said I probably didn't have anything to worry about, but it might be a good idea if I were a little extra careful about what I put in my mouth for the next couple of days.

"My stomach's a little upset," I admitted. "And I tend to jump at loud noises. But apart from that, no. I'm glad to be alive, though. That bullet practically parted my hair before it killed the TV."

Diana nodded. "I'm sorry."

"It wasn't your fault. It was all Araminta."

"I gave you this job," Diana reminded me.

"Yes, but all you wanted to know, was what Steven was up to. You didn't ask me to get involved in murder, and human trafficking, and kidnapping. I did all that on my own."

She smiled. "And I'm grateful you did."

"So you and Steven are going to be all right?"

She sounded surprised that I asked. "Of course."

Good to know. "What about Anastasia?"

"Steven's talking to the people at ICE," Diana said. "To see if she'll be allowed to stay while we figure things out."

"So you think she might be his daughter?"

"He thinks so," Diana said. "I figure he ought to know."

Probably so. "And how is it going?"

"If necessarily, we'll hire a lawyer," Diana said. "One who specializes in immigration cases. But Steven's making a good case. She's here legally, on some sort of tourist visa. There's nothing for her in Russia. Her mother's dead, and so are her grandparents. She has nothing to go back to. And she came all the way here to find him. This girl allowed herself to be trafficked so she could look for her father. So I'm fairly confident that things will work out, even without the lawyer."

It sounded like it might.

"What about the other Russian girls?" Zachary wanted to know.

Diana glanced at him and hid a wince. He still looked pretty colorful, but he was sitting up and in pretty good spirits, so he was obviously improving.

"I'm not sure what will happen to them," Diana said. "From what I understand, they're also here semi-legally, so they can't be deported. Although someone could make a case of them working illegally, I suppose. Although anyone who tried would likely be crucified in the media."

We all nodded.

"So they may be allowed to stay. If they want to. I think at least one of them does."

Zachary looked cheered. I guess he assumed, as I did, that the one who wanted to stay might be Tatiana.

"Happy endings all around," I said.

Diana nodded. She glanced around the kitchen. "I didn't think I'd see you back here. When you moved into the penthouse, I thought that was it."

"So did I. But this is temporary." Until Rachel got back on her feet again and could move home, and until we found Zachary somewhere else to live.

After a second I added, "The dog seems to like it."

Edwina opened an eye, slapped her stubby tail against the floor a couple of times, and went back to sleep.

"So I see." Diana sounded amused. "You're keeping her?"

I was. She was good company. I liked having her around. And giving her a happy home—while Araminta, who had wanted to give Edwina to the pound, spent the rest of her days in prison—seemed like poetic justice.

"Besides," I added, "David never would allow me to have a dog. He was always afraid it would scratch his floors and dig holes in his lawn. She's better company than David ever was. And I cheer every time she pees on the grass."

"Good for you," Diana said. "So you're continuing the business?"

Rachel and Zachary both looked at me, as if they were concerned about my answer. I had no idea why they would be.

"Of course I'm continuing the business. Just because Steven wasn't guilty of cheating, doesn't mean there isn't some other married bastard out there right now, running around behind his wife's back with some girl half his age."

Diana looked amused. "I'm sure there is."

"We're planning to have an open house next week. I'm inviting all the wives of David's old clients." There were plenty of trophy wives among them. Wives who were now hitting thirty-five and forty, whose husbands were probably looking to replace them with even younger models. "If you know anyone who might qualify, feel free to send them our way."

I gave her the day and time.

"I'll be sure to do that," Diana promised. She pushed back her chair and got to her feet. "I should be getting home."

I got up, too. "I'll walk you out."

We headed down the hallway in silence. At the door, she gave me a hug. "Thanks for everything, Gina."

"No problem," I said, squeezing back. "I'm glad it

all worked out." She hadn't lost a husband, she had gained a daughter.

Although until I knew a little more about how she felt, it was probably best not to say that out loud.

So I watched her get into her car and maneuver slowly down the driveway, and when she reached the bottom and disappeared down the road, I shut and locked the door and went back to the kitchen.

Zachary and Rachel were still at the table. Edwina looked up when I came in, decided I was no threat, and closed her eyes again. I sat back down.

A few seconds ticked by.

"You know," I said, "I don't think we did too badly for our first official case."

They both stared at me.

"OK, so you both ended up in the hospital. I almost did, too. And we almost got killed a couple of times."

They both nodded.

"And we didn't make any money."

Rachel winced. Zachary smirked.

"But we saved Diana's marriage." And all right, it probably would have saved itself, since Steven wasn't actually cheating. But that wasn't all. "We saved three Russian girls from prostitution. We helped solve a murder and get the murderer sent to prison. We stopped a human trafficking ring. And on top of that, we saved a little dog from the pound."

We all turned to look at her. She grinned back at us, stubby tail thumping.

"I think we did good," I said.

Nobody said anything for a moment. Then Zachary lifted his glass of Dr. Pepper. "To us."

I raised mine, and Rachel did the same. We clinked them together. "To us."

And we all drank. To us, and to our next case.

Hopefully not too far in the future.

# # #

About the Author

New York Times and *USA Today* bestselling author Jenna Bennett (Jennie Bentley) writes the Do It Yourself home renovation mysteries for Berkley Prime Crime and the Savannah Martin real estate mysteries for her own gratification. She also writes a variety of romance for a change of pace.

For more information, please visit Jenna's website:
www.JennaBennett.com

Made in the USA
Middletown, DE
19 July 2018